SHOR

by

Greta van der Rol

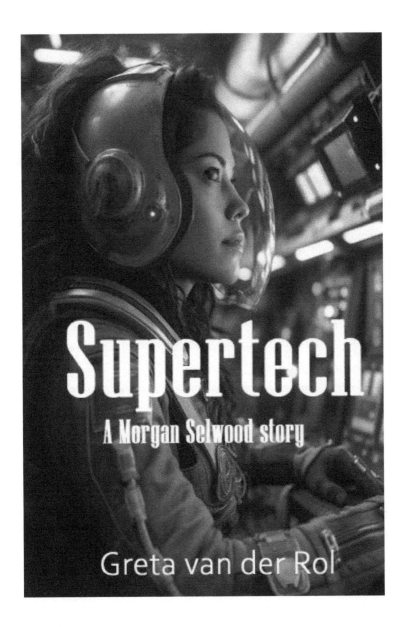

Supertech

A Morgan Selwood story

Greta van der Rol

Supertech

Supertech evolved while I was writing The Iron Admiral. I'd been at it for a while and reached that point where I threw the virtual manuscript at a virtual wall and snarled, "Nobody's going to want to read this rubbish!" The problem was that I felt my heroine in that story was drifting perilously close to fantasy. How did she acquire her abilities? This was supposed to be Sci-fi, not magic.

But writing doesn't like to let go of its victims and soon I was starting to imagine a somewhat different heroine who was born with special, unusual talents which qualified her to be nurtured as a Supertech. This was in the days when cyborgs weren't common, as they are today. I imagined Morgan as a feisty lady who hadn't asked to be a Supertech and refused to fit the mould.

She had been modified at birth to incorporate a super computer into her brain. Her eyes were replaced with sophisticated technology that enabled her to connect her massive computer capability wirelessly with any computer. She was a product of an age after the devastating Cyber Wars when Humanity was brought to the brink of extinction after a battle with the machines which had taken over the running of society. Humanity was thrown into a Dark Age.

When it recovered, it vowed to keep the workings of machine technology out of the hands of ordinary people. Supertechs built and modified all machines, and Supertechs were controlled.

But some Supertechs are more easily controlled than others.

So, this little story is an introduction to Morgan Selwood who is strong enough to thwart her programming. And that's how the Morgan Selwood series started. It has been published separately

By the way, I sorted out my Iron Admiral script. It's the first of six books in the Ptorix Empire series.

She's a Supertech, bioengineered from birth, fresh out of the Academy and tasked with designing a control system for an experimental fighter. Morgan's up for the challenge but there's more to the job than meets the eye. The Fleet invested in her education but did they train her for ... this?

Ensign Morgan Selwood was almost too good at her job and far too casual about Fleet rules and regulations. Tasked with designing a control system for an untested attack fighter seemed like a dream come true and a real career booster. But the specs and modules tell only part of the story—what Morgan discovers can put not just her career, but lives at risk.

MORGAN SLAPPED HER HAND ON THE PANEL that opened the door to the broom cupboard also known as her office. Lights flickered on as she entered. She really must bring in a broom and a bucket to finish the look. Another day in paradise. She flung her bag into its usual corner and sagged onto the chair. What riveting task would Cam have found for her today?

Concentrating on the dataport, she flicked the mental switch in her implant to meld with the base's computer system. The impersonal lens became a colored highway, transporting packets of data back and forth. Morgan sent her ID, on which she'd long since changed her security clearance to system administrator, and looked around for changes.

Ah. A new frigate up on Gens Brasna Two, the larger of the maintenance base's two orbital space stations. She sighed. Dead boring. Routine annual checkout and recalibration. They wouldn't even ask her to move her backside out of her chair for that. Nothing in her in-tray. She'd finished this week's work yesterday morning. Oh, well. Might as well play with the simulators.

She browsed the list of simulator scenarios for a star destroyer, meant for Fleet engineers, navigators or officers on advanced training. This one sounded good; Star destroyer in orbit around a planet, main drives failed, orbit decaying.

She'd barely started diagnosis when Commander Campbell's voice jolted her out of the system.

"Morgan. ENSIGN SELWOOD."

Damn. She hated being forced out of a meld. She sat back in her chair, eyes closed, waiting for the wooziness to pass as her brain reset itself for the physical world.

"Hi, Cam, what's up?" she said through her implant.

"Got something for you, Morgan. Stop playing simulators and get yourself into my office."

Heat rose to Morgan's face. She hadn't realized he knew. But then again, she'd never felt the need to hide the fact she played on the simulators. Besides, she could always call her activity research. Anything a Supertech wanted to know and then some. If they ever posted her somewhere worthwhile, the knowledge would be useful.

"On my way."

She stood, a glow of hope flooding through her, and hurried down the corridor to Campbell's office.

He sat behind his cluttered desk, top button of his rumpled uniform undone as usual. A sharp mind hid behind that scruffy exterior. He had little regard for regulation creases and mirror shine on shoes and that suited her fine. He pointed a finger at his visitor's chair. "Sit."

She sat. "What have you got? Another intermittent fault on that frigate upstairs?"

He grinned. "You enjoyed that, didn't you?"

"Yep. Took me all of six hours."

The smile faded from Campbell's face. "I wonder when they're going to see sense? You must have really, really upset Captain Jorvik, you know. Wasting a Supertech on a maintenance depot..." he shook his head. "I would have thought you'd been punished enough after six weeks."

Six weeks. Was that all? It felt like six months.

She shrugged. "I guess they sent me here because they couldn't send me to a prison planet with the rest of the no-hopers."

She stared at the window simulation in Campbell's office. Five levels above them drizzle fell from an overcast sky. Fat droplets collected on the virtual glass and ran down like tears. Jorvik's face rose in her mind, a malicious glint in his eyes as he presented her with her ensign's stripe and her first posting. Gens Brasna. High on minerals, low on weather and living conditions.

"I didn't think even a martinet like Jorvik would have been quite so stupid. You're too rare and valuable for that." Campbell ran a hand though thinning hair, making it stick out even more around his head. "Never mind that. Here's something that's certainly worthy of you."

He slid a datacube into the reader on his desk. A holovid display of a fighter rotated in the air between them. Streamlined and sleek, canards, and forward-sweeping wings.

"That's an SU-43," he said. "A brand new, versatile attack fighter, space and atmosphere capable, to be carried on star destroyers and deployed at ground bases. It's the replacement for the K-11. This is a prototype. They want you to build the fighter's control system."

Woohoo. A real job at last. She could have jumped up and kissed him. "Okaaaay. Thank you thank you thank you."

He laughed. "Happy now? Come on, Supertech. Let's see what you've got."

The day flew past as she collected background information and read up on fighter control systems.

After work she bounced into the apartment she shared with Brad.

"Hey. Had a great day, lover, how was yours?" She threw off her coat and flung it onto the nearest chair.

Brad grinned up at her from the couch and turned off the holovid. "That's a change. Tell me about it."

She pirouetted, landed on his lap and engulfed him in a kiss.

"I have to create a control system for a new fighter called the SU-43," she said when she came up for air.

The arm around her waist loosened. "Oh yes? What's an SU-43?"

"Don't tell me you're interested? You're never interested in what I do."

"In fighters, sure. That's what I do."

"It's a replacement for the K-11."

"I've flown K-11s. Quite a few times. How's it different?"

"Totally reconfigurable wings. Forward slanting with canards when you want maneuverability, backswept when you need stability, wing length can be changed, wings and canards can be joined together to create one smooth delta-wing surface. Wings and canards are retractable, so the craft can be stored in a smaller space. That's an improvement for a star destroyer."

"I guess. Weapons?"

"Laser cannons forward and aft and missile tubes under the fuselage."

"Are the missile launchers Techwares?"

"I don't know. Does the manufacturer matter?"

His hand stroked her back, up and down, but absently. "Guess not. But Techwares are solid, problem-free and accurate."

"I can find out for you."

He grinned and hugged her shoulder. "I know you can, babe. But let's not bother right now. A celebration is in order. Let's go out for dinner and then on to the dance club. We can show each other some moves."

She sat up. "Sounds good. And then we can come home and practise some more horizontal moves."

He laughed. "That sounds even better. Go get changed, then."

She skipped off to the bedroom and pulled out her red dress while Brad changed into grey pants and a dark blue jacket. She liked his body, fit and strong. The scar still showed on his left leg, a long white line but he hardly limped at all and the injury certainly hadn't stopped his ability to dance. Vertically or horizontally.

Gens Brasna may be the armpit of the Fleet, but at least she'd met Brad here. Nothing was irrevocably bad. And Captain Jorvik could put that small fact wherever he'd like it, with her compliments.

She slipped on dancing shoes, the heels high enough for elegance without causing nose-bleed. "What did the doctor say?"

His fingers stopped in the act of buttoning his coat. "Another month and they'll consider sending me back to my squadron."

A month. Her heart almost stopped. But he was a fighter pilot, only here on Gens Brasna to recuperate, regain his skills flying refurbished ships as a final check before they went back to active duty. She knew that. Now the knowledge transformed into a hand around her heart, squeezing.

"Hey." He crossed the few steps between them and took her face in his hands. "This new assignment is a good sign. Do a good job and you'll be out of here, too. Love you."

He kissed her lightly then pulled her into his arms and clamped his mouth over hers. She molded against him, eyes closed.

He pushed away at last. "Come on, we need to eat first."

She managed a laugh. "Guess so."

"And who knows? Maybe they'll post you to *Leviathan*."

Yes, maybe they would. She'd been a good girl so far, hadn't put a foot wrong since she landed here. The last thing she wanted was to lose her commission. If Gens Brasna was bad, the prospect of going home to Sal Moneo with her tail between her legs... No. She'd never do that.

Morgan almost skipped into work the following day, bubbling with barely suppressed joy. A job, a real job. She connected with the computer, called up the schematics for the SU-43 and began to design the control system. She'd spent some time yesterday checking the controllers for the K-11s and a number of other fighters and reading up on the literature. The system would be a closed-loop neural network, collecting input data from sensors within the machine and modifying the flight characteristics accordingly.

So many variables to consider; drag, flex, angles, external wind speed and temperature in atmosphere and the absence of those elements in space and a heap of others. The existing tech was a good jumping-off point. She could innovate a little more after she'd seen what the SU-43 would do with something similar to what was already out there.

First things first; a whole slew of parameters to set up, all depending on what the aircraft was supposed to be able to do. She went back to the contract documents, entering minima and maxima which would define the best the aircraft could be expected to deliver.

A few days' work and she had a prototype ready to test in simulations.

Now to match the pie-in-the-sky with the real world. She went back to the contract to check the capabilities of the components.

Extron Avionics had won the tender to build the entire aircraft. Out of curiosity she looked the firm up. Five years old, never built a fighter before. Odd. Why would they give a contract to a new firm? She went back to the tender process itself. Four companies had responded, one of them Techware, the firm Brad had mentioned. Techware had built the K-11 and that company's design for the new fighter was very similar to the older ship. Extron's bid was certainly far and away the cheapest, by a good twenty-five percent. The company trumpeted a new material, lightweight, strong and cheap, and a radical design. But the main reason for the reduced quote was that Fleet was going to supply the control system.

Alarms bells tinkled in her head. A control system supplied by her. And a brand-new product called 'durafibe' for the fuselage, a composite from a recently discovered plant fiber reinforced with carbon. It hadn't been used anywhere else before. Uh-oh. Durafibe was still experimental. Her feeling of unease growing, she followed the data trail to the test results. Oh shit. The material tested to well below the maxima Fleet required. But the company set out assurances that the new substance was undergoing further development to improve its behavioral characteristics which would be finished in time for a production run in the following year.

Morgan leaned back in her chair and broke the meld with the computer system.

They couldn't be serious. They couldn't possibly be planning to build a brand-new aircraft with experimental materials. Surely.

She'd have to talk to Campbell.

She found the Commander in his office. He swiveled around from his monitor when she knocked on the doorframe. "You look worried. What's up?"

She perched on the edge of his visitor's chair.

"Aircraft design isn't my specialty, Cam, but this SU-43 business bothers me."

"In what respect?"

"The design will work. I'm just worried about this Extron crowd who won the tender."

The two lines between Campbell's brows deepened. "So? I expect they tendered a lower price."

"Yes, they did. Cam, this crowd has never built anything for a space-faring aircraft before. They're contracted to build the whole damn ship and this durafibe stuff they're going to use for the hull is still experimental."

"Morgan, it's not your problem. You're a Supertech. You build information systems, not aircraft. And you don't write contracts."

"Sure, Cam. But my partner is a fighter pilot. He flies those aircraft and yes, I'm very interested. I took a look at the tender. I'm no lawyer, sure, but it seems to me we've got plenty of obligations to them and they have sod all to us, except to deliver a product that works. Eventually."

"So what's the problem?"

She stared at him. The lines in his face seemed deeper, his eyes sunken and the normal glint of humor had gone.

"They're giving us lots of assurances that this new material they're developing will be ready in time. But if it isn't, we just wait. No penalties, no compensation. And the control system I build will revert to them. They'll own it." She shoved a hand through her hair. "They owe us nothing. We fit in with them. So I looked at the Techware tender to see what they offered. It'll work."

Campbell shrugged. "I've seen Techware's design. It's just an upgrade of the K-11. Safe but unimaginative."

"That's right. Safe. Not quite as fast, not quite as maneuverable, but —"

"You're saying you can't make this prototype safe?"

Morgan looked away. "Yes, I can make it safe. Provided nobody pushes it too hard."

"Well then. Just do your job, Morgan. Build what's asked of you." Campbell's hands had clenched into fists, the knuckles white.

A tingle of alarm wriggled down her spine. "What don't I know, Cam?"

"Admiral Makasa is pushing this thing. It's his baby."

"Who's he?"

"Morgan, he's the boss of the whole munitions section." Campbell glanced around nervously as though his every word was being recorded for playback to the admiral.

"Well, does he know about the tenders? Maybe we should tell him."

Campbell slammed his hand flat down on the desk. "No. Do your job. Design a control system. You have the model, you have the simulation test bed. You said you wanted a challenge. Get on with it."

Morgan sat back in her chair, her eyes closed. *Do your job... do as you're told. You're a Supertech. Do as you're told.* She heard the words. Saw them seared across her senses. Supertechs did as they were told, in spite of anything. It was part of her programming even if she tried to override it. Her body tried to make her stand and leave, go back to her office.

She rose to her feet.

No. She forced the impulse away and took a deep breath, steadying the pounding of her heart. Do as she was told, yes, but raise issues, surely. The compulsion faded to a dull ache.

"Look, I can program the control system. But if the wings fall off, what do you want me to do about it?" She leant over the desk at him, letting her anger rise to push the compulsion back even further. "You know what they're gonna say? Oh, sorry about the pilot. Here's a new ship. And there's nothing we can do about it.

Campbell tried to meet her eyes and looked away. "Don't blast me with your mercury glare, Ensign. This is bigger than both of us. Get on and do your job. What you were built for."

Built for. The words seared her soul. Modified at birth, she carried more computing power in her implants than all the processors on a battle cruiser. But nobody could see that. She was just another woman, except for her eyes. They were artificial, able to connect to dataports and yet still see what a human brain saw. To people like Campbell they looked like they were made of mercury; silvery, fluid; a nice, obvious reminder to all that she was different, strange. He couldn't match her gaze; not many people could.

Morgan pushed herself upright and slouched back to her broom cupboard. Cam hadn't called her Ensign since a day after she'd arrived on Gens Brasna. This Makasa fellow had to be pushing him hard.

Do your job. Design a control system. Obey. The urge to obey pushed at her.

Well, maybe Makasa didn't know about the faults in the contract. Sometimes senior officers were told what they wanted to hear, not what they should hear. Besides, compliance was part of the design job, surely?

She checked all the tenders, listed the problems as she saw them, asked questions about the quality of the components and returned to Commander Campbell with a report.

"It *is* my problem, Cam. I can design a control system constrained by the limitations of the materials but if they don't come up to specification—"

"Then you've done what was asked of you. We'll go back to the manufacturers and hold them to account." Campbell played with a laserpen, turning it over in his fingers.

Morgan folded her arms. "I told you I'd tell it like it is. Isn't that part of my job?"

He shook his head. "No, it's not. You build information systems. That is your job. You'll have to learn to work *with* the system, Morgan."

Obey orders. The compulsion had always been there, as long as Morgan could remember but it was stronger now than it had ever been before. At the Academy she'd sometimes had to shrug it off but now it felt like a physical pressure. With an effort, she said, "I never have before, which is why I'm here. Why start now?"

"Well, you might want to be somewhere else, for a start. Maybe this is a test." Campbell looked at a point just above the bridge of her nose, still absently twirling the laserpen. "You *could* get yourself taken off the project. Do you think that would help? Either the project or you?"

"Me? Why?"

"Put up too much argument and they'll get someone else to build the control system. You'll be stuck here, recalibrating information systems on ships brought in for routine maintenance. The thing will be built, with you or without you. Might as well go with the flow, get yourself out of here."

It was true. She could see that. If not her, then somebody else. Yes, another Supertech. And she wouldn't want that, would she? *It would be easy. Go back to your office and build the system.*

"Cam, there's something wrong here." She forced the words out. "They're throwing something together on the cheap, putting pilot's lives on the line by cutting corners. It's the same with the control system. I checked that, too. Firms like Techware have their own Supertech employed to build control systems. But the contract with Extron specifically excludes the control system. It will be supplied by Fleet. Me. Straight out of the Academy. Ensign Selwood."

Campbell shrugged. "Why not? You have the skill. You topped your course—in fact, the Academy's historical records—for all the technical subjects. You're sitting here twiddling your neurons. Why not use them?"

"And save the cost of that module. Why not indeed?" It was true. He was right. She shook her head. "You have more confidence in me than I have. They just should... not... be... doing... this." She glared at him, punctuating each word with a jabbing finger. "At least not until that material is delivered on spec."

"Makasa needs funding to build the ship. Funding hat must be agreed now," Campbell countered. "Morgan, you just have to make the best of these things."

"Will you at least send Makasa my report?"

His face hardened. "No."

Wimp. Useless, spineless wimp. "Why not?"

His lips tightened. "Because it's not part of your brief. I, for one, am not going to offend Makasa."

"Why? What's Makasa got to do with it? Surely he'd want the best machine he can get?"

Campbell closed his eyes and shook his head slowly from side to side. "Leave me alone, Ensign, please."

He looked old and tired. Dispirited. Harassed. She didn't care.

"Oh, and when did pulling rank last work with me? If you don't tell me I'll find out."

Campbell rubbed his hands over his face. "Dammit, Morgan, he's a three-star admiral. Makasa can ruin your career. He can ruin Brad's. He can ruin mine. Brad wants to go back to an active squadron; I'm expecting to retire next year on a good pension. Three-star admirals can influence those decisions. And just remember," he added, raising his voice slightly and pointing a finger at her, "you want out of here. Let it go. Do the best you can. It's your job to obey orders."

He turned back to his console, indicating the discussion was over.

With that last sentence repeating softly in her mind, Morgan spun around and marched off, wishing she could slam the door.

Back in her office she slumped into her chair, still fuming. The anger helped, suppressing the siren song telling her to get on and do her job. Campbell might think the discussion was over. She didn't. And it *was* part of the job, whatever he might say. It *was*.

First thing to do was to make sure she could prove her allegations with facts and dates. Why hadn't she made meticulous copies all along? Too trusting. She never expected to have to explain herself to her own. That was something she'd learnt.

Morgan slid her mind into the system, accessed her work space and looked for the report. Odd. It was gone. She opened the backups. Not there, either. A tingle of alarm spread through her nerves. Deleted? Yes, completely, utterly and irretrievably, even for her. Nothing in the archives and no audit trail.

When she told Brad that evening he frowned. "That's strange, Morgan. Who could have done that?"

"Easy enough for a Supertech."

"You're the only Supertech here."

"Don't be naïve, Brad. People like Campbell and no doubt others would have the authority to run a function built by a Supertech at HQ to delete stuff."

"Yes, silly of me." He paused in thought for a moment. "Didn't you have a copy of the document at home?"

She brightened. "I did. I'll take a look."

Nothing. A whole squadron of butterflies took wing in her stomach. She met Brad's gaze.

"Look, be careful, babe. You don't want to piss off Fleet. It's bigger than both of us."

"I'm starting to feel like I'm being shuffled into a cage, Brad. It's clear Campbell will go along with whatever Makasa tells him, so I'm in a corner on that one. And even if I had an old copy of the report, it would be my word against an admiral's."

Brad put his arms around her, settling her comfortably into the curve of his shoulder. "Look on the bright side. The ship's not a complete eggshell. The simulations were good most of the time, weren't they?"

"Yes, but... The control system is all about parameters set within the structural constraints of the material. This durafibe is flexible and strong, but it's very thin to make it even lighter and the wings will tear under too much pressure. So I've limited the amount of force the aircraft can pull, which affects performance. That in itself is dangerous." She put her arms around his waist.

Brad stroked her hair. "If the ship can't exceed limits, it's safe enough, isn't it?"

"I guess. Provided I've factored in all the variables correctly. What if I haven't?"

"Look, you said yourself that Extron is producing an improved product. Fleet isn't in the business of sending pilots out in sub-standard craft. It costs too much."

"Maybe. But pilots shouldn't have to worry about the possibility of bits falling apart in the sky. There's got to be something I can do."

"I can think of something you can do," said Brad, turning her face up to his. "It's nothing to do with a fighter, though." He drew her closer towards him and kissed her.

"Publicity," she said over breakfast the next morning as she poured cereal into a bowl.

"What do you mean?" Brad asked, his spoon held stationary halfway to his mouth.

"I'll just do a letter to the editor, asking a few questions about the equipment tender. I can disguise it so it won't involve me."

Brad shook his head. "You don't imagine it'll occur to them that you might have written it?" He went back to eating, crunching on his grain flakes.

"I can cover my trail."

He swallowed, shaking his head. "Let it go, babe. You can't win, but you can certainly lose. Big time. Remember what I said. It's not in Fleet's interest to buy sub-standard craft and they won't."

Morgan kissed him and headed off for work. Not even Brad was on her side.

The compulsion to obey hovered over her shoulder but Morgan found she could muffle it with unrelated work. An hour of research revealed that prominent civilian weapons expert Professor Wenisant regularly sent letters to the editor and to some of the senior supply officers in Fleet, criticizing tender documents. She grinned over some of his letters. Sarcastic as sin and he certainly didn't miss anybody. Perfect.

The morning Professor Wenisant's scathing letter about the SU-43 appeared in the *Galaxy News* a grim-faced Campbell stopped Morgan before she even reached her door. "My office."

She followed meekly, ensuring her face was a picture of innocence. That was one thing she'd learnt at the Academy. She'd out-fenced masters at face-reading. Silver eyes had one advantage; nobody could read what was going on behind them.

"Have you seen this letter?" He tossed a sheet displaying the letters to the editor section of the *Galaxy News* in front of her before he'd even sat down behind his desk.

"Any one in particular?"

"The one entitled 'What happens if the wings fall off?' The headline letter. Professor Wenisant."

"Good questions," she said when she'd read the letter through. Much better than she could have done and pretty funny, too. "This Professor Wenisant knows his stuff." She smiled and returned the sheet to a scowling Campbell.

"Where did he get the detailed information about the project, do you think?"

She shrugged. "Who knows? He has a reputation, doesn't he? I guess he has his sources."

"Not you?"

"Me? No. Why would I? It's been made very clear to me that I'm just building a control system. Although he mentions that, too. Did you notice?"

Campbell positively bared his teeth. It was all she could do not to laugh. "Yes. I noticed. Makasa will not be happy." He leaned at her, over the desk. "If you've had anything to do with this, Ensign, you will be in serious trouble. Serious trouble. Clear?"

"Never clearer. Sir." She stood. "If that'll be all? I have test results to check."

"Dismissed."

Brad and Morgan sat together on their couch and watched the *Galaxy News* interview with Admiral Makasa as he answered every question in Professor Wenisant's letter. He lounged on a sofa, a mountain of a man, the gold-encrusted collar of his admiral's uniform seemingly embedded in the rolls of fat around his neck.

"The dangers are grossly exaggerated," he said, his voice deep and rich. "My administrative people have checked Extron's credentials. It's true they don't have a track record with delivery of aircraft but they have an enviable reputation with mag lev trains and various types of industrial equipment. I spoke to the CEO just yesterday and he explained they'd hired experienced people who had worked in the space avionics industry to augment their pool of engineers."

"The Professor mentions stress issues with the materials. What if the wings fall off was his question. What if they do, Admiral?"

Makasa waved a fat hand in dismissal. "It is a new substance. Rest assured thorough tests will be carried out before the aircraft is released. Yes, we can expect some tweaking. That is normal."

"What about the control system. It's vital, isn't it?"

"Of course. But we have our own Supertechs. Why pay the astronomical rates the designers charge if we can do the work internally? I must say, I'm a little surprised that on the one hand you criticize us for misuse of funds and now, when we try to reduce costs, you criticize us for that." He chuckled, sending his stomach bouncing. "It's hard to win that sort of game."

"But the person building the control system is apparently inexperienced."

"The Supertech building the system has the skills. Our Supertech program ensures that only the very best make it through the system. Nothing more needs to be said. It is not my intention to discuss staff selection with Professor Wenisant or, indeed, the general public."

"He's smooth," Morgan said.

Damn and blast. Smooth enough to convince the reporter. She hoped the prof would stay on the case.

"Seems he's a prince, third son of the king on the planet he comes from," Brad said. "He probably learned how to do this sort of thing before he learnt how to walk."

"Huh."

"You leaked, didn't you?" Brad scowled at her, brows knitted. "Morgan, please. Let it go. This is Fleet. And look, I'll be honest with you, Makasa's answers sounded pretty reasonable to me. He's got it under control." His expression softened and he put his arm around her, pulling her against him. "You and me, that's all that's important."

She wished she could agree with him.

Three days later, immediately she arrived at work, Commander Campbell summoned Morgan to his office. He was standing when she arrived, looking abnormally formal despite his characteristically rumpled uniform, his hands clasped behind his back.

"You're to report to Captain Liemen's office, Ensign," he said. "Immediately."

The base commanding officer. A squadron of butterflies performed barrel rolls in her stomach. But then, what had she expected? They had no proof. All she had to do was keep calm.

"Liemen wants to talk to me about the SU-43?"

"No. Admiral Makasa does."

The butterflies in her stomach carried out a starburst. He must have taken a flight to Gens Brasna as soon as the interview with *Galaxy News* was over. This could prove interesting. *Keep cool, Morgan. You can do this. Just like another round in the ring with Warrant Officer Dubik.*

She made her way through the corridors and up the lifts to the reception area of the Captain's office on the first floor.

"Ensign Selwood." The captain's adjutant glowered at her. "I believe you've been making a fuss."

"Not that I know of, sir." Morgan said.

The adjutant announced her arrival and sent her in with a gesture.

Morgan marched into the office, came to attention and saluted. She'd known he was a big man from the broadcast but seeing Makasa in the flesh simply enhanced his bulk. He overflowed the seat behind the desk, a vast black man with a mass of tightly curled black hair. Dark eyes under thick brows assessed her. Three gold stars gleamed on his shoulder boards. Several gold rings glinted on both of the hands clasped together on the desk in front of him. His gaze passed over her like a searchlight. The silence grew. A barely audible knock in the climate conditioning became an insistent percussion section.

She stared back at him, keeping her face impassive. If he thought she'd break down and blab to fill the vacuum, he could think again.

"We don't often have the benefit of a Supertech on Gens Brasna, Ensign."

His voice was even more beautiful than on the newscast, deep and musical and rich. He tried to meet her gaze, but looked down in seconds. Morgan grinned inwardly. At least she still had that weapon at her disposal.

"I've been looking at your record. It's an interesting mix. You topped your course in all technical subjects. Remarkable, outstanding results. But you were quite deplorable at a good many other subjects. Fails in military law, drill, military history, administration. Bare passes in man-management and instruction."

"Yes, sir."

"Your instructors' comments are interesting, too. 'Recalcitrant' appears more than once. So does 'difficult' and 'uncooperative'. Even the instructors of subjects where you achieved spectacular results have not always been flattering. I see Captain Jorvik tried on more than one occasion to set you straight."

"Yes, sir."

What did he want her to say? She couldn't be bothered with the boring stuff. It wouldn't be part of her career. Who wanted to waste time marching or polishing buttons or making a bed you could bounce coins on? She'd done well at the subjects that mattered, sometimes despite the instructor.

"So... here you are at Gens Brasna." He paused to make the point. "Commander Campbell is happy enough with your application since you've been here, I'm pleased to say. And indeed, may I congratulate you on your work on the SU-43? You did a wonderful job. The tests so far are impressive, to say the least."

A warning tingle slid down her spine. "Thank you, sir. But they're still only computer simulations." *Keep calm. He has no proof.*

"You are probably aware that questions were asked in the news about the aircraft?" He wasn't really expecting an answer. "Of course you are. Given the knowledge of the project displayed in the letter, someone from your section must have leaked information."

Gosh, what a surprise. Breathe in... breathe out.

"I've been able to dispel any fears, Ensign," Makasa continued, "but I'm afraid that Commander Campbell, as commanding officer, will have to take responsibility for his lax discipline."

Campbell? Campbell would take the rap? She hadn't expected that. Heart thudding, she forced herself to remain expressionless.

Makasa stretched fat lips in a mockery of a smile. "He's due for retirement next year. Subject to approval, of course."

Bastard. Devious bastard. He probably thought she'd admit her guilt. Well, he could think again.

Makasa levered himself out of the chair and walked around the desk to stand in front of her. His two-meter frame loomed over her like a wall. He wore some sort of cologne, sweet, cloying and incongruous.

"Ensign, this project is important to us. The K-11 has been a wonderful servant for a long time; too long, really. The fleet has aged and is well overdue for retirement. We wish to roll out its replacement as soon as possible. Give me a positive result as I know you can, and I shall be willing to forgive and forget. In fact, I'm told your partner is due to be transferred back to his unit on the *Leviathan*. I've arranged for him to remain here for a little longer so that he can act as test pilot for the SU-43. You'd like that, I expect?"

"Yes, sir." Brad as test pilot on the SU-43? She didn't like the sound of that at all but at least she'd be here to protect him. "To have Brad around longer, yes."

"Good. When this project is finished, I expect there will be a clamor to claim your services on something a little more fitting for someone with your skills. Maybe Supertech on the *Leviathan*?"

Anger bubbled in her gut. She kept her eyes fixed on the buttons of his uniform. He was dangling a bribe but the bribe had barbs in the form of Brad and of Campbell. Make this work and you'll be rewarded. If it doesn't work... it won't be just you that suffers. Bastard. He'd backed her into a corner. She let the anger rise to drown out the compulsion to obey.

"Commander Campbell?" she said.

"What about him?" Makasa had clasped his hands behind his back and rocked from heel to toe.

"I'm sure he would have had no control over the information leak, sir."

His slab of a stomach shifted as he sucked in a satisfied breath. "Perhaps, Ensign. I could be magnanimous and overlook the matter. But I can't give a guarantee. Leaks are regarded very seriously within the Fleet's development structure. Court martial with loss of all entitlements is the usual thing."

He waddled back around to Captain Liemen's chair and sat. The chair creaked as it took his weight.

She'd virtually admitted her guilt even if she hadn't said 'I did it'. Oh, well. In for a brick, in for a boulder. She couldn't compromise Campbell's retirement. He might be a spineless wimp but he'd been good to her.

"But this is a maintenance unit, not a development center, sir. Commander Campbell is a good officer. I would be grateful if you would grant him the benefit of the doubt and exempt him from prosecution." She made sure she looked at his forehead.

"A demand, Ensign?" he said softly, his eyes narrowed. They were almost porcine in his fat face.

"A request, sir. It would clear my mind, make me better able to perform my duties."

He chuckled. The poisonous, smart bastard chuckled.

"A small price to pay to focus your mind *completely* on the task required of you. Agreed."

His tone was light but Morgan didn't miss the menace behind the words.

"But." He raised the index finger of his left hand in an unmistakable warning gesture. "Judgement is suspended, not revoked. It is revoked if... no, when... you deliver."

"Thank you, sir." She kept her voice deadpan, while her mind shouted obscenities.

The admiral considered the desktop for a moment, then said in conversational tones, "By the way, Ensign, I know Professor Wenisant quite well. He told me he received his SU-43 information from an anonymous source. It seems he tried to trace the origin, but he couldn't. Neither could our intelligence people. Isn't that interesting?"

He glanced at her face. His eyes sparkled with almost contemptuous triumph.

"The prototype SU-43 will be delivered to this station next week. From then, you have three weeks, Ensign. I look forward to the launch demonstration. Dismissed."

She saluted, performed an impeccable parade ground about face and left the room, feeling like a rodent in a cage. With a large black feline circling around it.

Brad was waiting for her when she came home, standing in the living room with his arms folded. "Makasa was here for you?"

"Yes."

The two lines between his eyebrows drew closer together. "I told you not to do it."

"It's, okay, it's okay. I give up. You all win."

Damn, it rankled. She'd tried a simulation with the stress factors set a little higher just yesterday. The wings really had torn off.

"You'll do as you're asked?" Brad searched her face, his hands on her shoulders.

"Yes." But she didn't have to like it.

"Great." He pulled her into his arms. "If you'd kept on with this... I don't know what I would have done. But look on the bright side. We get to stay together for another few weeks."

She pulled away. "What do you mean, what you would have done?"

He flushed. Her heart froze.

"I've got a career, too, babe."

"Oh, so behave or I'm out, is that it?"

"Don't be like that. I love you."

"You love me but? I'm being set up and there's fuck all I can do about it." She blinked away the tears pricking at her eyes.

"Sweetheart, at least you'll be able to make it work."

She shrugged him off and pushed past him, into the bedroom. "Yeah. Until I'm not there to help and the wings tear off."

"Babe—"

"Leave me alone. Just leave me alone."

The disassembled SU-43 arrived on schedule at Gens Brasna Two. The engineers put the aircraft together, ran their stress tests and sent Morgan the results. She calibrated the control system accordingly.

Brad ran the first test flight, a routine take-off, a trip around the base and a landing. The engineers pronounced themselves satisfied with the aircraft's behavior and with the results of a close examination of the components.

"That went well," Brad said. "The ship handles beautifully. You done good." He planted an affectionate kiss on her lips.

"Good. We'll put it under a bit more pressure over the next few days."

Minute signs of stress started to show where the wings and canards extended from the fuselage.

"We should can this, sir," she told the chief engineer, Senior Commander Fleming.

He shook his head. "Not a chance. Makasa wants this passed to get funding. Reset the parameters lower so it isn't a problem for the demonstration. We can fiddle with the details later."

"The details? Sir?" He couldn't be serious. But he was. The rage spewed out. "This is the fucking airframe we're talking about, not the décor."

Fleming sucked air into his lungs, blowing himself up like a barrage balloon. "You will not talk to me in that manner, Ensign, Supertech or not. You will do as you are told. Or you can explain yourself to Admiral Makasa."

In her mind's eye the black cat prowling around the cage grinned. She reset the parameters and loathed herself for weakness.

The bedside clock's red letters showed 0250 hours. Morgan lay awake, staring at the low ceiling, listening to Brad snoring gently beside her. *Look at the choices. I endorse an unsafe fighter that's okay ninety-five percent of the time. And the Galactic Spirit help whoever's flying it the other five percent. And if I don't, Brad's for the scrapheap, Cam doesn't get his comfortable retirement and I... I'm checking weapons calibrations on frigates in for annual service. If I'm lucky.*

Moving carefully, Morgan eased herself out of bed and made herself a cup of coffee in the apartment's tiny kitchen. Makasa. A big, black cat with a paw full of strings attached to Extron, Campbell, Fleming, Brad, her. He had them all dancing to his direction.

For something to do, she looked up his profile on the information system. Yes, a prince, third son of a king. Probably bought his commission. Married, three wives, eleven children. Good grief. Maybe he was slimmer when he was younger. He'd put her off sex altogether. Imagine that on top of you. You'd need a reinforced bed.

She scrolled through to the next section, listing his career postings and business affiliations. He was even on the board of a couple of philanthropic organizations. Where did he get the time?

She stared at the wall, sipping her coffee. She'd never felt so impotent. And so wrong.

"Whatchadoin?"

She started. Brad stood in the doorway in his sleeping shorts, blinking sleep from his eyes.

"Just looking at Makasa's background."

"You're not getting any wrong ideas?" His voice held a warning note that was starting to grate on her nerves.

"Don't worry, your career's safe. I'm just curious."

He gestured at the holovid. "How about sharing?"

"Sure." She directed the images onto the screen instead of viewing them on her retina.

"That's interesting," he said, lowering himself down on the couch beside her. "He's on the board of Galaxy Vision."

"Why's that interesting?"

"Galaxy Vision's a philanthropic organization that helps refugees and war victims. There was some fuss about them getting money from some of the large weapons manufacturers. The religious lobby said that was wrong."

An alarm bell tinkled in her mind. "Weapons companies? Which weapons companies? Extron?"

"Naw. Don't think so." Brad yawned. "Come back to bed."

"You go, I'll just finish my coffee."

He wandered off.

Morgan looked up Extron, Galaxy Vision and Makasa.

The morning of the launch demonstration dawned overcast and drizzly, a normal day on Gens Brasna.

Makasa himself turned up with an entourage, including several other tame admirals and politicians. A reviewing stand with a roof was set up on the parade ground so that the dignitaries could watch the SU-43 go through its paces in comfort. They set up an enormous holovid so the visitors could watch Brad's fighter in space and in atmosphere up close, as well as seeing it roar past on its final, triumphant run. As Supertech on the project Morgan was, of course, expected to attend. She put on her dress uniform, white pants, white jacket. The stylised eye, symbol for a Supertech, gleamed on the upper sleeves. They could take away the symbol but not the knowledge, not her talent. That hard-won stripe on her shoulder; that was another matter altogether.

She'd weighed the odds, searched her conscience. The day of reckoning had come. It should be fine. If she could get her stomach to stop carrying on like a stew on the stove.

Resisting the urge to go to the toilet one more time, she straightened her shoulders, winked at herself in the mirror and headed off to watch the demo.

Brad took off and blasted up through the clouds into space. The aircraft disappeared but they'd sent up a K-11 to capture the action on the holovid. All eyes turned to the screen. The wings and canards had retracted. The silver cylinder that was the SU-43 pivoted, spun on its axis, traversed a square. The audience hardly reacted. This was only what they expected. Then Brad took the machine back into the atmosphere. The fighter streaked down from space, the protective force field for re-entry glowing white-hot. Wings and canards deployed, the SU-43 dived down below the clouds and performed high speed loops and rolls and some low-speed runs with the wings reconfigured.

Perched up in the back row Morgan curled her lip as Makasa graciously soaked up congratulations from another admiral and the Confederacy Minister for Defense. Toadies. Makasa looked around for her, his smile exultant as he gave her a tiny nod.

Morgan's face twisted in revulsion. Creep. So he thought he had her beaten, did he? Well, she hoped he'd enjoyed the show. Now it was her turn. For better or for worse.

The SU-43 had disappeared again, building up speed for the final run. She took out her comlink, set to the ship's data port, and concentrated. Brad had straightened the machine up, wings parallel to the ground, low and fast. Maybe she should have warned him. Too late now. Closer... a little closer... Now. Her brain linked with the fighter's control system.

The engines purred, running easily, well below capacity, as fast as the control system let it. She adjusted the permitted output parameter and the purr turned to a growl. The tachometer slammed on another ten percent.

Level with the reviewing stand she set a ninety-degree course alteration. The wings and canards responded. Its engines howling, the fighter arced around the right angle and streaked straight up.

Gauges recorded overloads. Error routines generated warnings. Alarms flashed in the control system. They'd be braying in the cockpit but she couldn't hear them. *Sorry, Brad. They have to know the shortcomings.* She sensed him wrestling for control, trying to override to manual. Not this time.

The cockpit display showed the graphic of the fuselage, the stress fracture red and growing. She'd protected the wings and canards. But not the missile launchers hanging off the machine's hull.

Slowly, gracefully, one missile launcher tore off the body, tumbling down towards the ground in leisurely arcs. Morgan slowed the fighter down, reset the parameters and allowed the control system to balance the forces. Time to go home.

She withdrew.

Eyes closed, she let her body sag back against the seat, sucking air into her lungs. The breeze felt cool on her face, drying the sweat. She'd done the right thing. Maybe Brad would see it that way. In time. Maybe.

Silence.

Or perhaps not. Someone stood beside her. She opened her eyes.

Makasa towered over her, resplendent in his white dress uniform, his face contorted with rage. On the lower steps of the reviewing stand faces turned to watch the spectacle, oblivious to the holovid where the SU-43 had shaped to land.

"Can you explain this fiasco, Ensign?"

Steady Morgan. Other people's careers are riding on what you say in public right now.

She kept her voice low. "You're not going to use me. Get your experimental material right before you throw lives at it."

Makasa swelled, glowering down at her with all the weight of his authority, his black skin darkening to purple in his fury. "You dare to speak to me, a senior admiral of the Confederacy Fleet, in that manner? I'll have you arrested."

"You can arrest me if you want to but you'd better check your comlink before you go any further." Her heart might be beating too fast but she'd kept her cool.

He pulled his comlink from his belt. Emotions flowed over his face, quickly controlled and suppressed for the public audience. His eyes flicked over her face, unable to match her stare. If anything, it made him angrier.

"I will need to discuss this matter with you in private, Ensign. Report to Captain Liemen's office and wait for me there while I attend to our guests."

Without another word, he stalked down the central walkway and turned to speak with the Minister for Defense. The lackeys crowded around him. Morgan stumbled off the reviewing stand, a wave of exhaustion washing over her as much from the clash with Makasa as from flying the SU-43.

"You okay, Brad?" she said into her comlink.

"Yes. No thanks to you. That was you up there, wasn't it? What the fuck were you playing at?"

"Sorry, Brad. I just couldn't let them get away with it. I'll explain later."

He ended the call before she'd spoken the last word.

Her eyes pricked and her throat filled. She'd done it for him; in a way; him and the other fighter pilots. Why didn't he understand?

Her heart heavy, she dragged herself to Liemen's office and waited outside the door until Makasa arrived, grateful for the opportunity to regroup. This interview would be the real challenge. She'd done her homework. She went over the data once more in her mind. She was taking on a three-star admiral, with the full force of the Fleet behind him. Talk about the little boy with his finger in the dam. One mistake and she'd disappear in the flood.

Makasa came through the door and gestured with a jerk of his head to follow him into Liemen's office.

"And what do you hope to achieve, Ensign?" The Admiral filled Liemen's chair, hands steepled on the desk in front of him. His eyelids were half closed, his expression unreadable.

Morgan stood, legs apart, hands behind her back. "This isn't about the SU-43. You knew that material wasn't ready. It's been tried before. Only the results weren't released."

"True. I had hoped you could do a better job."

"I'm not sure about that. I've been doing some digging. I found out that through a raft of front companies, you own Extron. I have proof, and it will be provided to everybody that matters if anything happens to Brad or me. I figure you already have Commander Campbell in your pocket.

"You know, as I was checking through all this, I got to wondering what it was really all about. I checked the personnel records; *you* got me this post, not Jorvik; *you* put me with Campbell. The orders are there; your office, your signature. Then I got to thinking. Would you really go to all this trouble and risk your career to sell a few fighters? Given you're already a multi-billionaire?" She shook her head. "Nah, I didn't think so."

Makasa's face had become a mask, impenetrable. "Go on."

"I'm a bio-engineered intelligence. People like me are rare as hens' teeth. I can't imagine the cost of modifying my brain as a baby. And then on top of that you've put me through the Fleet Academy.

I've cost the Fleet a lot of money to be stuck in an armpit like Gens Brasna. So now, at last, I asked myself why? Why wasn't I just kicked out to start a career in a design works somewhere? So I considered the differences between me and the other Supertechs I've met and the difference is that they behave themselves. So then I thought, what if that was it? I didn't behave myself? And I got to thinking what a Supertech with imagination and a criminal mind could do? And the answer is control anything that's run by a computer. I could clean out a bank, hold a city to ransom, bring a star destroyer to a halt, destroy a planet's economy."

She grinned across the table at the fat admiral. "That's what you wanted. My mind set is different. You saw that from my academy results. What you want is a Supertech who'll do naughty things under your direction."

He shifted his bulk and the chair protested. His lips turned up slightly in a smile that didn't reach his eyes.

"Very good, Ensign. Now consider the possibilities. You're clever and you have initiative. I can make you rich. With your talents, we can manipulate the stock market, hit the casinos — anything. You'll be very, very well paid for your efforts. You can buy a house on one of the resort islands, or maybe the whole island. Take your lover along with you. Do whatever you want in between occasional assignments. What do you say?"

"You can make me rich?" She snorted. "*I* can make *you* rich. Richer. No thanks. I won't be manipulated."

"Do you think so?" His beautiful voice was soft and dangerous.

"If you hurt me or Brad, I've fixed it so that the story will come out in all its sordid glory, to the media, the High Command, the Government and everybody else I could think of. Trust me on this. Even your worm program that deleted my original report won't stop this one. And by the way, that includes killing me or causing me an incapacitating injury. Remember, I'm better than a tame Supertech because I'm sneaky. What you are going to do is cancel this project and send Brad and me to *Leviathan*."

Her heart thundered. Just like that. Demand laid on the table. Over to you, fat bastard.

He'd make a good poker player. "I'll consider your request, Ensign."

"No. You'll agree now, or find yourself out of a job. Trust me, Admiral, I'll take you down."

Makasa tilted his head so all she saw was tight black curls. The climate conditioner knocked softly, a counterpoint to the thudding of her heart. But she'd won; he'd have to give in.

When he looked up at her again a smile was beginning to work its way over his face.

"Congratulations, Ensign Selwood. You've just saved your life."

Her jaw dropped. "What?"

"You've worked out a number of things," Makasa said. "As you say, a bent Supertech is very, very dangerous. When the implant is fitted the brain is modified to ensure obedience and conformity to a certain level of ethics. But, although it's very rare, sometimes those changes are unsuccessful. We keep track of our creations from the day the modifications are made, partly for that reason. We usually... ah... dispense with individuals we feel we cannot trust. You were different. Not as malleable as you should have been, but without the criminal streak that had been evident early in the other cases. So we decided to test you.

"You were recalcitrant at the Academy and that's vanishingly rare. The bent Supertechs tended to conform in public and try to keep their devious behavior secret. I'll not deny we had our doubts and some urged me not to take a risk but you became a superb Supertech; a superlative Supertech. So we sent you to Gens Brasna. Bored you stupid to see what you did. Commander Campbell has been keeping a close eye on you in your time here. If we'd seen any sign of a criminal bent — well..." Makasa waved a fat hand.

Morgan recalled Bashir, who died in an accident six months into their academy course. She hadn't thought much about it before. But then there had been Irvan. He'd been expelled but she heard later he'd died, too, another tragic accident. Same with Sylvara. She shivered.

"So the SU-43 thing?" she asked. "How did that fit?"

"I wanted to see how you would react with your commanding officer, who you liked, and your lover, being set up if you did not perform," said Makasa. "You went outside the military system several times to try to prevent something you didn't approve of from going ahead, but you never actually did anything particularly illegal. Then, at the end, you exposed the flaw in rather dramatic fashion."

"Was Brad involved in this?" The final insult if he was. Brought in to set her up. Oh, please, no.

"No. His involvement was a happy coincidence."

Happy for them. For her? How do you deal with a broken heart? It hadn't been on the curriculum.

"What about the SU-43? What will you do with that?"

"At this stage we've done a good job of testing the new material. It is a viable product for space craft. We have engineers in a number of labs working on developing the fiber further. Your work won't be wasted. When we're happy with its strength and resilience, we'll move on."

"With Extron?"

"Perhaps. Extron is well placed to work hand-in-glove with Fleet. Techware has become distressingly hide-bound, reactionary and complacent. I'm sure you'll check that information for yourself."

"Now what?" said Morgan. "Supertech on the *Leviathan*?"

Makasa laughed. His stomach wobbled. "I cannot imagine what you would be like as Supertech on a star destroyer. You'd drive the captain mad and yourself insane through boredom. No, your career as a military officer is over, Ms Selwood. I am rescinding your commission."

She swallowed, her knees turned to jelly. Since she started school she'd always known what she was going to be; a Fleet officer. She'd seen herself up there, on the bridge of a star destroyer, balancing its systems as it shaped for battle. There were civilian Supertechs; she would be given another role. But what? Designing control systems for aircraft? It had been fun but not as a career.

"You'll be a civilian contractor, but we'll look after the contracts you can carry out – secretly of course. You'll work through our sub-contracting organization, Tech Types. When we need a Supertech with your special skills, you'll be called upon. I assure you, you'll find the work interesting and varied."

"Illegal?"

"Sometimes, in a way. For instance, we might wish to know about the contents of a political rival's database. But sometimes you will work with top secret, experimental projects."

Wow. That sounded like fun.

"Brad will be all right?"

Makasa shrugged. "Of course. He's a useful enough pilot. But you can't tell him anything."

He wouldn't be listening. But that was none of Makasa's business.

"I take it I have not, in fact, got anything against you?"

The admiral smiled, shaking his head. His jowls wobbled. "Nothing you can use, no. Fleet knows I own Extron. At least, my family does. I keep that connection at arm's length."

He pushed a sheet across the desk. "Sign this. You'll come with me when I leave tomorrow morning."

'I, Morgan Selwood, resign my commission as a Fleet Officer...'

Morgan sighed. My illustrious career. Four years, three months, six days.

She signed.

A Victory Celebration

A Morgan Selwood story

Greta van der Rol

A Victory Celebration

I wrote 'A Victory Celebration' some time after 'Morgan's Choice' was published. People asked me for more about the relationship between Morgan and Admiral Ravindra. I never imagined that would have been standard, 'happily ever after' stuff. He is a product of his culture and she is an independent soul with a very different background. At some stage, sparks would fly. I had some fun with this little story, involving jealousy from both directions.

A Victory Celebration has been published separately.

What's good for the gander has to be good for the goose ... or so Morgan thinks. The fleet has won a major battle and Ravindra's doing his celebratory thing with his officers. Morgan gets a rare invite for a girls' night out.

Dinner, a little dancing, a little jealous pining... And a whole lot of trouble when Ravindra discovers his lady is out 'n about... without protection. What started as an innocent night on the town turns into something very, very different.

"I'M NOT GOING," SAID MORGAN.

Ravindra's holographic image, transmitted from the presidential palace on the planet the battle cruiser orbited, frowned. "I would like you to be there. Without your assistance this war would still be tearing the planet apart."

"Look, I just tweaked a few gadgets, improved your technology. It's my job, what I was..."

'Designed'.

Damn, she hated that word. Even if it was true. "It's what I do. Your troops did the job."

He still glowered at her. Not happy, not at all. "But you provided the answer. Without your 'gadgets', we'd still be looking for the rebels." He used his fingers to put the inverted commas around the word.

"I just did my job." She shrugged. "Admiral, this is your job, not mine. You know me; I don't like crowds and pompous presidential speeches. I'll probably offend somebody."

Quirking his lips he nodded. "All right."

Yes. She'd won that round.

His eyes narrowed and his chin lifted. "I shall expect you to attend the ball tomorrow night, though."

"Fine." She'd cross that bridge when she reached it.

"So you will stay on *Vidhvansaka*?" His eyes searched her face.

"Of course. I thought I'd get back to working on the experimental shift drive."

"Ah." His head jerked up. "The tests were successful?"

I wish. "No. The model never arrived at its destination. My guess is whatever happened to *Curlew* also happened to it."

"What makes you so sure?"

She raised a shoulder. "Proven engine design. The model made the distance with a standard drive. This time it disappeared. I think

I'll crawl all over the model one more time. I'm sure I can make this work."

She met his gaze, those fierce amber eyes reflective as he tapped the tops of his fingers together. Ravindra wanted that shift drive, a design capable of slashing the time taken to travel from one system to another.

He gazed at her for a moment longer, then blew out a breath. "I'll see you tomorrow."

Morgan's spirits soared. She'd won. "I'm looking forward to it. You enjoy yourself." She flicked him a kiss with her fingertips and turned off the transmission.

Then she dropped onto the couch. She'd won too easily. Maybe he was getting tired of her? All of a sudden her state room on the battle cruiser seemed empty and lonely. Sure, she and Ravindra shared her bed or his most nights when they were together, but they didn't advertise their relationship. An alien and a Fleet admiral? She knew, much as she loved him, that the day would come when he'd agree to one of these arranged marriages with some daughter of another Fleet admiral.

As for tonight... she'd heard about these victory celebrations. The hosts provided 'entertainment' to all senior officers, take your pick of nubile wenches. She'd heard stories of Ravindra's prowess when they thought she couldn't hear. One girl wasn't always enough, it seemed. Mind you, that was before she and Ravindra had come to an understanding, but then again, she hadn't seen much of him the past few weeks. She had no illusions about men, especially senior officers. For the first time in an age she wished she was twenty-five again. She should have stuck to hot-shot pilots like Coreb, not fallen in love.

What the hell. She hadn't thought about Coreb in an age. He'd been fun, a good dancer, not bad in bed. But not like Ravindra.

Oh, for pity's sake. She jumped off the sofa. The best thing she could do was go and work.

The battle cruiser felt like a ghost ship. She rattled around corridors normally busy with people coming and going. Only once did she encounter a group of fleeters in dress uniform, laughing and joking as they made their way down to the hangar bays where the transports ferried the crew down to the surface. She glanced over her shoulder at them as they filled the lift she'd just left. They looked like a bunch of college kids. She grinned. It wasn't a bad analogy; the ship was like a college during the summer vacation.

She strode on, her footfalls loud in the quiet. Down in the bowels of the ship, the door to the engineering section slid aside as she approached. Two bored techs sat at work stations, probably playing games judging by their quick movements to cover up whatever they were doing. The benches gleamed, devoid of tools and equipment, and empty chairs stood in front of blank screens.

The duty officer looked up from his office in the corner, eyebrows arching in surprise. "Morgan. What brings you here?" He came out to meet her.

"I thought I might go over the model again."

"You've thought of something?"

She smiled at the look of hope that spread over his face. He was one of the engineers who jostled for a chance to learn from her. "Not really. But if I take another look I might think of something."

"Did you know we brought your ship out of quarantine?" He stepped back and gestured over his shoulder through the window overlooking the hangar where ships undergoing maintenance were kept.

Curlew sat, squat and ugly, in a bay in the corner. Morgan's heart skipped a beat. She'd been here in Manesai space for a little over a year, by Manesai reckoning. A year since the experimental shift drive in that little freighter had malfunctioned, throwing her out of everything she had ever known into a distant place, another universe, another time. She swallowed the lump in her throat. Seeing it again brought back memories. Her last meeting with her boss, Admiral Makasa, as they ate dinner at a restaurant by the sea. She almost heard his dark chocolate voice telling her about the ship's experimental drive. *"Put it through its paces, Morgan. If this works, we can go anywhere in the galaxy; anywhere at all."* She'd put it through its paces, all right. The drive had been playing up before they'd reached Belsun Station, she didn't get a chance to finish fixing it there because of Jones and Tariq and their hare-brained smuggling scheme. And then they'd disappeared. But although the drive had malfunctioned, she was sure that the techs who had built the system were on the right track. If she could fix the drive, maybe she could even go... home. A shiver shimmied down her spine. She hadn't thought about home in months. Not that she wanted to go back there forever, but it would be nice to see Torreno again, meet some of her few friends.

Jarman's voice startled her. "I'd be happy to help. There's not much doing here." He looked like a puppy wanting to go for a walk. All he needed was the lead dangling out of his mouth.

She rested her hand on his shoulder for a moment. "I'll be sure to involve you where I can, Jarman." Then she pulled out a chair at a workstation. The gas hissed as she sat, accentuating the silence. She'd come here for some company. Oh, well. A final check of the model, then she might crawl over *Curlew* again. Maybe Lieutenant Jarman would like that.

She focused her attention on the data port, opening the connection with the processor in her brain. Part of her consciousness became a bright data highway, a procession of packets holding digital information. A thought brought up the schematic for the shift drive. For Jarman's benefit she directed the output to the visual projector in the lab where the device appeared in 3D detail. Hanging in midair, it looked so simple. But then, the best devices were simple, with few moving parts and elegant design. This one was no different, but somewhere, somehow, it was flawed. First things first. Check, yet again, that all the specs were right, the materials strong enough, the calculations correct.

As the processor in her implant worked on the calculations, her mind drifted, reliving old times. The beach at Torreno, night clubs with her friend Ella, her wedding to Alby. Huh. That had been a mistake. She'd learnt to dance on Miranda during one leave and then practiced with Coreb. She wondered where he'd be now, if he even knew she had gone missing somewhere out beyond the nebula they called Calisto's Veil. And then she'd met Ravindra. The love of her life. She shivered at the memory of his fingers on her skin, his lips on hers, his touch. She squirmed, her breath shortening.

Oh, bloody hell. I just can't concentrate.

The model hung in midair, motionless. Morgan broke the connection to the data port, leaned back in the chair and flung the nearest object to hand across the room. "Shit."

"Morgan?" Leila Peris stared at her, a data cube in her raised hand.

Oh, shit. That must've been what she'd thrown. "You caught that?"

Leila nodded.

"Sorry." Morgan lifted a hand. "Just letting out some frustration. What are you doing here? I thought you were on leave?"

Leila put the data cube back on Morgan's desk, leaning forward so she could lower her voice. "I heard you were still on the ship. You won't be joining the admiral?"

Morgan glanced at the two techs. They were bent over their screens. Not that it mattered. The whole ship had to be aware that she and Ravindra were a bit more than friends.

"Not tonight. He'll be celebrating with his men."

"Aren't you jealous?" Leila asked, propping a hip on the desk. They'd become friends, after a fashion. Leila was a promising engineer who had been involved in building and testing the model ship. She wasn't afraid to ask questions and wasn't afraid of Morgan.

Of course I'm not jealous. "No. I'm not the only woman in his life; never was, never will be. That's the way it is." Maybe a little bit jealous. But she was nothing if not pragmatic.

"Why don't you come with us? Girls' night out? We're going out for a really expensive dinner and then maybe to a club to do some dancing. All the local girls will be off trying to latch on to a fleeter so there are plenty of local guys to dance with. And don't worry if you can't dance. We can teach you."

Female company, a good dinner, some dancing. Yes, better than working by herself, mooning about Ravindra. Dancing. Yes, she could dance. The memory made her smile. Would Ravindra mind? Then again, did she care if he did? A resounding 'no' to that one. He lived his life, she lived hers.

"It sounds like fun, actually," she said at last. "Who else is going?"

"Bella Chantriss. You know her."

Morgan nodded. The doctor who'd treated her after her illness on Krystor.

"And two friends of mine, one from logistics and one from catering. Don't worry, I'll tell them not to ask too many questions."

Too many questions about her, or Ravindra. Leila had learnt that lesson in the past few weeks. She was a good sort. So a party of five, a girls' night out. "Okay. Let's do it."

"Great." Beaming, Leila stood. "We're meeting at bay B-14. Wear something pretty you can dance in."

"I'll be there."

Morgan watched her leave. Dinner and dancing. That's what she needed; to get away from here, do something different, recharge. And right now, she needed a shower and to pick an outfit.

She waved her fingers at Jarman as she bounced out of Engineering.

Back in her quarters she riffled through the dresses. All too staid and boring, designed for stuffy officers' messes, not for partying. She'd wear her flexi-dress, then she could adjust if she had to.

She connected her implant to the dress's tiny processor and selected blue, the color of the sky at dusk. The reflectors in the fabric shifted as instructed. For good measure she faded the color from dark at the neckline to a few shades lighter at the hem. She added some silver sprinkles here and there about the bodice. Mid-calf seemed to be the prevailing fashion, fitted at the waist, scoop neckline. She spun around in front of the mirror, watching the skirt flare. Fantastic. She was going to enjoy this. Clutching a purse, she headed for the door. Her comunit lay on the table. She paused, chewing on her lower lip.

Should she call him? And say what? I'm going out with a bunch of girls, will that be all right? *Oh, get real, Morgan. He's probably picking out his fancy right now. Let him have his rut with the rest of the boys.*

In bay B-14 Leila stood next to the airlock, looking out for her. "Come on, quick. Everybody else is in."

They closed the airlock hatch behind her before she'd even reached the ramp.

President Assarta had finally stopped speaking. Ravindra stood up to make the acceptance speech on behalf of the fleet. He'd be brief. Nobody wanted to listen to him, either.

"We are pleased to have been instrumental in ridding your planet of the threat you faced," he said. "And now I know my officers look forward to enjoying your hospitality."

He sat down to thunderous applause.

Ravindra glanced around the rectangle of tables at rows of men in white uniforms, talking and laughing, with many a look towards the main entrance to the room, where the dancers would enter. They were looking forward to it and they deserved it. Once the main rebel stronghold had been located, thanks to Morgan's stealth satellite technology, the campaign had been swift and brutal. A short war was a good war.

He swirled his glass, watching the liquor cling to the sides. Strange. Not so long ago he would have enjoyed one of these functions as much as the next man. Now? Morgan was up there, messing with a shift drive. He was sure she'd solve the problem, would have earlier if he hadn't diverted her skills onto the stealth technology. He was beginning to wish he'd insisted she come with him. They hadn't spent all that much time together in the last few weeks, what with the campaign. He understood her reluctance; she would have been one of the few women here and yes, most of them were a bunch of boring, self-important toadies. And after dinner, of course, all the women had left. All, that is, except the entertainers. They pranced in now, scantily dressed young women carrying scarves, pirouetting to a soft musical accompaniment.

He waved off the steward offering to refill his glass and watched dispassionately as they swayed and spun, weaving their scarves around their bodies, lithe and seductive. They didn't leave much to the imagination. Could Morgan dance? He didn't know, there had never been an opportunity.

Captain Lomandra leaned towards him. "Which one do you fancy?"

Ravindra turned to him, noting the glint in his eye, the way his thumb caressed the glass he held. The captain, at least, couldn't wait. "I hadn't really thought about it."

Lomandra's eyebrows shot up. He lifted one shoulder and turned away to watch the girls. They sprang in unison, backs arched, breasts straining against their gowns while their scarves floated behind them.

He should have brought her with him. They could have been in a hotel room by now, or back on the flagship making their own fun. He pulled his comunit off his belt and selected her ID. One of the dancers tried to wind a scarf around his neck. He waved her away and she ran her fingers through Lomandra's hair instead, insinuating herself onto his lap as she did so.

The call rang out.

He gazed at the unit in his hand. Poor connection? He stood and strode towards the exit.

Morgan gazed out of the taxi at tall towers ablaze with lights. Pedestrians jostled on the walkways and vehicles crawled along the streets. Quite a few uniforms were sprinkled amongst the crowd. The local businesses would be booming with a fleet this size in town. Everywhere advertising hoardings added their color. A vibrant city full of life and vigor, showing no signs of the civil war that had wracked the planet for years. That would be out in the back blocks, where the poorer people lived. The taxi passed an advertisement showing a new skimmer with a scantily-dressed young woman draped over the seats. Some things never changed whichever planet you were on, whichever society you were in. She wondered what the dancing girls would be wearing at Ravindra's boys own session. A damn sight less than the girl in the advertisement, she'd guess.

Their taxi pulled up outside an elegant two-story building not far from the central business district. Morgan waited on the pavement with the others while Bella paid the driver. A group of girls, their hair curled and striped in colors to match their short, tight dresses, minced past them.

"They'll be on their way to pick up a fleeter," said Madra, the lass from Catering.

Leila sighed, gazing after them. "I wish we could dye our hair in the Fleet."

Bella snorted. "It would cost you a fortune, especially if you went for yellow. Let's go eat." She led the way up the stairs, talking as she walked. "I looked up a few reviews of this place. It's won all sorts of prizes for food and wine and the service is meant to be the best."

An attractive young man wearing a dark red suit led them up the stairs to a private balcony on the first floor. A slight breeze stirred the potted plants, bringing with it the smells of food, perfume, foliage. So different from scrubbed, space ship air.

"Why don't we do the tasting menu?" Bella said. "I haven't eaten this world's food before. Has anybody else?" She looked around the table.

"That sounds like a great idea," Leila said. "Little bits of everything with matching wines."

Bella glanced through the wine list. "Everybody okay with white to start with?" She beckoned the hovering waiter. "We'll have one of those." She pointed at one of the entries.

"Here's to us, ladies," said Nali, raising her glass when the wine had been poured. Morgan remembered she was from logistics. Everybody raised their glass and drank. The wine was pleasant, fruity and fragrant.

"Is there wine where you come from?" Nali asked.

"Oh, yes," said Morgan. "Our cultures are similar in many respects. I'm looking forward to trying the food." Many, many respects. She rested her chin on her fist, remembering dinners shared with Makasa, and her good friend Carissa. She wondered where they were, what they were doing? Had Makasa found someone to replace her? Had Carissa made captain yet? She deserved to.

Morgan sat back and listened to the women talk about boyfriends and clothes and home worlds, so normal, so human. The sound of the city murmured a muted accompaniment, now and then highlighted by the whine of a vehicle passing by. All the while, the food came, small servings, exquisitely presented, with a different small glass of wine. Each time a new morsel came it generated discussion amongst the group, comparing and rating the food, deciding how it was prepared. Morgan drank moderately, conscious of the fact that they were going dancing later, and drank lots of water. The others did the same.

They split the bill between them, each of them transferring their share to Bella's card so she could pay. It had been a marvelous meal and, as the reviews had said, the service had been wonderful, attentive without being obtrusive. Bella asked the house master to organize a taxi for them, thanked him and left a generous tip.

"We're going to *Trimpathi's*," Leila said to the driver when the women had settled in the taxi. The fellow nodded, then entered the location into the skimmer's control. "It's a top dance club," Leila explained, "and uniforms are not allowed."

Morgan grinned. "Sounds good to me."

The taxi stopped outside an ornate pavilion, a spectacular concoction of curves and arches all glowing with color that rippled like water. The name *Trimpathi's* flashed and danced, letter by letter, across the arch. Very large men wearing beautifully cut suits stood discreetly near the doorway. Morgan was about to step forward when Bella caught her arm. "Hang on. Let's not get involved in that."

One of the doormen placed a massive hand on the shoulder of a uniformed fleeter approaching the entrance. "No uniforms. Sorry."

"What, d'you mean we can't go in?" The sergeant had had more than enough to drink, slurring his words.

"See the sign? No uniforms."

"Get your hands off me." The drunk squirmed, trying to shrug off the doorman's grip, his face contorted with effort. Without the big man seeming to do more than flick his hand, the fleeter sprawled backwards onto the pavement. "You bastard." He struggled up, his face red, his hands clenched into fists.

This was starting to look ugly. "Maybe we should do something," Morgan said.

Bella held her back, shaking her head.

The second fleeter had more sense and grabbed his companion's arm. "Let's go. There's plenty of other places that'll take our money."

Bella smiled, watching them weave their way down the street. "They'll have a headache tomorrow." She stepped forward. "Come on. Time for some dancing."

The bouncers stared at Morgan, eyes flicking over her golden-brown skin and silver eyes. Yes, different; unusual. She'd bet these two fellows were ex-troopers. They reminded her of Chief Abu Prakesh and his platoon on Krystor. She smiled up at both of them as she walked past them into the club.

Infectious dance music assailed her ears, accompanied by lights that changed with the beat, sweeping colored beams over the handful of couples gyrating on the dance floor at the bottom of a wide staircase. At this relatively early hour, the place was busy without being crowded, so the women were able to find an unoccupied booth on the top level, not too far from the stairs.

"Let's dance," said Leila, taking Morgan's hand.

Morgan tripped down the stairs with the others and took some impromptu lessons from Leila. Dancing was dancing, after all. She'd been a very good dancer back home. These were just new steps. She let the rhythm flow through her body, move her legs, her feet, her arms.

Leila leaned toward her, eyes sparkling. "Gee, you're good."

Morgan grinned as the joy of the dance rippled through her being. She pranced, then spun, tight and fast. The music paused and she stopped, panting, waiting for the next tune.

"Care to dance, *Suri*?"

Morgan looked up at a good-looking young man with green eyes. Why not? That was why she'd come, after all. This was fun.

In the foyer Ravindra tried again. The call connected but she didn't answer. What the hell was she doing? Pacing the floor, he switched the call to his security guard on *Vidhvansaka*.

"Check her room."

The reply came back in minutes. "She's not there, *Srimana*, but we found her comunit on the table."

This wasn't right. If anything had happened to her... But how could it? She worked on the ship surrounded by people she knew.

"Go and find her. Now."

He should have made her come with him. Perhaps something had happened. There were always *Bunyada* sympathizers on ships. What if they'd waylaid her, drugged her, smuggled her off the ship?

A call from the ship interrupted his thoughts.

"Well?" His heart beat faster.

"She's left the ship, *Srimana*, with a group of officers. They went planetside about three hours ago."

Three hours? Three blasted hours? After telling him she was going to work on the shift drive. Oh, she'd be sorry. But then again... Sick apprehension replaced anger. Last time she'd gone down to a planet without permission she'd been abducted.

"Which officers?"

"There's a list on your comunit, *Srimana*."

Ravindra's eyes flicked over the list as it appeared. All female. The most senior was Bella Chantriss, a commander in the medical center.

"Have you tried calling them?"

"Yes, *Srimana*, I have. No reply from Commander Chantriss. I thought it best not to try too many of them."

No. If anything has happened to her, he'd rather the abductors didn't know that people were searching. *Oh, Morgan, you foolish, foolish idiot.*

"Find out where they are."

"We're on that already, *Srimana*. If you'll hold, we're analyzing the coordinates now."

He waited, his mind filled with images. Morgan drugged, carted off who knew where. Asbarthi might be dead but his movement lived on. Worse, the knowledge about the Krystor Temple had leaked. One of the leaders of the uprising here had been adamant. Proof that the Vesha were the equals of the Mirka, somewhere on Krystor. They didn't have the details but the knowledge couldn't be kept quiet forever. That 'Orionar Queen' tag hadn't gone away, either. He'd been asked about it several times at the civic reception.

"Commander Chantriss's comunit is in a dance club in Vestro's entertainment district. It's called *Trimpathi's*."

"Have it checked. Use the locals. Find out if *Suri* Selwood is there and what might be happening."

When he got his hands on her, he'd he'd... If she was all right. If she wasn't, he'd find somebody to kill.

He caught the eye of the lieutenant in charge of his personal guard unit. "Get me a skimmer and ten troopers, Lieutenant. Immediately. And put a gunship on alert." Ravindra started towards the door. "We're heading for a place called *Trimpathi's*."

"The dance club, *Srimana*?"

"We're not going dancing."

Ravindra ordered the skimmer stopped in a street close to the club. He sat in the back seat, drumming his fingers irritably on the arm rest. Local, plain clothes agents had moved immediately to enter the premises.

His comunit chirped.

"Yes?"

"They're all here, Admiral. It appears to be above board. She's on the floor, dancing."

He let out a breath, relief flooding through him. Safe. Safe and well. Thank the spirit. But dancing. With somebody? With another man?

"Dancing? Who with?"

"A local. Do you want us to detain him?"

"No. I'll deal with it myself."

He closed the comunit with a snap and ordered the skimmer to the club, his body hot and tense. She lied to him, saw him off with a story and skulked off with a bunch of women to party. The car had hardly stopped moving when he was out, striding toward the entrance to the club.

"Sorry friend, no uniforms." The bouncer peeled himself away from the wall, one massive arm outstretched.

Ravindra skewered the fellow with a glare. "Get out of my way."

The man blinked, hesitated, his arm still outstretched to block. Ravindra slapped his arm away and kept walking. He heard the click of an assault rifle being readied and one of his guards said, "I'm sure the admiral won't be long."

Music assaulted Ravindra's ears, pulsing into his brain. How they could stand this noise for any time was beyond him. Standing at the top of the stairs for a moment to get used to the strobing lights, he scanned the crowd below.

She was dancing with some fellow, holding his hand, his arm around her waist. Smiling, having fun. And where was that to have ended? Well, it was going to end now.

He stalked down the steps onto the dance floor, and shoved through the crowd to Morgan. The blue dress swirled about her as she laughed with the young man who held her hand. He scooped her up with one arm around her waist. She resisted for a moment but even before she'd looked up at him, startled, she'd relaxed in his grip, recognizing who was holding her.

"Hey, she's with me," said the boy she'd been dancing with.

"Is that so?" He flicked a glance at one of the troopers who'd followed him.

The trooper pointed his weapon at the lad. "Upstairs."

"Oh, don't," Morgan said. "He's just a kid I was dancing with."

"You can explain on the way back to *Vidhvansaka*." He grasped her wrist in a none-too-gentle grip and towed her towards the stairs.

Outside the club the young man who had been dancing with Morgan waited next to the skimmer, tense and nervous. Spectators had gathered, surrounding the vehicle at a respectful distance. Curious club-goers who had followed them up the stairs swelled the ranks.

Ravindra released his grip on Morgan and, arms folded, stared down at the youth. He wasn't much more than a kid, round-eyed, his chest rising and falling rapidly, lips parted, his eyes shifting from time to time to the assault rifle in the guard's hands. She could prefer this stripling to him?

"So. She's with you is she?"

"Look, I just danced with her. I only just met her. I don't even know her name." He babbled the words.

"Oh, for pity's sake. He's not involved in this." Morgan's fingers gripped his arm. "I was just dancing with him. Let him go. Please."

"Dancing... and then what? A victory party?" The very thought bubbled in his gut, bitter as bile. Morgan with this. With anybody.

"Oh, you don't think..." She gasped. "You do. You think I'd..." Her brows lowered, her back straightened and the ice fire blazed in her silver eyes.

She leaned towards him, her voice lowered. "You think I'd, I'd... have it off with this... this kid." She was as furious as he was now. "This is between you and me. It's got nothing to do with him."

She jabbed her finger at the young man. "Let him go and deal with me!" She pointed her finger back at herself.

"Oh, I'll deal with you."

She was right. He was venting his fury on a victim of circumstance.

"Get in the skimmer," he snapped at Morgan.

Her nostrils flared, her lips a straight line. She didn't move, her eyes fixed on his, a picture of insolence.

"Now."

Still scowling, she slipped into the back seat.

Now for this young pup, shaking in his boots. "You have his details?" he asked the lieutenant, jerking his head at the young man.

"*Srimana.*"

"Release him."

The lad scurried off, walking as fast as he could and almost running around the nearest corner.

"Lieutenant, we return to *Vidhvansaka*." Ravindra followed Morgan into the back of the vehicle.

She sat stony faced, arms folded.

Ravindra made sure the privacy screen was turned on. "Well?"

"Well what? Can't I go out and have dinner with the girls?"

"*Not* without telling me. *Not* after you'd told me you were staying on the ship and *certainly not* without taking your comunit with you."

She just glared at him, her jaw set.

"And it wasn't just dinner with the girls. How was this dancing party meant to end? Hmm?"

"I can't believe you'd seriously think that I'd have a casual fuck with that... kid. I'm hardly desperate."

"How should I know? We haven't had much time together lately, have we?" It was low. He could hardly believe he'd said the words.

Her nostrils flared. "And whose fault is that?"

"There was a war on. Don't change the subject. You sell me a story about not liking crowds and there you are in the middle of a crowd denser than the market place at Hrkensa on a fair day."

"I was dancing. That's all. After a lovely dinner with a bunch of *your* female officers. I do not see your problem." She rasped the words out between gritted teeth.

Recalcitrant, contrary, obstinate, unreasonable bitch.

"Do you have any notion what I've been through in the last hour? Do you remember what happened at Electra when you took a little unscheduled visit to a planet without permission? Do you? I sure as hell do. It was months before I got you back. Months. Do you think that because Asbarthi is dead that *Bunyada* is finished? I've been sick with worry and you come out with some half-assed rubbish about a night with the girls."

"But it's all right for you to enjoy yourself with a couple of grateful virgins young enough to be your daughter?" She sneered. "I've heard about these things."

He leaned back. "I asked you to come with me. I wanted you to come with me."

She tossed her head. "Oh, sure. I knew better than to get in your way."

"What do you mean get in my way?"

"You know. The male bonding thing. The victory celebration. Boys being boys. Allowing the ladies to show their gratitude."

She stared straight ahead, her lips a straight line.

So that was it. The anger drained away, just a little. "If you weren't here, I probably would have joined in with the rest, yes."

"There you are. That's what I mean. I have no hold over you. There's no reason why you shouldn't. And there's no reason why

I shouldn't have a night out with the girls." She looked away, the fingers of her right hand clenching and unclenching on her left arm. He took a deep breath. Anger wasn't going to work, not with her.

"Yes, you can have a night with the girls. But tell me, Morgan. Or better still, next time come with me. We could have been having our own dance party in a hotel room by now. You think I'd rather screw some nameless whore than make love with you?"

The skimmer drifted to a halt outside the entrance to the space port and the doors slid apart with a soft sigh. The waiting guards slammed to attention.

She hesitated, pulling at her lip with her teeth. "You didn't? You didn't even want to?"

He sighed. "I love you. Why do you find that so hard to understand? I know I don't always tell you. I'm a man. But believe me, it's true."

She nodded, a half smile curving her lips. "Looks like I owe you an apology." She slid out of the car.

Ravindra alighted from his side and joined her, putting a possessive arm around her waist. This was sounding a little better.

"Be assured, my dear," he said, leaning close over her, "you'll be apologizing more than once."

"Give me ten minutes?" Morgan asked when they arrived at the door of his quarters.

"What for?"

"I just want to freshen up, change."

"Why?"

"Well, I thought maybe, since you were interrupted while the girls were dancing, you might like me to dance for you." A hint of a smile lurked around her lips, a glint lit her silver eyes.

"You can dance? Like that?"

She nodded. "I learnt how. Just for fun. Some of my, er... boyfriends enjoyed the show. You might, too."

Oh, my word. He could imagine her doing something like that. She certainly had the body, lithe and athletic. But to dance like the girls at the Presidential Palace, light and fluttery? Somehow he didn't think so. A sensual shiver slithered down into his groin. This could be interesting.

"Ten minutes. I'll be counting."

He watched her until the door closed behind her before he entered his own quarters. Ten minutes. He kicked off his boots, hung up his jacket and poured himself a brandy, stiff with anticipation. Glass in hand, he settled on the couch in his shirt sleeves. He was looking forward to this.

She stepped inside two minutes late.

She wore a robe over the dress and when she took it off he could see why. It was translucent and clung to her body, sculpting it and softening the outlines although she was quite obviously naked beneath it. He squirmed in his seat. Right now all he wanted was sex.

"You don't have to dance."

She smiled at him, her eyes sultry and seductive. "I want to. It'll be worth it."

The music began. Tribal, primeval, its rhythm the double beat of a heart, steady and repetitive: da dum... da dum... da dum, the tempo slow.

Standing on her toes she arched her back, ran her hands up and through her hair, and let it fall through her fingers in a heavy cascade. She swayed, her body becoming an instrument for the music, fluid and graceful. The tempo built up, a sensual, erotic melody overlay the heart beat beneath. She flowed with the phrasing, sensual and seductive, weaving a pattern around herself with hands and hips, belly and thighs and breasts. The dance promised and whispered, beckoned and teased. Her hands slid down her thighs or up the back of her neck, where she pushed her hair up, to let it flow down around her shoulders. Her fingers wove their own tapestry.

The garment was open at the front, held in place only by a silver belt at the waist. He could see the curve of her breasts, her nipples taut against the translucent material, a tantalizing flash of bare thigh as she moved, silk on tawny skin. The soft mound between her thighs beckoned.

He swallowed and stirred in his seat, his breath shortening. His cock was so hard it hurt, shoving against his trousers. Much more of this and he'd come in his pants. *Oh, gods, Morgan, enough.* He stood, ripped his shirt off and reached out for her. He'd fuck her here, here on the couch, fuck her senseless.

She danced on, aware of his presence but ignoring him.

No. His chest heaved as he sucked air into his lungs. No, this wasn't about a casual fuck, however passionate. It wasn't what he wanted from her. She was no houri dancing for any man's whim; she danced for him, giving herself to him to do with as he willed. This dance was an apology and a surrender, woven into an erotic fantasy. He would make her quiver, make her ache with lust just as she had done to him.

His hands on her thighs, he drew her against him so that her back was to his chest, and slid his hands slowly up her body, pushing the dress aside, her silk smooth skin beneath his fingers. Her body tightened at his touch. When he cupped her breasts she gasped and leant her head back against his shoulder. Fondling her erect nipples, he buried his mouth against her neck underneath the thick, dark hair. Lust raged through him as he rubbed himself against her. Careful. Too much of this and he'd be finished.

He turned her to face him and lifted her up from the waist, holding her so that his lips could touch her belly, then lowered her, tasting the salt tang of her skin all the way, until his mouth closed over her nipple, sucking and flicking with his tongue. She groaned in response, murmured his name, fingers clutching his hair. He let her slip a little lower until, clutching her tightly against his hips, he could kiss her. She clung to him, legs, arms, lips. They swayed together, the music throbbing in his brain.

He carried her to the bedroom, where he slipped the dress off her body and shrugged off the rest of his clothes. He knelt on the bed, buttocks on his heels and pulled her towards him. Facing him, knees on each side of his thighs, she lowered herself onto him. Delicious. Warm and slippery wet. He fought the urge to thrust. Not yet; not yet.

She whispered something in her own language and then his mouth closed over hers. The music continued its rhythm, sensual and erotic and he let it flow through him as it had flowed through her, moving them both in an ancient dance with intricate steps and delicious harmonies, her arms wrapped around him, her voice sighing her pleasure, her fingers tracing his body.

He owned her, he possessed her, she was his. The music changed and he leaned her backwards until she lay on the bed looking up at him. The rhythm became faster, deeper, her fingers gripping tighter, her body arching harder. Now he thrust deep, as deep as he could. She raised her knees, gripped his body with her thighs. Oh, yes. Deeper. The blood pounded in his brain, matching the music. She gasped, moaned, writhed beneath him as the flood gates of passion burst for them both.

It was a long time before either of them stirred.

"That's not what I expected," she murmured at last.

"Is that a complaint?" He rolled onto his side, supporting his head on an elbow.

"No. That was very, very beautiful."

He stroked her face with his fingers and she moved her head to brush his fingertips with her lips. This certainly beat a quick fuck with a dancing girl. But then... she'd danced before, she said. He didn't like that notion. Not at all.

"How many times have you done this dance?"

"Once. But it wasn't like this. This was very special. With Coreb it was nice but..." she shook her head.

"Coreb." He almost snarled the word.

She smiled. "His name is Coreb Jenson and he's ten years younger than me. He's quite tall, but not as tall as you, black skin, broad nose, thick lips, black, curly hair, not a bad body and he's pretty good at sex. Apart from that we had absolutely nothing in common. I didn't love him, he didn't love me."

His stomach squirmed with jealousy. Morgan doing something like this with another man. "How could you do this dance for a man you didn't love?"

Morgan was silent for a moment. "Oh, you can. The dance is different every time you do it. You try to discern what your man wants and you give it to him. Coreb wanted fast fun."

"And what did I want?"

She smiled, looking deep into his eyes. "You wanted to dominate me, own me. And I guess I was apologizing..." she paused, searching for words. "I was wrong about a number of things. To be honest, I expected it to be out there on the sofa, fast and furious."

"It did cross my mind," he admitted. "But I wanted rather more than a quick release." He wanted to own her. He wanted for her never, ever to countenance dancing for anyone but him.

"So I gathered. I love you, Ashkar. But you'll never own me. What I give you, I give willingly."

He nodded. "So you'll marry me?"

She half sat up, staring at him. "Marry you?"

"Yes. It's a Manesai custom. A man and a woman bind themselves to each other in front of family and friends." He couldn't keep the irony out of his voice.

"But your marriages are arranged. Family to family. It's got nothing to do with love."

He shook his head. "I'm a grown man, my parents have no say in who I wish to marry now my wife has passed on. And I've done my duty to the family line, produced a son and a daughter. I want to marry you."

She sank back onto the bed. "I love you desperately, Ashkar. But I'd be the wrong wife for you. You'd offend all those admirals offering you their daughters."

"I've already done that."

"Oh."

"Yes. Three out-and-out proposals. And I've ignored quite a number of indirect propositions. I'm not in the market." He grinned. He'd said those words and they were so right. The woman he loved lay beside him.

"Ashkar, you can't be married to an alien. Imagine what a field day the gossip mongers would have."

"I don't care."

She tilted her body so she could meet his gaze. "I do. You'll be grand admiral, I'm sure of it. If I'm not holding you back. Look, they accept our relationship because we don't advertize it. But marriage?"

He slid an arm around her, holding her tight to his side. She smelled of sex and sweat and a hint of her favorite perfume. He'd never loved her more. "They'll get over it."

"Please, let it go. I'm very happy with how things stand. Please?"

He felt the tension in her body. She meant what she said. But so did he. This was a subtle form of warfare, or perhaps diplomacy. He would have to persuade her, win her over to his position. Time to retire gracefully, and regroup. He gathered her up, aware of parted lips close to his, her breast against his chest, her beautiful, silver eyes imploring him. "If you're happy, I'm happy."

He met those luscious lips with his own.

Ravindra stretched his shoulders and wished the chairs in these conference rooms were a bit more comfortable. He'd fielded the questions from his senior admirals, anxious to know what had happened the previous evening. He hadn't gone into detail but the knowing smirks said it all. They were happy; only President Assarta to go. Speaking of which, here was the man himself with his entourage of lackeys. Ravindra stood and bowed.

"Good morning to you, Admiral," said Assarta, returning the gesture. "I trust you all enjoyed your evening, officers," he said to the room at large. "And I understand you retrieved your lady safely?"

"I did, Mister President."

"There was some... ah... fuss, I understand? Armed troops in an innocent nightclub?" He waited, clever eyes on Ravindra's face. He already knew all this.

If he was expecting an apology it would not be forthcoming. "Unfortunate, I know. We had reason to believe that *Suri* Selwood was in danger. But my public relations people have already explained this have they not? And apologized for the inconvenience caused?"

"Mister Trimpathi—the owner of the nightclub—is a well-respected businessman here." Assarta's voice held a note of reproach.

And a generous supporter of Assarta's Mirka faction. "I assure you, his business won't suffer. Quite the reverse. The place will have added popularity. And the lads *Suri* Selwood danced with... they'll have a story to tell their grandchildren."

"True," conceded Assarta, lips pursed. "Not every man can claim to have danced with the Orionar Queen." His eyes glittered with a hint of malice. He knew what had happened on Krystor and he probably knew about the temple, too. So many leaks.

"Without her your local war would still be unfinished."

Assarta raised an eyebrow. "And when will we have the opportunity to meet this remarkable woman?"

"She'll be joining me for this evening's ball."

"Ah. Excellent. Well now. Let's move on to the agenda items."

Ravindra took the opportunity for a quiet word with Prasad during the morning break, leading him away from the other delegates and out onto a balcony with a murmured excuse. The city basked in sunshine, the sky clear and transparent, a slight breeze stirring the flags on their poles. A far off glitter betrayed the snow caps on the distant peaks, and a bright glare low on the horizon was the second of this system's twin suns.

Ravindra leaned on the balustrade, one foot propped up on the lower rail. "I want you to investigate, Prasad. This whole business with Morgan smells wrong."

"How did she get off the ship without an escort?"

Ravindra grunted. "It seems Morgan explained that she was going out with a group of Fleet officers and wasn't that escort enough?"

"Ah. That was a mistake."

"Not one those troopers will make again. They're already off the ship. After what happened last time she went off on her own..." He took in a deep breath and blew it out again, then shifted his position, turning so that he had his back to the railing, his arms folded. "It all seems to have been very innocent but..." he shook his head and frowned. "Look at anything you can lay your hands on about that night—the restaurant, the nightclub, the shuttle flight down." He gazed out across the city. "I don't know. Maybe I'm being paranoid, but she's such a prize. We've only just started to scratch the surface of what she can do. Asbarthi may be dead but *Bunyada* isn't."

"She is. I think if I was *Bunyada*, I'd be trying again."

Chairs scraped in the conference room. "Report to me as soon as you have something."

"*Srimana*." Prasad bowed.

Ravindra returned to the conference as the intelligence chief slipped out the doors.

Eyes still closed, Morgan wiggled her nose and breathed in deeply. Ravindra's bed, but he was gone. She sighed, stretched and yawned. What a night. What a spectacular, magnificent night it had been. After that first glorious union, she had slept until, aroused and wanting, he had woken her with kisses and caresses from erotic dreams into reality. Her orgasm had rippled through her body like a seismic wave, shaking her to her core, as she gasped beneath him, arms around his shoulders.

She sat up in bed and put her arms around her knees, her hair hanging down around her face. She still felt stupid and guilty about her night out with the girls and yet she'd been touched more than she realized by the depth of his concern. She had to admit that she wouldn't have imagined he'd care so much. Enough to want to marry her. That would have been silly. He deserved to be their grand admiral but with her as his consort... She shook her head. No. Even though they both knew she wasn't really an alien, nobody was going to believe it. They'd point at her hair and her eyes and how weak she was. She was glad they'd put *that* notion to bed.

She stretched her shoulders, wincing a little as sore muscles complained. Out of practice. Still, the dance had been a spectacular success, two bodies moving together, working to the music in a way she could never have imagined. The routine had certainly never been designed as a duet.

"Oh."

That was it. The shift drive. What if the interlocking parts of the motivator didn't quite dance to the same tune? She leapt out of bed. This was something she could work on.

Morgan ran a hand through her hair as she walked along the passage to Ravindra's office. She'd been summoned, but by his clerk. And he wasn't taking her calls. He wasn't even supposed to be here. What the hell was going on? Oh, well. She'd find out soon enough. And at least she could tell him they were almost ready for another test of the shift drive. She grinned. And this time she reckoned it would work.

Ravindra's office door opened as she approached. He sat behind his desk, his hands steepled in front of him. Prasad, standing facing the door, offered her a neck bow.

"What's going on?" she asked. "I thought you were staying planetside for the ball?"

"I want you to be present for a small ceremony." Ravindra rose and walked around to stand behind her. A glance at his face was enough to tell her not to ask questions.

A moment later Leila Peris entered, flanked by two guards. Her eyes slid to Morgan for a moment and then she saluted Ravindra, head respectfully bowed. "*Srimana.*"

She was nervous, but then you'd expect she would be, dragged into the admiral's office.

Prasad stood in front of the girl. "Lieutenant Peris, you are under arrest for treason against the Manesai Union, in particular for conspiring to kidnap *Suri* Selwood."

Morgan started. "What are you saying? That's ridiculous."

She made to step forward but Ravindra laid his hand on her shoulder. "It's true. Watch."

Judging by Leila's reaction, it was true. The fear beamed off her, bright as a beacon but she managed to shake her head. "That's rubbish."

Prasad put a data card into the reader on Ravindra's desk. "Is it?"

Morgan recognized the nightclub, *Trimpathi's*. The grainy security footage showed Ravindra shoving through the dancers to collect Morgan, showed the crowd following behind as he dragged her up the stairs. A few moments later, the people returned, coming back down in small groups, chatting and laughing. Morgan recognized all the women from the group she had been with, saw them collect their things and leave.

"I was fetched, they left. So what?"

"Keep watching," said Ravindra.

Leila, coming back. Leila meeting someone, someone who put an arm around her.

Morgan turned to stare up at Ravindra. "So she met somebody. I still don't see the point?"

"It's *who* she met," he said. "This man is a local *Bunyada* operative. We found out about him from the rebel data we obtained when we seized their headquarters."

Bunyada. Again. Morgan's legs trembled. It was all she could do not to sway.

"He is under arrest," said Prasad softly, smiling slightly, a nasty, satisfied smile as Leila started. "We caught him yesterday."

The room fell silent, except for the sound of Morgan's breathing, her chest heaving. Leila stared at the floor.

"I thought we were friends," Morgan said. "I guess I should have known better." The disappointment was a bitter taste in her mouth.

"We are friends." Leila raised her chin, staring at Ravindra for a moment. "I don't care what you do to me. But you, Morgan. You don't want to work for them, these Mirka oppressors. All we want is freedom to govern ourselves. We're equals, we Vesha and the Mirka. We know you found evidence on Krystor." She flung out an arm pointing a finger at Ravindra. "But he... he has covered it up. You must see. They're trying to hide our past from us, prevent us from learning the—"

"That's enough," Ravindra snapped. "Prasad. Take her away."

The guards gripped Leila's arms, one on each side, and marched her out, Prasad following.

Morgan leaned back against Ravindra's chest, feeling the warmth of his body. He slid an arm around her waist. "All right?"

"Yes. Huh. And here I was thinking she really liked me."

"Perhaps she did. But the point is, my love, you are a target. And you will continue to be."

"Yes, yes. Point made and understood. Was it just her? Not the others?"

"Just her. And her boyfriend."

That at least offered a small sense of relief.

"What was the plan?" she asked, turning to look at him.

"They were going to drug you—all of you, spike your drinks so you appeared to be drunk."

"All of us?"

"Except Peris, of course. Then she and her friend would have helped you out of the place."

"And then?"

"We can only guess."

She sighed. "When did you know all this?"

"Today. Prasad contacted me when they'd caught Peris's friend." He urged her toward the door to his quarters. "Come. I'll pour you a drink."

They sat on the couch together, Morgan's head on his shoulder, grateful for his warmth, his hard strength. "At least I have some good news. I think I've solved the problem with the shift drive."

She felt him straighten. "Have you indeed."

"Mmm. Have you really been keeping all the Krystor Temple revelations from the people?"

He sipped his brandy. "There's so little to go on. You've seen what happens if the wrong people get even a sniff of something they can use. The Orionar Queen?"

She snorted.

"And yet," he said softly, "our people should know where they came from. If we can find the evidence to show them. Maybe forge links with their ancestors. If you've fixed that remarkable shift drive, perhaps we have the means as well as a route to follow."

Morgan put her glass back on the table and turned to gaze into his eyes. "You want to go back."

He nodded. "Follow the trail. Backtrack Artemis and take it from there. We *must* come from the same stock."

She still had lingering regrets that they'd had to destroy Artemis, the massive ship with its fabled Artificial Intelligence. She could have learnt so much if the AI hadn't been insane. But Artemis had shown her the route she'd taken through the galaxy, from what became the Coalition. Morgan had the data in her implant. It would take too long with a normal shift drive, but with the one she was developing?

Excitement bubbled. Go home, at least to see. "Will you come?"

He nodded. "I'll persuade the High Command or I'll take leave of absence. We can find out where Artemis came from and maybe track down the man in the temple."

Maybe. A man thousands of years dead. But they had some clues; the star system in the temple, the man's DNA, the feline.

"Oh, man." She flung her arms around his neck and kissed him, molding against his body. He shifted, sliding his fingers into her hair, his tongue thrusting between her lips. He tasted of brandy.

He dragged himself away with a groan. "We have a ball to attend." Panting, he waved her away. "Go and get ready. We're going to have a lot to talk about in bed."

She stood and smiled down at him. "Talk?"

He rose and smacked her gently on the butt. "In due course. Off you go. And that's an order."

Grinning, she bowed her head. "As you order, *Srimana.*"

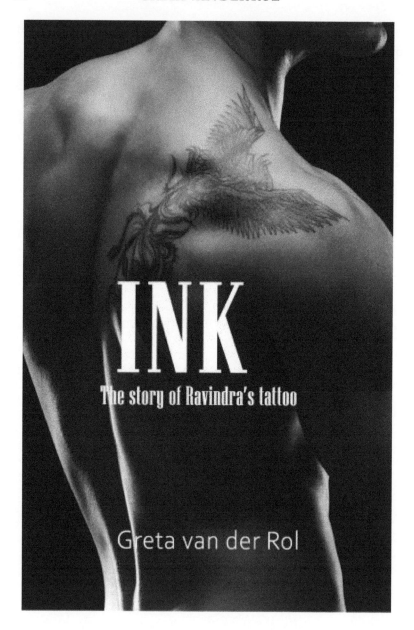

INK

The story of Ravindra's tattoo

Greta van der Rol

Ink

Admiral Ravindra was always an unconventional officer. That was why he'd been banished to the outer parts of Manesai space where he encountered Morgan Selwood in her disabled ship. He has an excellent pedigree and is very good at his job, but he has ignored convention. For instance, he has a tattoo, something a man of his class should never, never have.

This story gave me an opportunity to consider Ravindra's origins, just as I had for Morgan in Supertech. How did Ravindra acquire that tattoo?

I have to say – I love this story. I hope you do, too.

Ink has been published separately.

Life's good for 18-year-old Ashkar Ravindra. School's over, and he's been accepted into the Fleet Academy. There's time for one last trip up into the mountains in the brand new flitter his father gave him as a graduation present, before his real life, the one he's been groomed for from the day he was born, begins in earnest.

Up in the mountains not everyone is pleased to see the privileged admiral's son. Jealousy and ulterior motives turn the pleasant hunting trip into an ordeal. Lives are a stake. If Ashkar makes the wrong decision, he will be the first to die.

Captain Torbane read through the charges one more time. Basically, it boiled down to conduct unbecoming. A senior cadet in hospital with concussion, four others with cuts and abrasions received in a brawl. Certainly Lieutenant Herssun was quite correct in meting out discipline, but his recommendation to expel the lad as unfit seemed totally out of proportion, especially when it was Admiral Shivu Ravindra's son. Torbane was beginning to wonder about Herrsun. The man was competent enough, if a little bit too wedded to 'tradition' and 'rules'. Torbane re-read the note at the bottom of the indictment. The fight had been about a tattoo. What in the Goddess's holy name would have possessed the son of a *Darya* family to get a tattoo? Herrsun hadn't given any explanation.

He sighed. Only one way to find out.

Holding down the intercom which connected him with his clerk in the reception area, he said, "Send him in."

Torbane sat back in his chair, fists lying on the desk in front of him, his gaze fixed on the door, which slid aside. The cadet marched in, a tall, rangy lad, not yet grown into his height. He performed an immaculate right turn, two steps forward, halted, then pivoted to stand precisely halfway along the length of Torbane's desk, facing the captain. The salute was absolutely regulation.

"Cadet Ravindra, sir."

The cadet's face was devoid of expression, his gaze directed at a point on the wall behind Torbane. The commandant deliberately kept that wall bare so there was nothing to look at, but Ravindra must have found a dust spot or something. High cheekbones, amber eyes, a finely sculpted mouth. His features might have been carved from stone.

Torbane looked down at the report on his desk, then up at the cadet. "You've managed to cause something of a fuss in the few short weeks you've been here."

"With respect, sir, I simply defended myself."

Deep voice, still no eye contact. Willing to take his punishment.

"Senior Cadet Peshwaran is in hospital with concussion."

A barely perceptible shrug. "I tried not to injure him. If he'd known how to fall, he wouldn't have been hurt."

Arrogant, but an uncontrived arrogance. No regret, a mere statement of fact. This boy had talent with a capital T. But Torbane couldn't avoid the issue of a tattoo. It wasn't in the rule book, but Mirka officers, especially those hoping to become senior officers, did not wear tattoos. More to the point, Ravindra had drawn attention to himself in the worst possible way. Bully boys like Peshwaran probably deserved a dive into a wall but there would be others. Always.

Still, perhaps Torbane could insist the tattoo be removed, or masked in some way. "Show me this tattoo."

For a moment Ravindra didn't move, his face still, then his lips jerked into a brief, humorless smile. He slid a hand down the fastenings on his long-sleeved shirt, then pulled the garment off and draped it around the back of the visitor's chair beside him. Bare from the waist he pivoted, graceful as a dancer, displaying wide shoulders tapering to a narrow waist. The whole of his right shoulder was covered in lines that trailed down his back.

Torbane shook his head. Brainless, stupid boy. He'd hoped for something subtle, something he could ignore, or accept with a reprimand. Although he couldn't argue the tattoo was a work of art, some sort of flying beast, its wings raised, a crested, cruel-beaked head looking to the right, the elaborate tail curving around Ravindra's back. The lines almost glowed against the lad's dark skin.

"About face."

Ravindra turned around, his gaze fixed on that spot above Torbane's head again. He stood at attention. No. Many cadets had stood at attention in that spot. Most had been rigid, about as flexible as a metal rod. This man/boy was calm, comfortable with his stance.

"What in the Goddess's holy name possessed you to have something like that done? You're the son of an admiral."

For the first time Ravindra's gaze met his, a deep, penetrating stare. "I know the unwritten rule, sir. But it is a tradition, not a rule."

Torbane leaned forward, his elbows on his desk, his fingers interlaced. He suspected this cadet knew exactly what he'd burdened himself with. But why? He unfolded his hands just long enough to point a finger at his visitor's chair. "Sit."

Ravindra blinked and Torbane suppressed a grin. At last, he'd managed to unsettle the lad. But the cadet did as he was told, seating himself with hands in his lap.

"Tell me about this tattoo. Where did you get it? Why? Because I'm sure you know that you've marked yourself for life as a rebel, somebody who doesn't toe the line."

Amber eyes stared at him. "It's a vulsaur, a beast that lives in —"

Torbane lifted his hand. "I don't care *what* it is. Why? Clearly after you had the medical for the Fleet Academy, because there's no mention of it."

Ravindra licked his lips.

"Just tell me the story, boy. Start at the beginning."

RAVINDRA GUNNED HIS BRAND NEW FLITTER around the winding river valley, dodging fallen logs and spurs of rock, the adrenalin spiking with each jerk of the steering column. Steady, now. He settled his heart rate and slowed the little vehicle down. Razza had warned him more than once about roaring into the village like a river monster's spawn. When he reached the waterfall he veered right, over the wide expanse of water to the clearing where the Kotara village stood beside the lake, a cluster of squat stone buildings, the melting frost on the slate roofs glinting in the early morning sunlight.

He landed the flitter in the clearing between the trees, collected his pack from the seat and vaulted onto the grass. The last flowers of springtime littered the ground, a few more drifted in the air from branches thick with bright golden leaves. School was over. Six more weeks and his real life would begin, a cadet at the Fleet Academy. For now, he'd have one last trek with Razza, one last journey up the mountain, a fitting farewell to boyhood.

The grin on his face matching the joy in his heart, he half walked, half jogged into the village. He hadn't quite reached the outskirts when a figured stepped into his path from behind a tree. He had to shuffle through his memories to remember the fellow's name. Jaddu, that was it. The powerfully built young hunter was a year or two older than him, not quite as tall but more than making up for it in bulk and muscle. He stood with his arms folded, his eyes narrowed.

"What are you doing here? Shouldn't you be at school with the rest of your Mirka princelings?"

Ravindra slowed to a halt. Jaddu wasn't alone. Three smirking youths lounged in the shadows behind him, pretending nonchalance, spoiling for a fight. "I've finished with school." He stepped sideways, intending to move around Jaddu.

The other man mirrored his move, blocking his way. "Here to see Selinel, I expect. I think you should leave our women alone and bugger off back to your manor house."

Selinel. Last summer she'd shared his bed at Razza's house, and then he'd seen her a few times in school breaks. It had been her idea, although he hadn't needed much persuasion. She was pretty, he'd enjoyed himself but she was starting to become too clingy. Even so, it had nothing to do with this young lout. "Your women make their own choices. Get out of my way. I'm here to see Razza."

"Yeah?" Jaddu dropped the casual stance, flicking out a brawny arm to stop Ravindra. Behind him, his three friends straightened. "You get back in your fancy flitter, and I'll tell Razza Daddy called you away."

When you must fight, make your attack fast and meaningful. Ravindra had that lesson banged into him in his self-defense classes at school. Grasping Jaddu's arm with both hands, he pivoted, swinging his opponent over his shoulder and onto the ground. He swung around, blocking a punch from a second attacker, and managed to trip a third but four was one too many. A fist landed in his gut, leaving him winded. A kick to the back of the knee toppled him, ugly laughter ringing in his ears. A boot struck his back, just below the rib cage. He rolled, trying to protect his head.

"Let him be, let him be." Jaddu shouted to be heard. Hands hauled Ravindra to his feet.

Held between the two larger men, tasting blood and grit in his mouth, Ravindra glowered at Jaddu. The Kotaran fisherman's lips were twisted in a snarl, his yellow eyes slitted. "Let the prick go. I'm going to beat his pretty face to a pulp."

The hands holding him fell away. More people had joined the audience, some boys, some older men, even a few girls, forming a ring with him and Jaddu in the middle, circling each other. He needed to end this quickly. His stomach hurt and he was gasping for air.

Jaddu charged, his fist swinging. Ravindra flicked his head aside, but evasion wouldn't be enough. Tire him out, frustrate him and Jaddu would make mistakes. Then Ravindra could use the man's own weight against him. Ravindra dodged, circled, dodged again.

Jaddu whirled, his face purple. "Stand still, you bastard. Fight like a man."

And have my face pulped? No thanks. Ravindra kept moving, deflecting the aimed blows. Shouts rose around him. 'Come on you coward, fight. You show him, Jaddu. Thinks he's better'n us.'

Jaddu lunged, his fists raised but at the last moment he shifted his weight onto one hip. Ravindra danced backwards, caught Jaddu's leg as it kicked and sent the fisherman thudding onto his back.

"Enough."

Razza walked through the crowd. The old shaman didn't have to shout, or push his way. They parted before him, like water before a ship's prow. Jaddu clambered slowly to his feet. Ravindra swallowed his sigh of relief.

"What is this?" Razza said, looking between the two men.

For a moment Ravindra exchanged a glance with Jaddu. They would never like each other but he wasn't going to tell tales. "A disagreement, Razza. I'm sure it's over."

"He doesn't belong here, Razza," Jaddu said. "He comes here to mess with our women, then when he's had his fun, he disappears back to his manor house." He accompanied the words with a wave of his hand in the direction of the Ravindra estate.

Razza didn't raise his voice, but one eyebrow lifted. "You talk like a harmara in rut. Leave your mating challenge to another time."

The tension broke as the watchers sniggered and Jaddu looked away, his skin darkening. Ravindra chuckled. Harmara, the great, six-legged mountain deer which grazed in the high meadows, went into rut in the Fall, when their bellows echoed in the valleys as they fought for a harem of females.

Razza fixed Ravindra with a narrow-eyed stare. "You find this funny?"

Ravindra's muscles tightened as a wave of amusement rippled around the watching crowd. He'd been put in his place and he didn't like it. Jaddu knew it, too, his lips jerking in a grin laced with disdain.

"No." The response sounded petulant, even to Ravindra.

Razza's eyebrows cocked over a gimlet stare.

"No, *Srimana*." Humiliation burned but the old man had earned his respect years ago, when he'd saved Ravindra from the river.

Razza nodded, then gazed around the spectators. "You have nothing to do but gawk at a pair of young bucks? Go about your business."

Amid cleared throats, people shuffled off. Jaddu couldn't resist one last glare at Ravindra before he straggled off with his friends.

Razza clapped a hand on Ravindra's shoulder. "What was this about?"

Ravindra shrugged. "He resents my status." He hadn't advertised his liaisons with Selinel. After all, it was just a bit of fun. He hadn't seen her since last break, a good six weeks ago, when he fobbed her off with some excuse.

The old man pursed his lips, searching Ravindra's face. "Hmm." For a moment Ravindra thought Razza would say something more about the incident, but he didn't. "Wait for me outside the tavern. I have some things to collect."

Razza strode off. Ravindra slung his pack over his shoulder, wincing when the edge caught the place on his back where he'd been kicked. He'd have a bruise there, for sure. The back of his knee felt tender, too, but exercise would help. He ambled through the village, dodging around a hand cart and a couple of women on their way to the communal shop.

"Ashkar."

He slowed, glancing over his shoulder at a girl hurrying toward him down an alley. His heart sank. Selinel.

"Hello, Selinel. I have to catch up with Razza." He glanced at the tavern, which dominated the small main square. No sign of the old shaman yet.

The girl stared up at him, searching his face. "I heard Jaddu and his gang bashed you."

Her white blouse with its scooped, embroidered neckline showed off the cleft between her breasts. Resisting the invitation to stare, he said, "Not much, as you can see. A few scratches is all." He took a step back. "Razza will be waiting."

"You'll be coming back? Maybe we could spend some time together." She curled a lock of dark hair around her finger, a coy smile on her lips. "I've missed you."

She looked so hopeful, it made him feel bad. "Selinel, it was fun, but it's over. I'll be leaving soon. Best you move on, consider some of your own men."

Oh, for pity's sake. Her lip trembled and her eyes began to fill. He glanced up at the tavern again, looking for Razza's tall figure. Thank goodness. He'd just arrived. "I have to go." Breathing a sigh of relief, he jogged off.

Razza came to meet him, a pack on his back and his old hunting rifle slung across his shoulders. Together, they walked across the cobblestoned square to the path leading down to the lake. On the way they passed Selinel. Jaddu stood with her, his hand on her shoulder, comforting her. That hadn't taken long. The young hunter glowered at Ravindra, mouthing the word 'bastard'. The look on Selinel's face wasn't exactly friendly, either, but at least the tears were gone. She'd get over it.

The slight twinge in his knee as he clattered down the steps between the cottages gave him something else to think about. At the bottom he waited for the old hunter to catch up with him.

"Is that what the fight was about? A girl?" Razza said, a smile twitching his lips.

Ravindra cleared his throat. He really didn't want to talk about it. She'd pursued him and, well, he was a man, wasn't he? "She offered. I didn't say no. That's your way, isn't it? The woman chooses her man and she's free to experiment until she's made a choice. Men from outside the village are welcome, isn't that right?"

Razza's stare pierced him. "Not men outside her class. You've toyed with her."

Heat rose into Ravindra's face. "It was a few nights, that's all. It was just sex, a bit of fun with no risk of pregnancy for her."

"Hmm. I doubt she sees it that way, even if she knows it's true."

"I'm Mirka, she's Shuba. It's obvious."

The deep lines in Razza's face hardened. "She's still a person, with feelings. You would be wise to remember that when you command people from all classes."

Oh, stars. Ravindra shook his head. The old man was taking it far too seriously. The girl wouldn't be that stupid, surely?

Razza treated him to one more piercing stare. "For you it was a fling, free sex. But Jaddu has been chasing Selinel for the last couple of years, hoping for marriage. He's been sullen of late, so I thought there must have been another man, someone from outside the village. I would not have imagined it would be you." He let the words hang in the air between them for a moment, then shrugged. "We'll say no more of it."

That suited Ravindra. Without another word he walked beside Razza along the gently sloping path leading through a meadow of grasses and wild flowers down to the lake. Four fishing boats drifted at anchor, their shapes mirrored in the dark water. Beyond the lake the mountains rose into an azure sky. For once, the snow-covered peaks were not burdened with the usual expanse of cloud. Golden-leafed forest edged the far side of the lake. Higher up, evergreens covered the lower slopes, and above them, the sun glinted off dark cliffs too steep to hold the snow.

Razza led the way along a wooden jetty jutting out into the lake and jumped into his boat moored at the end. Ravindra wasn't overly keen on boats. He stepped gingerly into the vessel, compensating for the rocking.

Razza slipped the painter out of its metal ring, pushed the boat off with an oar and made himself comfortable in the stern of the small craft, handing the oar to Ravindra. "There's no wind, so you'll have to row."

So this was his punishment, was it? Ravindra had rowed with Razza a few times and although he was no expert, he knew the drill. Water splashed over the side as he struggled with the oars, doing his best to ignore Razza's smirk. After a few lurches, he settled into the rhythm, despite the occasional twinge from the bruise in his back.

As they neared the opposite shore, Razza said, "Ship the oars and let her drift." When the little boat bumped against the simple jetty, Razza jumped up and tied the painter to an upright. Balancing in the rocking boat, Ravindra handed up their packs and Razza's rifle.

Razza slipped his heavy pack onto his shoulders with practiced ease, and hefted his rifle. "I want to make the high meadows by nightfall. Let's go."

Past the jetty the well-defined path under the trees was invisible beneath a thick carpet of decaying flowers that swallowed the sound of footsteps. The crisp air of the lake gave way to the rich scent of earth and mold. Ravindra walked in the hunter's wake, listening to the forest. Here, the rustle of some startled creature in the bushes, there, the shrill alarm call of a bird. Between the pale grey trunks the last of the spring flowers enjoyed the sunshine filtering through the leaves.

After several hours they stopped to eat, snacking on cheese and bread brought from the village. The bread was fresh and coarse, full of natural grains, and the cheese golden yellow, sharp and crumbly. Leaning against the smooth trunk of a tree, Ravindra closed his eyes and savored the food, as good as anything he'd ever eaten in the fancy, five course meals at dinner parties at home.

"Have you met your betrothed yet?"

Ravindra's eyes snapped open at the sound of Razza's voice. The old hunter sat on an outcrop nearby, a questioning smile on his lips. What a way to bring a man back to earth with a thud. "No."

"Has she been selected?"

Ravindra sighed. "Yes. She's *Darya*, of course. Admiral Narra's daughter. I haven't met her in the flesh. I've spoken with her on the nets. She'll do." He supposed. Good looking enough. She'd play the part as expected. Although he got the idea she was as happy about the match as he was. That suited him. They'd do their mutual duty, meanwhile, he'd get on with his career and she could do whatever took her fancy.

"And when is the marriage?"

"Not until I've earned my commission." He rose to his feet, dusting off his hands. "Hadn't we better be moving along?"

His eyes twinkling, Razza rose and set his pack back on his shoulders.

They trudged on, up a path now becoming steep and rocky. The forest changed as the land rose, the drifts of flowers replaced by low, tough bushes beneath the reddish mountain spires, their wide branches with their fleshy leaves spiraling up the trunk.

Razza called a brief halt, pointing up at the peak. "There's a hollow where the trail goes around the cliff. We'll make camp there."

The sunlight had turned orange when they reached the hollow. Ravindra slipped his pack off with a sigh of relief. Amazing how heavy a light pack could become. Not two body lengths away, the mountainside dropped into a distant valley. He grinned. The view was almost as good as he'd get in his flitter, except in a flitter he could move in the sky. He'd have to bring his wonderful new machine up here before he went home. It would perform magnificently up here.

Speaking of which... he stepped to the edge of the cliff, shaded his eyes and peered. A prickle of anticipation shimmied down his back. If it was what he thought it was...

"A vulsaur." Razza's voice was deep and soft. "She's big."

She certainly was. The wingspan must have been as wide as the wings on an atmosphere-capable, T-700 fighter. The underside of her hide was basically white or pale gray, her legs tucked neatly underneath her. When she turned, the mottled brown-bronze of the upper wings almost disappeared into the rocks. Perfect camouflage coloring. He wondered how the creature could fly, and didn't realize he'd said the words aloud.

"Vulsaurs are different," Razza said. "Their bones... well, they don't have bones, not like ours. They are native to this planet. Not like us. I've read that their structure resembles the carbon fiber used in spaceships, light and incredibly strong. Their wings are made of the same stuff, with three powerful muscles pumping blood through their bodies."

Ravindra watched the creature soar, then bank and drop, then soar again. So large, so graceful. No wonder the Kotara worshipped them as the steed of the Great God Kotluk. Imagine that, to ride a vulsaur the way he drove his flitter, gliding with the air currents, swooping through the valleys.

The vulsaur flapped mighty wings once, twice and disappeared beyond a spur. The air seemed a little emptier, a little colder.

"Come, Ashkar, not so near the edge." Razza grasped his arm and drew him back to the path. "You're privileged to have seen her. There are not many left."

"Why?"

"They don't breed often, every five years or so. And for a long time, stealing an egg was a mark of a great warrior." He grinned. "A lot of men died trying that. They're very smart creatures." He clapped Ravindra on the shoulder. "Come. Help me get some firewood."

Ravindra searched the sky for a moment, then went to help Razza, bringing dry branches from under the small stand of trees in the hollow. He laid his burden on the ground for the shaman, who was blowing gently on a spark he'd lit in twigs. "Why is it here, now?"

A small flame flared. Razza sat back. "It's breeding time. That was a female here to lay its egg. She may already have done so."

Ravindra filled the small kettle and set it to boil water for a hot drink to go with the cold meats and bread they'd brought. As night fell the cold nipped harder. He wondered where the vulsaur was now, where it nested, what the nest looked like, if anyone other than Kotluk had ridden a vulsaur. "So no one has tamed a vulsaur?"

Razza put a larger log on the fire, causing sparks to dance up into the air. "People have tried. They say Kotluk tamed a vulsaur, so we should be able to."

"But Kotluk is a God."

"Mmm. But even Kotluk used the beast's egg to bargain with it. That is why stealing an egg was such a prestigious act."

"What did Kotluk do?"

"A thief had taken her egg. Kotluk told her if she'd carry him, he would return her egg. He did, and they cooperated from then on. But that's not why they take the eggs. They think that if they raise the creature from a chick, it will be their friend. It won't be. They don't like people." Razza yawned, and stretched. "Go to sleep, Ashkar. Tomorrow we hunt harmara."

Morning dawned cold and misty. After a breakfast of dried meat and cold tea, Razza strode out of the glen under the cliff and back onto the path. A deceptively gentle breeze curled around Ravindra's face, nipping at his nose and cheeks, and seeking to penetrate the cracks in his clothing. He rolled his shoulders to ease the pack, grateful for high tech jackets and boots. Mist roiled around in the deep valley, but here the sunlight on the snow caps dazzled the eyes.

Moving helped to get the circulation going. Ravindra walked steadily, glad the twinge in his knee had all but disappeared.

When Razza stopped, Ravindra nearly walked into him. "What."

The hunter pointed, his hand shading his eyes, his body tense. "The vulsaur."

Ravindra came up beside him, his nerves buzzing. The great beast jagged and jolted in the sky, its wings half-closed, the long neck arched. A shape no more than a third the vulsaur's size flew at the beast, then angled away. A flitter. He was sure of it. His heart jolted. "That's my flitter. Some bastard has stolen my flitter."

He'd never locked the ship down. He'd never had to. The Kotara didn't steal. But somebody had and he didn't have to think hard to put a name to him.

"Idiot." The lines in Razza's face deepened. "A vulsaur can out-fly a flitter."

The vulsaur wheeled, making to turn to the mountainside. The flitter darted down, then zipped up in front of the beast. The great beast flicked a wing, deliberately tipping the flitter's wingtip. The flitter rolled. "Keep it going," Ravindra muttered, "Set a barrel roll. Roll out of it."

But the pilot tried to correct. The vulsaur grabbed the craft in its claws and slung it away. So close to the cliff, the vehicle didn't stand a chance. The boom as it struck the rock face echoed around the valley, followed by jarring scraping that grated Ravindra's nerves as the wreckage slipped down the rocks, over a lip, then somersaulted into the valley. A distant boom echoed, followed by a finger of black smoke.

Ravindra watched, sadness fighting with anger. His flitter, stolen and destroyed. Whoever the pilot was had to be dead.

"Look. She's chasing someone." Razza pointed.

Ignoring the flitter, the vulsaur swooped down at a figure racing down the path toward a section where the cliff face formed a sort of half tunnel the Kotara called the overhang. The runner stumbled, fell, avoiding the vulsaur's clutching talons. As the creature flapped away from the cliff the figure rose and sprinted, making a last, ungainly dive to the relative safety of the overhang.

The creature's high-pitched hiss rattled Ravindra's eardrums. It rose, the flap of its wings booming, then it turned to land on a nearby outcrop. The figure stirred, creeping down along the path to the lower end of the overhang. He stopped, peering around. At this angle he couldn't see the huge beast perched above him, even when he looked up. He ventured out. One step, two.

Ravindra's stomach clenched. "She's waiting for him. If he goes any further, he's gone."

Razza ran, shouting in the thick Kotaran language. Ravindra had learned a few words, enough to get by on. "Stop, stop, stay where you are."

The figure looked up at the sound of the hunter's voice.

The vulsaur launched, screaming. The man skidded to a halt and turned around, stumbling for the shelter of the overhang. Razza had reached him, shoved him forward. The vulsaur was there, right behind them, the downdraft from its wings throwing up dirt and debris as it shrieked its fury. Razza staggered. The vulsaur swept around, preparing to launch a new attack on Razza.

Not while he was around. Ravindra raced down the path. His heart hammering, he grabbed the old man's shoulder and half dragged him under the protection of the overhang. The vulsaur screamed its frustration, huge wings beating as it took off, its talons, long as knives, spread wide. Ravindra heaved a sigh of relief, working to slow down his thudding heart. He glanced up at the man who'd caused all this. His pulse bounded again.

Jaddu. Fucking Jaddu.

Ravindra stared at Jaddu's pale face staring defiantly from within a long, harmara hide coat with a fur lined hood. He shoved the questions aside. Razza first. He knelt beside the old hunter, who waved him away. "I twisted my ankle, that's all."

"Twisted? Not broken?"

"No. It hurts, but not enough for that. Help me to the wall, Ashkar. I can't sit like this." The old man's eyes drooped, tired as well as in pain. Ravindra looped his arm around Razza's shoulders, hefted him as gently as he could against the rock face, and handed him his water bottle. "Drink."

The old man's throat bobbed as he swallowed. He handed the bottle back to Ravindra, then said to Jaddu, "What are you doing here?"

Ravindra rocked back on his haunches, anger rising in his gut. He'd like to hear the answer to that, too. He rose to his feet, his hands balled into fists. "Who stole my flitter? Why?"

A flush darkened Jaddu's cheeks.

"And tell us what you've done to attract the ire of a vulsaur," Razza added.

For a moment Jaddu glared at Ravindra, his lips pressed together. Then his face crumpled into sorrow. "I never meant it to end this way," he whispered.

"Jaddu." Razza spoke softly but with that tone a man obeyed. "Did you steal the vulsaur's egg?"

Ravindra's heart jolted. Steal a vulsaur's egg?

Jaddu nodded reluctantly.

Razza hissed, his lips bared. "You idiot. Where is it?"

No answer.

Razzu clenched his fist. "Answer me, stupid boy."

Jaddu pointed over his shoulder at his backpack.

"Why?" asked Ravindra. "Why would you steal a vulsaur's egg?"

Jaddu's eyebrows flicked together, but he said nothing.

"To impress Selinel." Razza shook his head sadly, his gaze fixed on the young hunter, whose face contorted in pain.

"I wanted to prove I was better than him." Jaddu spat the last word, hatred lacing his words, and glittering in his eyes as he stared at Ravindra.

Better than me? He thinks he's better than me? She obviously didn't think so.

"How did you get here before us?"

"We took your flitter. Terion and me." He tried a mocking smile that faded away. "I got Terion to drop me off this morning, just past the Chimney."

His flitter, in pieces down the mountain. A state of the art Camtron, his graduation present from his father. Ravindra forced himself to settle down. It hardly mattered now.

"The vulsaur nested on the top of the Chimney," Jaddu continued. "Terion buzzed her with the flitter to give me a chance to climb up to the nest." He stared into space, rubbing his chin with his knuckles.

Ravindra knew the place, a column of rock not far from here that had split away from the rest of the cliff but was connected at the base. Razza had told him once that vulsaurs nested there.

"Then what?" Ravindra asked. "Was Terion supposed to hold her off, come back for you? That's not going to happen now, is it?"

Hate-filled yellow eyes stared at him. "I've got nothing to say to you. Bastard."

Ravindra thrust out an arm, pointing at the column of black smoke curling into the air. "That's Terion down there. He's crashed. In *my* flitter. So *you* could impress a girl."

Jaddu's pallor deepened and his eyes glistened. "I was running for my life, so I didn't see it all. The vulsaur deliberately clipped the flitter's wing. The last I saw the flitter was still in the air." He squeezed his eyes shut and licked his lips.

Ravindra shoved down his anger. Served him right. Maybe now he'd realize what he'd done, caused a crash that killed his best friend.

"So. We're stuck here," murmured Razza. "She won't let us out of here. We can't contact the village." True enough. Ravindra hadn't bothered bringing his communicator up here.

"She'll have to sleep," Jaddu said, some of the bravado coming back. "We can sneak out then."

Razza shook his head. "They don't sleep. Not really. You won't get past her."

"Well, what, then?" Jaddu looked around him wildly, then scooped up Razza's rifle. "We'll have to kill it."

Razza lifted a hand. "No, Jaddu."

But the young man had leaped out onto the path, lifting the weapon toward where the vulsaur had come from before.

"Ashkar, get him back here," Razza said, his voice urgent despite the pain. "He can't kill her with a rifle."

Ravindra edged out onto the path. Jaddu stood with his legs apart, the rifle raised in a two handed grip, sighting along the barrel. The vulsaur had taken off, swinging around for the best run. Jaddu turned to follow her, the red dot of the sighting scope gleaming on the mottled, brown and bronze hide. Ravindra put a hand on the young man's arm. "Razza says you can't kill her."

"Piss off, Mirka bastard. I'm as good a man as you." Jaddu loosed off a shot.

The vulsaur dodged. Stars, the beast was fast. The dodge became a dive. "Jaddu, back off. Get back here," Ravindra said.

Jaddu shrugged him off. "Leave me alone. I'll get it coming down."

Ravindra let go. Let him try. It was hard to imagine the creature could survive a full-on shot like this. And that would solve all their problems.

"It'll bounce off," Razza said, a hint of desperation in his voice. "Jaddu, the shot is nowhere near powerful enough."

The red dot grew on the creature's forehead, just above the eyes. "Got you," Jaddu said through gritted teeth. The rifle barked.

The beam hit the vulsaur and deflected. She shook her head and came on, swiveling in the air to use her talons. Ravindra's heart hammered. She was aimed at Jaddu. As though in slow motion, Ravindra watched her legs swing down and forward, the great claws uncurl, the talons thrust out. No time. He slung an arm around Jaddu's waist and dragged him back toward the overhang. Jaddu struggled, dropped the rifle, which teetered for a moment on the edge of the cliff, then disappeared. Ravindra lurched back, pulling Jaddu, who finally seemed to realize his peril and turned to dive for cover. The vulsaur's talons reached out, curving around Jaddu's thigh. The hunter screamed. Ravindra pulled with all the strength he had. For a moment he thought she'd win, dragging them both out onto the path. He rammed his feet against a rock and hung on. Then he was falling, Jaddu's body on top of him. He lay on his back, winded, a hissing screech ringing in his ears, along with the snap of flapping wings and a sudden wind smelling of spices. The beast had let go, her bulk too close to the cliff.

Ravindra shoved Jaddu aside. The man slid awkwardly, staying on his stomach, where he lay, groaning. Ravindra pulled out a knife and slit Jaddu's trouser leg, revealing deep puncture wounds and a ragged scratch from mid-thigh to calf, oozing blood.

Razza help up a packet, extracted from his pack. "*Ronia* powder. Mix it with water and pour it on the wound."

Ravindra grabbed his water bottle, poured a measure into the lid, then added the powder. When the fizzing died down Ravindra drizzled the green fluid over Jaddu's wounds. The young man flinched, stifling a groan.

"Keep going," Razza said. "It stings at first, but that will settle."

Jaddu scrabbled at the rocky ground with his fingers, his head tilted back. This clearly hurt.

"He'll need a healer," Razza said. "This will only ease the pain for a little while. The puncture wound is deep. It's bound to become infected."

"Are their talons venomous?" Ravindra asked.

Razza shook his head. "Don't need to be. When they grab, they force whatever's on their claws deep. I saw it happen years ago, when I was young. An idiot trying to steal an egg. She clawed him, flung him off the nest. We found him a few days later, raving from the pain. The healers took his leg but he died anyway."

Ravindra sat down next to Razza, his back against the wall. Beyond the cliff the sun shone on the mountainside opposite. A waterfall tumbled down a deep ravine, a rainbow in the spray. "Jaddu, does anybody know where you've gone? Are they expecting you back?"

Jaddu shook his head. "We took your flitter, didn't say anything to anyone." Ravindra had to strain to hear the muffled words.

Razza and Jaddu both needed help and that vulsaur wasn't going to let them pass. He had to be able to do *something*. He still had his laser rifle in his pack. He pulled the gun out and showed it to Razza.

The old man smiled, shaking his head. "Think about it."

The momentary flare of hope ebbed away. Razza's hunting rifle hadn't made her flinch, his weapon wouldn't harm her, either. Even so. "Not even her wings?"

"Especially not her wings."

Ravindra rested his head against the cold stone. What to do, though? No one would miss any of them for days. They couldn't contact the village. They couldn't kill the vulsaur, she wouldn't go to sleep. If Jaddu didn't reach a healer soon, he could very possibly lose that leg, perhaps even die. Terion was sure to be dead already.

And all over a woman and an egg.

Stars, if he hadn't become involved with Selinel... But he wasn't *involved*. It was just a fling. He'd known years ago he'd marry a selected, *Darya* woman. Oh let's face it, he'd known for a few years who it would be, even if the match hadn't been announced. Selinel was just sex. She hadn't been the only one, for pity's sake. It wasn't his fault she'd become obsessed, pressing to see him more often. Even less his fault that Jaddu should see him as competition. Stupid. Maybe he should just throw Jaddu out and let the vulsaur do what she wanted.

But it is your fault. Actions have consequences. He could almost hear his father's voice.

This was all about the egg.

Ravindra turned to Razza. "What if we give the egg back? Will she take it and go?"

Jaddu turned his head but he didn't argue.

"From the cliff face?" The old man pursed his lips. "A nice idea, but I wonder if she could carry it gently enough. It's a very small egg for such a large creature and she'd have to grab it on the wing with not much space to maneuver."

Ravindra had to agree. The egg was all they had, the reason for their pain and what the vulsaur wanted most. That, and maybe the life of the thief. Razza's story of Kotluk and the vulsaur rose in his mind. Razza had said Kotluk had bargained with the vulsaur, returned her egg. But that was just a legend. True, but Razza also said that vulsaurs were smart, not dumb beasts like harmara. The vulsaur had demonstrated how smart she was, downing the flitter, trapping them under the overhang, waiting where she couldn't be seen.

He stood. Just the thought of what he was going to do threatened to turn his knees to jelly, but he had to try something.

Kneeling beside Jaddu, he opened the fisherman's backpack. Jaddu stiffened and tried to worm away. "What are you doing?"

"Taking the egg."

"No. I won't let you." Jaddu twisted, scrabbling sideways.

Anger rose from Ravindra's gut. This idiot was not going to stand in his way. "You will stay where you are and you will do as you are told."

Jaddu subsided, lying still while Ravindra removed the egg, wrapped in cloth, from the back pack. He pulled the material back to make sure the prize was undamaged. Its smallness surprised him, its smooth, leathery skin the same mottled brown and bronze colors of its parent.

"What are you going to do, Ashkar?" Razza asked, his tone wary.

Ravindra wrapped the egg up again. "I'm going to put it back. And hope that she forgives us."

Jaddu tried to sit up, his face a grimace of pain. "No. It's mine. If you put it back then all this, Terion, it was all for nothing."

"And if we all die up here? That makes it worthwhile?" Ravindra couldn't keep the contempt from his voice.

"Show it to her. Don't go too far. See how she reacts. If she attacks you..." Razza shrugged.

Ravindra sucked in a huge breath. This was it. His heart thundering in his chest, he walked up the slope to the edge of the overhang. Beyond, the narrow path was bathed in sunlight. One more step. He unwrapped the egg and walked forward; one stride, two. Not so far that he couldn't dive back if he had to. He turned, looking for the vulsaur, squinting in the sunlight. And there she was, wide wings curved to catch the wind, slowing down. She'd done what he would have, risen silently from her vantage point and dropped with the sun behind her. Smart. She'd had her talons out, ready to grab, but now she curled them underneath her body. Her wings arched over, holding her up in the air currents with little effort. Keen, cruel eyes flecked with gold gazed at him. A droplet of sweat slipped down the side of Ravindra's face. He raised both hands, showing her the egg.

"I'm going up there, up to your nest. I'm going to put it back."

She wouldn't understand but it felt good to say it. She angled a little, catching another updraft, hanging in the wind like an enormous glider. He risked a step forward. She hissed.

He could see the chimney from here, a splinter of rock sheered off from the main cliff. Someday it would lose its grip and tumble down into the valley hundreds of meters below. Hopefully not today. He pointed with both hands, the egg held between them. "Up there. Put it back."

She drifted beside him. One lunge now and he was dead. He took three more strides. Now, if she wanted to attack he couldn't get back to the overhang. He shot a glance back to that haven of safety. Razza was there, lying on his stomach, propped up on his elbows, watching. Perhaps the old man would see him die. Ravindra needed his hands now. Keeping his gaze on the vulsaur, he put down the egg, then slipped off his back pack. "I need my hands," he told her, wrapping the cloth around her egg. With trembling hands he pushed the egg down into the pack. The vulsaur rose again, steadied, swooped back down, hissing softly. Ravindra stood and slipped the back pack over his shoulders, securing the straps.

"I'm going now." He walked slowly up the path, the vulsaur shadowing his progress. His world had shrunk to the rocks of the mountain, the yawning, cloud-filled chasm to his right and the vulsaur riding the air currents a wing span away. The Chimney towered ahead of him, a spire of rock fifty meters tall. At the base, he stopped, staring up the pinnacle. There didn't seem to be a lot of hand holds, but Jaddu had climbed it, so he could, too.

The slap of giant wings startled him. She soared to the top of the Chimney and settled, staring down at him, the sunlight catching the golden flecks in her eyes. Ravindra knelt to take off his boots. They wouldn't help him on his climb. Perhaps he should have thought to take Jaddu's light, flexible, climbing shoes. Too late now.

Coldness seeped into the soles of his feet. One final check to make sure the back pack was secure, then he stepped up to the first, easy foothold on the cracked surface, searching with his fingers for a hand hold. Hang on tight. Find somewhere to put his left foot. Pull up. Find a finger hold to take his weight. Up again. The vulsaur had taken off again. He saw her swing around to his line of vision, then she was out of his sight. His nerves jangled. What about Razza's other story? The thief the vulsaur had taken from the nest and dropped? The one who died? But no, he had the egg. His relief was short lived as another thought crowded in. What if she'd decided to take him up there, drop him on her nest and keep his body to feed to her chick when it hatched? His back prickled, expecting any second the sharp bite of talons.

Don't be an idiot. She could have done that a hundred times. Keep climbing.

He reached out, his fingers fumbling for another grip. He pulled. His fingers slipped and he slid back, jabbing his toes for somewhere to stand. Pain stabbed up from his feet into his leg. The back of his knee, where one of Jaddu's mates had landed a kick, twinged. He steadied, clinging on like a rock spider until his nerves settled. Down in the valley the mist had begun to burn away. He caught a glimpse of a ribbon of silver snaking across a green meadow. The air whooshed beside him and his nerves twanged. The vulsaur, her head angled to watch him as she swooped past.

Only a couple more body lengths to go and he'd make the top. Ignoring the ache in his fingers and toes, he climbed on. Don't think. Climb. Find a handhold. Find a foothold. And another. And another.

At last, he heaved himself over the edge onto the flattish platform on top. For a few moments he lay there, panting. The vulsaur called, a short, sharp whistle. She'd perched on the cliff where the Chimney would have been attached. He could almost hear the words. "I'm watching you."

Ravindra crawled forward to a messy nest built of branches and twigs. The vulsaur had lined the middle with feathers and fur taken from her kills. The stink of dead animals cloyed his throat. On his knees Ravindra slipped the back pack off, took out the egg and placed it, with the material beneath it, in the central hollow. Rocking back on his heels, he said, "Here you are, ma'am. Your egg."

Automatically, he put the pack on again, barely aware of the vulsaur gliding across the gap between the cliff and the chimney. She landed with a gust of wind, a clatter of claws and a waft of her scent. Her wings half furled, she swayed over to the nest and bent her head, inspecting, rolling the egg with her beak while making creeling noises in her throat. So close, she was even bigger than he'd thought. Her mottled hide gleamed softly in the sunlight, like polished leather.

Time to go. Crouching, he crawled sideways to the edge of the pinnacle. The vulsaur paid him no heed, tending to her egg. She'd pulled up the edge of the wrapping he'd placed in the nest, and draped it over the egg, like a blanket. *Goodbye, ma'am.* He said the words in his head, his aching toes seeking the first foothold. He didn't really want to attract her attention now.

The top part was the hardest. The muscles in his fingers and toes screamed complaint, his sinews felt like fraying rope. He stopped when he could get a decent place to stand and risked a glance down. Too far to jump for the path and if he missed, he could count the seconds until he hit the meadow, where harmara grazed. They'd get one hell of a fright.

A sudden rush of spice-scented wind was his only warning. He was plucked off the rock wall while huge wings slapped like sails. His scream of terror mingled with the vulsaur's cry as he hung by the straps of his backpack. Oh, stars. What a way to die, flattened on a mountain or eaten by a vulsaur's chick. The ground swung beneath him, the silver thread of the river, a splash of red where mountain spires grew, the distant gleam of the lake, the anonymous dots of grazing harmara. He'd seen all this from his flitter but he hadn't had the wind blowing in his face, bringing tears to his eyes.

In the middle of the valley, the vulsaur let go.

Falling, Ravindra spread out his arms and legs, keeping his body steady. The wind rushed past, grabbing the air from his mouth as he tried to breathe. This was it. Finished. Now they'd all be dead. Razza, Jaddu, Terion and prospective officer cadet Ashkar Ravindra. *Sorry, father. I got it wrong.*

His body slammed into the straps of his backpack, sending searing pain through already stressed muscles. But at least he was still alive. So far. The harmara, formerly just dark colored specks on the grass, had resolved into a herd of panicked creatures fleeing for the safety of the trees. What now? Ravindra didn't believe in any sort of god, but if the Kotaran God Kotluk, who rode a vulsaur, could help him now, he'd pray. *Please. I'm too young to die.*

The vulsaur's wings beat the air as she swept down the valley toward the lake, losing height as she went. Ravindra noticed a few fishing smacks out on the water, and Razza's little boat tied up at the jetty. Perhaps she wanted to drown him, or simply drop him in the lake. He could swim, but it wasn't his greatest skill. She slowed, back winging, descending. Ravindra watched the ground rising to meet him. Just handspans above the ground she let him go. He fell, flexing his legs as best he could. His bare feet, cold and battered from the climb up the Chimney, slammed onto the dirt. He tucked and rolled, taking most of the momentum on his shoulders. It hurt. All of him hurt. But he was alive and she'd let him go. He sat up. She'd landed, crouched on the jetty, her gold-flecked gaze fixed on him.

"Thank you." What else do you say to a vulsaur? And thank Kotluk?

He could have sworn she nodded. Then she raised her wings straight up above her head and leaped high into the air. The downdraft from her wings sent ripples dancing in the shallows. Razza's little boat bobbed like a cork. She banked and soared away, back up the valley. Back to her nest.

Ravindra watched her until she was out of sight. Trembling, he collapsed, his head between his knees. Sobs wracked his body. Every part of him ached. His fingers and toes were bruised and bleeding. His shoulders felt like they'd been cut to ribbons by the straps. But he was alive and he'd struck a bargain with a vulsaur.

A hand touched his shoulder. "Young Ravindra?"

He looked up into the eyes of a fisherman. "Razza and Jaddu need help. Up on the mountain path in the overhang near the Chimney. They're both injured."

The man nodded. "What about you? What happened? A vulsaur carried you here." Awe and curiosity fought for dominance in his expression.

What to tell the fisherman and his crewman, who hovered, round-eyed, nearby? Ravindra swallowed. "It's a long story." He waved a hand across the lake in the direction of the village. "Can you get me there? And get them to send a flitter for Razza and Jaddu?"

"Of course." The fisherman helped Ravindra to stand, and supported his shoulders as he limped to the vessel now tied to the jetty.

Ravindra kept his feet up on a bench while the boat chugged across the lake. The fisherman called ahead, alerting the village council to the need for help for Razza and Jaddu. By the time they reached the other side Ravindra's muscles had seized and his feet and hands were throbbing. The fisherman and his mate carried him to Razza's home in a makeshift stretcher, where the village medic, old and experienced, tutted over his feet and hands.

"Nothing too serious, young man," she said when she'd finished cleaning and bandaging. Lying on the bed, he felt a sharp sting in his hand. He gazed at the healer, whose face was beginning to blur. "It will help to ease the pain and get you to sleep."

The smell of fresh bread and tea woke Ravindra. A laden tray had been placed on the low table beside his bed.

Razza, smiling, sat on a chair. "Welcome back, Ashkar."

Ravindra sat up. The old man looked tired but well enough. A stick leaned against his chair. "You're all right?"

"A twisted ankle. Mirrenel strapped it for me and I have a stick and orders not to do much. Jaddu is much worse off. He'll live, but that leg will never be the same again. If he doesn't lose it. We've sent him to the hospital in the city."

With clumsy, bandaged hands Ravindra managed to pick up a stone mug and sip tea, feeling its warmth spread through his body. "Have they found Terion?"

"Yes. They're preparing him for his last journey." Razza shook his head. "Such a waste."

Ravindra wolfed down a warm bread roll before he spoke again. "Have you told my mother?"

"I have. I've explained you are not badly damaged and we'll see you home safely tomorrow. She wanted to send a flitter immediately but I persuaded her not to do that." He raised a finger. "You must call her, though."

Mothers. He was fine. Well enough, anyway. She'd fuss and have the servants fuss and call doctors. "Thanks," he said as soon as he'd finished another roll.

Razza sat back, making himself comfortable. "Now then, do you feel up to telling me what happened? I saw some of it. You climbing the Chimney, and starting back down. My heart nearly stopped when she plucked you off like some sort of insect."

Ravindra chuckled. "*Your* heart nearly stopped? I nearly wet myself." He sipped some more tea, then gazed into the reddish depths, reliving that incredible flight in his mind. "I thought I was dead, so many times. She dropped me once."

Razza gasped.

"She caught me again. I think that was to tell me she could kill me. Easily. And never to forget that."

"No, I expect you never will," the old man said softly.

A slight breeze wafted through the window near the bed, bringing with it the chill of snow. Ravindra finished his tea and set the mug aside. No, he never would forget. So much had happened in a day. And he could tell that Razza had something more to say, but didn't know how to start. "What else, *Srimana*?"

Razza grinned. "You're older than you were a day ago." He paused, chewing on his lip, then looked up. "This business with the vulsaur has had a profound effect in the village. The story has done the rounds many times already. Torbald, the fisherman who brought you across the lake, hasn't bought a beer since he walked into the tavern yesterday, and he's drunk as a lord. The thing is, they want to make you a warrior, a valued member of the Kotara clan. In fact, they insist. A man who has bargained with a vulsaur."

Ravindra shrugged. It would be an honor, he supposed.

"The thing is, you'd have to wear a tattoo." Razza waited for that to sink in.

"Like the bear you have on your shoulder?"

The old hunter nodded. "The tattoo would look like this." He drew a silver clasp from a pocket in his battered coat and handed it to Ravindra. "My great-grandfather made this."

Ravindra turned the brooch over in his fingers, admiring the graceful lines, the beautiful detail, right down to the tiny, gold-flecked eyes set in the head. The wings were raised, half furled, just as she had been before she jumped for that final lift off at the lake.

Mirka didn't have tattoos. *Darya* especially didn't have tattoos. His father would be furious, or disgusted, or both. Razza knew that.

He looked up at Razza, who was gazing down at him with a look of compassion. "I'll understand if you say no. And I'll have that," he pointed at the clasp, "made into a hair clasp for you, so when you graduate and can wear a *coti*, you can use this to tie it back."

Ravindra brushed the short hair at the back of his neck. As a Mirka officer he would wear a *coti*, a long hank of hair showing his status. He'd expected to use a family design, but this was so much better. "Thank you. I'd appreciate that. Very much." He handed the clasp back to Razza.

Nodding, Razza put the brooch back where it came from, then stood. "I understand. I'll—"

"No. I'll have the tattoo."

Razza's eyes widened, then, frowning, he pursed his lips. "Your father won't—"

"No, my father won't. Neither will my mother. I'd like it done soon, please."

The old man grinned, approval shining in his eyes. "I'll talk to the tattoo artist. You can change your mind anytime until he pushes the first ink under your skin."

"Yes. Thank you." But Ravindra wouldn't be changing his mind. He felt an elation greater than any he had felt before. The image of the vulsaur appeared, her gold-flecked gaze fixed on him as she nodded. This felt right.

Razza had his stick in his hand, dithering. "One more thing. Selinel wants to see you."

One more thing indeed. Ravindra didn't want to see her, but he knew he should, if only to draw a line under everything that had happened. "Yes, send her in."

She arrived a few moments later, pushing the door open, her long, black hair tied back in a thick braid, the green dress she wore complimenting the green of her eyes. He noted it wasn't the sort of dress the women wore for ordinary days, low cut to show half her breasts. His groin tightened.

"I'm so glad you're recovered." She leaned over the bed as if to kiss him. He raised his hand to stop her and she straightened, her eyes narrowing for a moment.

"Sit, Selinel."

She sank down gracefully on the chair. "You were so brave. I've heard all about it." Her eyes sparkled.

He cringed. The last thing he wanted was hero-worship from her. "Selinel, stop. You have no future with me. I'm betrothed, now."

She nodded. "I know. But... it doesn't matter, does it? You could be married to someone of your own class and still... you know. Lots of men do it."

Ravindra's head hurt. "You want to be my mistress? Oh, come on. No family, no children. Is that what you want? Jaddu loves you. He wants to make a future with you. He went and stole that egg—a vulsaur's egg—to impress you."

"Oh, a vulsaur's egg." She dismissed the effort with a wave of an elegant hand. "I don't want to be here. I don't want to gut fish, raise children, grow old before my time. I never thought he'd—"

Her expression changed again, to pretty entreaty. "I want to be with you."

I never thought he'd— The words reverberated in Ravindra's brain. Anger boiled inside him. "You *asked* him to do that? Asked him to prove himself with a vulsaur's egg?"

She licked her lips, fear flaring in her lovely green eyes. "Ashkar—"

"Did you?"

She sagged in the chair. "You have to understand. He kept on at me. Said he was a better man than you'd ever be. Fine, prove it, I told him. Bring me a vulsaur's egg." Her eyes filled, one drop suspended from an eyelash. "I never thought he'd actually do it."

Ravindra's stomach lurched. "And now Terion is dead, and Jaddu has an injury he will carry for life."

She sobbed prettily, her fingers meshing together in her lap. "I didn't mean it to be like this."

"Go." Ravindra pointed at the door. "Get out. If you don't want to be here, go to the town. You might find somebody who wants a kept woman."

She scowled. Stars, the woman changed expressions to rival the best actors. His heart jolted. An actor, that was what she was. She'd used him, seen him as nothing more than a ticket to a richer life. And he, fool that he was, hadn't seen through her.

Selinel stood, nostrils flared, lip snarling. "Bastard. Mirka bastard." She whirled, the gown swirling around with her, and flounced out of the room, leaving a hint of her favorite perfume.

"That's quite a story," Commandant Torbane said. In fact, it was an incredible story. "But why didn't you just accept the clasp and have done with it?"

Cadet Ravindra sat upright, his hands in his lap. "May I speak freely, sir?"

"Of course."

"I am *Darya*. From the day I was born, my life was mapped out for me. I would excel at school, then I would enter the Fleet academy. In time, I would marry a *Darya* daughter and we would have children to continue the tradition. I will be an admiral. All of that I am happy to do."

He smiled, going off somewhere in his mind, no doubt a steep mountainside. "But my encounter with the vulsaur was, as you say, incredible. I learned to trust my instincts, to overcome my fear and to take responsibility for my actions. And also, to take credit where it is due. It would have been an insult to the Kotara, and an insult to Razza in spite of what he said, to refuse this huge honor. I had bargained with a vulsaur. Only their legendary God had done that. Why shouldn't I be proud to wear her image on my skin? So I agreed to the tattoo," he leaned forward, a finger pointed at his own chest, "for me." He sat back, impassive again.

This boy would go far. Oh yes, Torbane could already see the admiral's insignia on his shoulders. But he would have to fight every inch of the way. "You've chosen a difficult path, Cadet. All through your career you will encounter people like Senior Cadet Peshwaran who will point at that tattoo and call you weak, no better than a trooper."

Ravindra pulled back his lips in a wide smile. "If they point at my tattoo as a sign of weakness, sir, they have underestimated me. And is that not a tactical advantage?"

Torbane swallowed his smile. "I will have no brawling in my Academy, Cadet. I don't care who caused it. You're confined to barracks for the next four leave periods. Consider yourself warned. Dismissed."

Ravindra rose to his feet, saluted and marched out.

Torbane glanced at the charge sheet on his desk, with the recommendation for dismissal. Lieutenant Herssun hadn't even asked Ravindra where the tattoo came from. Unfit, hmmm? He opened a new document on his desktop, recommending Herrsun's transfer.

Lucky Chance

Greta van der Rol

Lucky Chance

This is a very short story I wrote for a competition. It didn't win, but I like it anyway.

CHRISTIE STEPPED ASIDE AS A FEW MORE laughing workers bounced down the steps into the freedom of a Friday night. She looked at her phone and checked the time. Quarter past. It wasn't like Darren to be late. Maybe she should call him.

She'd found his number and was about to press 'call' when he appeared, glowering. "Sorry," he said, clattering down the steps. "Hanson went on and on and on."

Christie knew what that was like. The boss in full spate was hard to shut up.

Darren grasped Christie's arm. "Let's go. I don't want to be late for this party. There might be a job opportunity in it for me."

Christie fell into step beside him, hurrying along the footpath. Stopped by the traffic lights Darren dithered, bouncing on his heels as the cars went by, throwing up a fine spray from the wet road.

A tiny wail caught Christie's attention. "That sounded like a kitten." She gazed around. Nothing but wet pavement. But there it was again, somewhere low down. Staring around she spotted a storm water drain, still gurgling with the last of the shower's runoff. Crouched down she peered between the bars of the grid and made out a bundle in the corner, the light reflecting from huge eyes. "We've got to get it out."

"What are you talking about?" Darren grated. "We have to go."

"It's a kitten. It's trapped. It'll drown."

He rolled his eyes. "It's just a bloody cat. Thousands of the things are put down every day."

Christie stared up at his scowling face. He wasn't quite so cute and handsome from this angle. Heartless bastard. "Go. I might see you later."

"Sure." He stormed off across the road. Ignoring the fading thud of boots, Christie pulled at the bars.

"What's up?"

Christie peered up at the man standing beside her. Pete, the senior software engineer where she worked, a nice enough guy, but quiet, a bit stand-offish. His hair flopped into his face as usual. Just as well he wore glasses. "There's a kitten trapped down here." As she spoke the tiny creature meowed again.

Frowning, Pete pushed his hair aside and crouched beside her, inspecting the grille. "If I can get my fingers under here..." He reached between the bars and heaved. Once. Twice. With a squelch the grid lifted and slid aside. Together they peered down into the darkness, while the kitten yowled again, its voice barely audible above the drip of water and the sound of passing cars. The pit was deep, Christie judged deeper than she was tall.

Pete stood. "I'll go. You'll get dirty."

Before Pete could climb into the pit Christie grabbed his leg. "I'll go. I'm lighter than you. I won't be able to pull you up."

He chewed his lip for a moment, then nodded. "Get yourself over. I'll lower you down."

Holding her wrists he lowered her until her feet sank into ooze that made her flesh crawl. The kitten crouched in the corner, all wet fur and huge, frightened eyes. Her heart melting, Christie picked up the tiny body, cradling it in both hands. Poor little thing, wet and trembling. She wondered how long it had been there.

"Hand it up here, Christie." Pete's face was a dark oval, silhouetted against the evening sky.

She placed the kitten into his waiting hands.

"Poor little puss," he murmured as he put the little creature in his jacket pocket. That done, he reached down for her hands and dragged her, muddy and bedraggled, out of the drain. "Okay?" he asked as he steadied her with a hand on her hip.

She nodded. "Kitten?"

Pete lifted the kitten out of his pocket, stroking its head with one finger. She could hear the purr from here. The look on the man's face hit Christie right in the heart.

"I think you're one life down, little fella, one very lucky little cat." The grin on his face morphed into something else she couldn't quite pick. "Do you mind if I keep him?" he asked. "I mean, if you want him..."

Grinning, she blinked away the incipient tears. "No. I'd like to, but I can't." She'd been afraid he was going to suggest the council pound.

Pete looked her up and down, making her aware of her damp, filthy clothes. "Um... I can give you a lift home. If you don't mind stopping at the supermarket so I can pick up some kitty litter and food?"

Pete had lovely blue eyes behind his glasses. Wiping her nose with her grubby hand, she said, "We'd better stop at the pizza joint, too. Looks like I won't be going out to dinner, after all."

"I'm a good cook. If pasta and a salad would suit?"

"I'd like that. Then I can help you clean up Lucky."

He had a lovely smile. "Lucky it is."

Into the Dark

Once upon a time there was a website called Authonomy, where writers would gather and spruik their wares to the Great God Harper-Collins, who owned the site, hoping to have their opus selected for publication. Many tried, many failed, many made long lasting friendships. During my time there, one of our number floated the idea of an anthology of short stories, each written to match a randomly selected song. I joined in the fun and I was allocated (I will follow you) Into the Dark a song by Death Cab for Cutie.

I'd never heard of the band, or the song. But I had a listen and enjoyed the lilting tune.

Now something interesting happened. I wrote a story a long time before, for a contest or something. It wasn't selected. But that story really fitted the song. Deja vu? Who knows?

I've modified the story very slightly from the version in the anthology titled Words to Music. It wasn't ever a best-seller. We donated any earnings to charity. As so often happens in the publishing game, it's not about the money. Anyway, here's my contribution. Enjoy.

RICHARD NEWBY PUT THE RAZOR BACK down on the wash stand. There didn't seem much point in shaving, really. It wouldn't matter anymore. Not where he was going.

He sidled out of the ensuite, taking care not to disturb Mary. He paused and looked down at her as he passed the bed. They'd been married for fifty-four years; she'd been his companion, his soul mate. Perhaps he should tell her what he was about to do? He shook his head. He'd been through this, agonised over the decision. Best he kept it to himself.

Richard moved on, closed the bedroom door softly behind him and went into his study. He spent most of his time here, sitting in front of his computer, surfing the net or fiddling. Mary told him he should walk or play golf, and she was probably right. But he'd been in IT all his life, and the doctors told you to keep your brain active, didn't they? Find something you love and do it. That's what he'd done

He eased himself into his chair and turned the machine on, a slight smile playing around his mouth as the operating system loaded. He licked his lips, a tremor of anticipation... or maybe apprehension... running through his body. One way or another his life would never be the same again.

He loaded the song and listened one more time. It had been his inspiration, gentle and lilting. He smiled. Heaven and Hell displaying a 'no vacancy' sign.

The helmet was on a stand next to him, already plugged in. Richard slipped it over his head and pulled the visor down over his eyes. It fitted exactly, which was understandable. That was how he'd built it.

"Into the Dark," he said.

Mary came in an hour later with his cup of tea and two biscuits.

"Here's your tea, dear," she said, putting the cup on the desk. "Are you going to take that thing off your head?" She shook his shoulder.

His body slumped sideways in the chair, the left arm dangling almost to the floor, the right on his lap.

Mary's hands flew to her face. "Richard?"

She lifted his right hand, her fingers slipping around his wrist to feel for a pulse.

"Mary? Mary, over here."

Mary frowned and peered at the helmet. "Where?"

"The computer, hunbun. Behind you."

Mary peered at the screen, her expression wary. "Is this a joke?" she whispered. "Because it isn't funny."

"No, it's me." Richard pointed at his chest. "That thing there," he pointed at the body in the chair, "that's just a hulk. I'm not there anymore."

Mary gasped. "You're dead?"

"It depends what you mean, hunbun. The body out there doesn't work anymore because the operating system has turned off. But I'm fine here, in the cyber world."

Her eyes widened. "You're in the computer?"

"You might say that. Sort of. See that helmet on my—its—head? I worked out a way to transfer myself—my thoughts, my memories, my mind—into data sets. I've loaded all of that into this." His hands swept down his sides to indicate himself, the being she could see on the screen. "What do you think?"

He was young again, of course. But better looking, fitter, more athletic, like one of those lifesavers at the beach. No need for the glasses he'd worn all his life. And he'd given himself a nose job and wavy, dark brown hair. And of course the tumour, that malignant thing in his chest, sapping his strength, turning his lungs to mash, that was gone, too.

"You look wonderful," murmured Mary. "But... what about us? Why didn't you say? When are you coming back?"

"I'm not coming back, darling. This was a one way trip. And I didn't want to say anything in case it didn't work. But it has and I want you to come, too."

Another avatar appeared next to him. Mary at twenty five. Only with bigger breasts and thinner thighs. He'd given her thicker, longer hair and full, luscious lips.

"Remember her, hunbun? Wouldn't you like to be her again?"

Hope and longing shone in her eyes. Of course she'd want to be twenty-five again.

"How? What do I have to do?"

"Put on the helmet and pull the visor down over your eyes."

Mary frowned. "Will I die?"

"Only your body. You will be here, with me."

"But what if somebody turns off the computer? They will, you know."

"Won't matter." Richard waved his hand. "We'll be out there in cyberspace, riding the net. There's always a server switched on somewhere."

"What about food and... and going to the bathroom and such?"

Richard dismissed it with a snort. "All bodily things. They won't concern you anymore. Neither will arthritis and bad knees. We'll live forever and never grow old."

She chewed her lip. "What about the children? They'll be upset."

"They're hardly children anymore. They've got their own lives. And really, we'll be saving them a lot of pain. The doctor said the lump was getting bigger. He gave me six, eight months."

"Oh." Her gaze lingered on the corpse in the chair and then lifted back to the screen. "The lump's gone?"

"Of course. And here, it can't come back. Go on, Mary, take the helmet off the body. There's a clip under my—its—chin."

She hesitated, staring at the computer screen as if trying to see inside, beyond the glass. "I'm frightened, Richard."

"Mary... hun... we've talked about this. You don't believe in heaven or in hell."

She almost smiled. "No. Of course not."

"So the option is... darkness. One day, the operating system fails and it's over. For all eternity."

She rubbed her hand across her mouth. She always did that when she was nervous. "And then I'd be..." She sighed. "Alone."

"And so would I, Mary. Come on. Darkness isn't the only option."

She stood a little straighter, head cocked to one side, considering. "What will we do?"

"Anything you like. You'd be amazed at the sorts of things you can find in cyberspace. Visit anywhere in the world, sample all sorts of places, do..." He sniggered. "Do some things we haven't done for a long time."

She blushed and smiled. A series of expressions flitted across her face. He knew what she was thinking; the things she'd be giving up. The children, the bowls club and her friends. He crossed his fingers. *Please, Mary, please.*

Mary sucked in a deep breath. "All right."

Richard watched her take the helmet off the... his body. There was a smile on its face and its eyes were open. Mary closed them with her fingers. She stood for a moment with the helmet in her hands, pressing her lips together.

"Come on, hun," he whispered. "Push the... me... out of the chair and sit down."

Mary reached out with a tentative left hand. A push, little more than a tap on the shoulder. Richard's bodily remains slumped a little more, but remained in the chair. Mary sucked in a deep breath, swallowed, and pushed harder. The body slid sideways out of the chair and collapsed into an untidy heap on the floor. She sat down, gripped the helmet in her hands and placed it firmly over her head. It was a little bit loose, but that was all right. She fastened the clip and stared at him, a sparkle in her dark eyes.

"Now put down the visor and say 'Into the Dark.'"

A nervous flick of her tongue across her lips and then she slid the visor down over her face. "Into the Dark."

Richard saw her body stiffen and then relax and sag, almost as if it was deflating.

Beside him, Mary's avatar looked down at her new body and laughed. "How about a kiss, big boy?"

Little Red Pebbles

Greta van der Rol

Little Red Pebbles

This is one of the earliest stories I wrote although it has been modified quite a bit from the first version. I've often wondered how humans would react if they encountered an intelligent life form that didn't fit their expectations.

"WELL, WE'RE HERE," BILL SAID. He used the cameras to scan the hollow where the lander had put down. Red scoria, the trademark landscape of Mars, surrounded them. Dust blasted up by the retro-jets drifted lazily in the thin air. On the rim of the valley, a willy-willy flared up and drifted away. "Why here, I'm not sure. I can't imagine how anything could live in this god-forsaken terrain."

Jason unbuckled his harness and came to look over Bill's shoulder. "Reckon you're right," he said. "Ah well. Maybe we'll find some microbes. We're here for five days. Better get the first experiments set up."

He took his survival suit out of the rack and started putting it on.

The grand vizier slowed down and rolled into Her Majesty's throne room, balancing haste with the dignity befitting his position.

"Your Majesty," he said, "there has been a new Appearance."

The queen sighed. "Oh bother, not another one. You'd better call the council together."

"How many is that now?" the queen asked the assembled council. "Has anybody been keeping count?"

"Er... let's see..." the senior ranger muttered. "I think the first time it was just funny junk falling from the sky..."

"Yes, that's right. And then that ... thingummy... appeared out on the plain," the grand vizier added.

"Yes, whirring and making funny noises – but we soon put paid to *that*," the general said.

"I think we were very fortunate that the thing moved along under a ridge so we could roll a boulder down on it," the grand vizier said. "But it worked."

"I hope you all remember I warned you against that action then," the high priest said, his voice dark and ominous.

"Yes, you did," the queen said. "But I'm still not sure that I see these things as something sent by the Gods, High Priest. After all, they haven't actually done anything for us have they?"

"Oh, I don't know," the general muttered, too quietly for the queen to hear. "The next one scooped up and devoured the last High Priest." He exchanged a glance with the grand vizier.

"A warning to the blasphemous," the high priest said, undeterred. "He'd always been too forward."

"If you'll recall," the grand vizier said, "another time we lost a number of soldiers as well as priests when one of these things just rolled over the top of them."

"Gods act in mysterious ways," the high priest said. "You'll see. Have you noticed the pattern? Each time they come they do more. They are preparing the way for the return of the Gods. We should see the signs and accept them as a warning." His voice rang ominously in the chamber.

"Yes, yes," the queen said. "You've made your point."

She turned to the rest of the council. "What do we know about this new arrival?"

They all looked at the senior ranger.

"Well, it just sort of appeared," he stammered. "I happened to be on a headland, looking over the plain. This big, shiny thing came down in a hollow over there. There was lots of noise and dust and then there was this ..." he searched for words to explain the unexplainable. "Well, taller than the others. It's a bit like the first one, but bigger. Not moving. Well, not around. There are things on it that move around if you see what I mean. But don't ask me what we do about it. I'm just a ranger." He looked pointedly at the grand vizier.

"I suppose we'd better go and take a look at it Your Majesty. We can't deal with something we don't understand," the grand vizier said.

"See to it," the queen said. "One can't let one's subjects be menaced by mindless monsters. You go too, General, with some soldiers and take the senior ranger along. Be careful."

"I should go too, ma'am," said the high priest jiggling up and down, "with some priests. The Gods would expect it."

"If you must," the queen said.

The Apparition stood in a valley, towering up into the sky. From the rim where the reconnaissance party was gathered, it looked like a small mountain.

"Hmmm," the grand vizier said. "This is certainly something different. I wonder if it will open up like the other ones did?"

The tower hissed as if in response and the watchers cowered. A vast section of wall detached from the main edifice and descended slowly to the ground.

The grand vizier was the first to master his fear. "That's interesting," he said. "The wall is still attached to the face, like the big slab in the canyon that balances on a rock."

Nothing happened for a moment, then a huge object came out of the tower onto the top of the slab. Hinged pillars moved the thing down the angled surface, sunlight glancing off its shiny covering. A pillar moved, and hit the ramp with a dull boom. Then the second pillar moved past the first. Boom... boom.

"What did I tell you?" said the high priest, bouncing up and down in excitement. "These are the Gods themselves. Come on priests, it's time we made ourselves known."

"Don't," the general called. "You don't know what you're dealing with."

"I have faith," the high priest said. He whirled down the slope towards the tower, the other priests following close behind.

Where the great slab met the ground the high priest's group collected into the traditional posture of greeting, understood and respected by all. Even across the distance and above the booming noises of the pillars hitting the slab, the watchers heard the high priest utter the traditional words of welcome "Hail to you, stranger," he shouted, "you are welcome in the lands of the...."

The pillar came down, off the end of the slab and crushed him before he could finish the words.

The general and the grand vizier looked at each other.

"How can we fight that?" said the general as the huge figures moved slowly away. "Those things have just destroyed fifty priests without even trying!"

"Or knowing," the grand vizier said. "I don't think they were actually looking for us. Perhaps if they had, they wouldn't have trampled us."

"Oh, please! You're not suggesting they're intelligent?"

"The senior ranger has had his people follow the things and see what they do. They go backwards and forwards between their tower and other places where they have built other things – some that look similar to the ones that came before."

"Even if they are intelligent, how do you imagine we can communicate with beings so different to us?"

"I think there's a way– but I'll need some help from your troops."

The first four days passed without incident. Each day, Bill and Jason donned their silver suits, shuffled down the ramp of the lander and walked the short distance to monitor the experiments they had set up, readjust the settings or to collect samples for testing. They spent the afternoon writing up their results and analysing data. It was as part of his analysis work, as he checked back through the hourly recordings of the landing site that Jason noticed the anomaly.

"Have you noticed the way the rocks move around, Bill?" asked Jason, indicating the image on his screen.

Bill looked up from his keyboard and grinned. "What, on little legs?" he asked.

"No, really. Have a look at this." He flicked back to a previous days' image as Bill leaned across to look over his shoulder. "These are hourly views of the hills over the days we've been here. When we first landed, that hill over there was empty." He pointed at one of the slopes of the hollow. "Then, a few hours later there were lots of little rocks there. All drawn up like an army. See?"

Bill snorted. "An army? Only if you cross your eyes." He grinned down at the top of Jason's head. ""Have you been smoking dope?"

"No, really, Bill. And see?" Jason flicked to a later image. "The next day they're gone. And today, there are little rocks up there again." He twisted round to look at his companion.

"Buddy, it's windy here", Bill said, patting his colleague on the shoulder. "Little rocks get blown around." He went back to check the test results for the presence of microbes in the soil.

On their last morning on Mars the two men set off as usual to check their equipment on the surface. Even after four days of practice, the walk down to the ground required patience. The ramp was steep, the suits were cumbersome and the way the helmet fitted meant they couldn't actually see their feet as they moved. Bill was already off to start the morning's checks when Jason finished edging his way to the bottom. He glanced over at the slope and stopped in stunned amazement.

Jason pointed at the hillside, his voice sparkling with excitement. "Bill! Look at that Bill!"

Bill sighed, and went back to where Jason stood. "What?" He looked at where Jason was pointing and his jaw dropped. "Well, I'll be..."

"You see it?"

"Yes."

"What does it look like?"

"Well...."

"Come on?"

"It looks like 'NASA'." Bill spoke the words slowly, reluctantly.

"Bill, they're moving!"

As the two men watched, the formations of pebbles swirled into the air and a moment later reformed into a fair semblance of an American flag.

"How do they... it... whatever... know what to form?" asked Bill, dumbfounded.

"Good question." Jason stared around. "The lander. They're copying what's on the lander!"

Bill's hand dropped on his shoulder. "Jas, you know what this means, Jas? There's life on Mars, Jas. You and me, we've found LIFE on MARS! And not just LIFE! INTELLIGENT LIFE! We'll be famous! In the history books! Bill McMasters and Jason Bell – first encounters with aliens! We'll be up there with Yuri Gagarin and Neil Armstrong!" His voice shook with excitement.

"Yeah." Jason stared at his colleague. "You're right. We'll get a medal. Or they'll put us on a stamp!" He stopped. "Hang on... let's think, now. We'll need proof. The experiments haven't shown anything and they won't believe us..."

"We've gotta get specimens," interrupted Bill. "I've got a jar – I'll get some. You go inside and get pictures."

"Yes, pictures." Jason turned back to the lander. Too quickly. His foot slipped on the rocks and he stumbled backward, saved from falling only by Bill's hand in his back.

"Take it easy, pal," said Bill. While Jason set off again, Bill put his specimen jar on the ground and leaned towards the pebbles, scoop in hand. They rolled out of his reach, wherever he tried to scoop them up. On the third attempt, he transferred the first pebble to his specimen jar.

"You were right," the general said, "they do seem to have some intelligence. But they didn't understand a single word we said. And now one of my soldiers has been captured."

"Yes. I fear it's time to leave."

"Not without my soldier."

"How can you fight these?"

"You saw. They are so large they can be unbalanced. While this one tries to capture more soldiers we'll have time to prepare." He turned to his assembled army. "Armoured brigade, follow me."

Bill clambered to his feet, picked up the container and headed for the lander. Four of the little buggers. He rattled the jar around a little, looking for feet or eyes. Anything to differentiate these things from the other rocks. But they rolled around, just like any other pebble. Amazing.

He set a booted foot on the ramp – and fell forward as his foot slid away, rolling on round rocks scattered on the metal surface. He arched his body, trying to keep his balance, waving his arms. Oh shit, the specimens. The jar had no lid and the four precious pebbles bounced around with his motion. He let himself fall. In this low gravity he wouldn't hurt himself. The container stayed upright all the way down. Until his elbow hit the ramp. The jar jerked out of his hand. Bill scrambled to his knees and lunged forward to grab it. Too late. The four pebbles spilled onto the red soil and rolled away, beyond the reach of his flailing hand.

Bill scrambled awkwardly to his knees, retrieved the jar and clambered to his feet. Moving more carefully this time, he went back to the slope and collected more specimens. Although they still moved to evade him it was a little easier this time and soon he had four pebbles in the jar. Clamping one hand firmly over the top, Bill cautiously returned to the lander, watching his feet as best he could.

"Here are the specimens," Bill said, holding up the jar for Jason to see. He took off his gloves and screwed on the lid. "How did you go with the pictures?"

Jason threw him a worried glance. "I did my best, but the camera wasn't on when we saw NASA and the flag and when I got back here there was no formation. Take a look."

Bill's frown cleared when he saw the footage of himself trying to collect specimens. "But you can see them trying to get away."

"Let's hope so," replied Jason with a twist of his lips. "But it is fairly windy today."

On the hill the general and the grand vizier watched Bill make his way up the ramp.

"I'll have to say I'm disappointed," the general said. "Not as intelligent as you might have thought."

"No." Disappointment coloured the grand vizier's single word. "We'd better go back and talk to the queen. Retreating to the mountains is looking like a really good option."

"Have you seen this from the Mars landing team?" General Anderson asked Doctor Sorrensen, indicating the report he was holding in his hand.

The Doctor flicked a well-groomed eyebrow. "I have."

"What did you make of it?"

"Pebbles making formations?" She shrugged. "If they want us to believe things like that, they should have sent evidence. The best they could do is a few computer images showing the same hillside covered with little pebbles in a kind of pattern one day and no pattern the next. Have a look." She brought the footage up on a screen.

General Anderson frowned at the pictures. "You know, if you look carefully at this one, you could almost imagine an army drawn up in companies."

"Really?" asked Doctor Sorrensen, the corners of her mouth drawn up in amusement. "And tell me General, when you were small did you see patterns in the clouds – rabbits and horses and castles and so on?"

"But didn't they send specimens?" he asked, ignoring her levity.

She gave him a sardonic grin. "Yes. And we tested them."

"And?"

"And they were little red pebbles. Just as you'd find in places like Australia."

Ella and the Admiral

I rarely dream – at least, not that I remember. But this particular night I woke with a fading vision in my head. There had been fireworks and crowds and panic and shooting. And the Muse stepped in and suggested I write a story along those lines. So I did. Not long after it was completed, a terrorist incident occurred in Nice, France on New Year's Eve.

Fireworks, crowds, death.

Just as well I don't believe in premonitions.

This is a short, stand-alone story set in my Dryden Universe. It has been published separately.

When Admiral Goran Chandler suddenly turns up in Ella's restaurant her comfortable world is thrown into turmoil. Ten years ago he'd been a senior commander, and captain of the frigate *Antelope*. She had been Lieutenant Bulich then, and he'd kicked her off his ship.

With unexpected danger threatening, and a killer stalking the corridors of the Hotel Majestic, Ella and the admiral must work together to escape with their lives before they can consider the events of ten years ago, and what they mean now.

ELLA PAUSED ON THE HOTEL'S BACK STAIRS and breathed in the gathering night. Thank goodness the day was done. The lunch service had been frantic, the restaurant full of revelers enjoying themselves before this evening's five hundredth anniversary celebrations. The city glowed with light, the red and gold festive decorations in the main square and surrounding boulevards obvious even from here. Music and voices drifted on the air, that unmistakable buzz of a crowd having fun. The festivities were starting already. She'd be out there, too, dancing in the streets, imbibing a drink or three, until the fireworks over the lake.

And tomorrow she'd hand in her resignation. She'd been here too long, taken on too much responsibility. Time to move on.

She started down the steps, but paused at the patter of running feet behind her.

"Ella. Ella, wait up."

Oh, stars and space. Ramira. What in hell would the restaurant manager want her for? If he tried to ask her out again... Plastering a smile on her face, she turned. "Is something wrong?"

He stopped, panting from the unusual activity. "Nothing's wrong. At least, not really." He licked his lips. "I need a favor."

Ella kept her eyebrow under control. Why in the world would Ramira think she owed him anything at all? Except maybe a kick in the balls. "I'm off duty." She turned to go.

"Please." Ramira raised a hand. "I know you're off duty. But I just got a call from the hospital. My mother is fading fast. They say she won't last the night." He paused, looking down at his feet, then gazed at her, his face a picture of entreaty. "Will you do my shift for me? Please?"

Shit. She'd been looking forward to kicking her heels up for a change. She'd promised herself. But then, she hadn't been there when her own mother died. That was something she'd regret for the rest of her life.

"Please, Ella. I'd ask someone else but there's nobody else close by and it's such an important night for the hotel." He was babbling, begging. "I'll make it up to you, I swear."

"All right."

He lunged toward her, hugging her. "Thank you. Thank you so much."

Ella strained away from him, fighting the urge to slam him onto his butt. "Just... go, okay? I can handle it."

With a last thank you he lumbered off, back up the stairs and into the hotel.

Ella stared up into the night sky. The fuzzy river of stars marking the galactic plane was starting to assert itself against the endless dark. There were times when she missed space. Quite often, really, if she was being honest with herself. She sighed. One more shift. Just one more, then she'd give her notice.

Peeling off her coat, she walked back up the stairs into the staff-only labyrinth. Calling on skills she'd learned at the Fleet Academy she took a quick shower, changed into a clean uniform, and went through the foyer and into the restaurant in a flat out five minutes.

The Majestic's crowning jewel, the Imperial Restaurant, was situated on the first floor at the back of the hotel, looking over the city's central lake and parklands. The hotel had been a palace many years ago, the dwelling of one of the tyrants who'd ruled the continent with an iron fist until he lost a battle with the Empire. Ella didn't know the details. He'd certainly spent money on this place. Floor to ceiling windows made up the back wall, with stunning views over the lake, its waters sparkling with the myriad colors of the city. Three tables for two were placed by the window, while the main area a step higher up contained tables for larger groups. Dark red tablecloths set off gold cutlery and the wine glasses glinted in the glow of soft lights hidden in the high ceiling.

Darius, the head table attendant, stood at one of the tables for two by the back window, checking the polish on the wine glasses. Ella joined him.

"All under control?"

Darius's eyebrows arched as he looked her up and down. "Where's Ramira?"

"His mother's dying. He asked me to take his shift."

Darius put the glass down. "Huh. That was nice of you." The man's lips jerked in a half smile. Darius was well aware of Ella's distaste for Ramira.

"Yeah well. Who's on tonight?" Ella strolled over to the entrance desk, next to the 'please wait to be seated' sign, and flicked on the screen.

Darius joined her. "We have a mix of old hands and a few extras to cover for those on leave. I put them through their paces earlier. With you here, we should be fine."

The Majestic Hotel's Imperial Restaurant sold itself on old-fashioned style and class, as well as fine food. The restaurant catered for no more than thirty guests, and promised an elegant, first class experience. While most restaurants had converted to inbuilt table menus and bot service, the Imperial used people: highly trained attendants who offered menu sheets and explained choices, who described complementary wines, and brought the food to the tables. They were taught to be attentive, friendly, yet unobtrusive. Ella knew the drill. She'd started off as a trainee here, and in a few months ended up running the place.

The restaurant was booked out. It usually was, despite the price tag. You had to be well-heeled to eat at the Imperial. Either that, or splurge your year's entertainment budget on one evening. She recognized a few names; Cosimo Themazoren and his wife were regulars, and it seemed they'd invited a few friends. Somebody called Ibbotson had booked the other table for eight. Herv Sands the holovid star and his latest squeeze had one of the twos, and wasn't Emile Zoran that airball player who just scored the billion credit contract? He'd booked a four. They would start to arrive at seven.

Ella had Darius bring in his crew. They trooped in, four women and five men, all wearing their Imperial uniforms of black pants and dark red jackets. She checked uniforms, hair, cleanliness, and while she was at it quizzed them on tonight's menu and the suggested wine list. She knew most of them, had worked with them.

She smiled at the two new staff, a tall older man and a young woman. "Liam and Sara, are you ready to go? Any questions?"

Sara seemed composed, standing comfortably with her hands at her sides, but Liam's Adam's apple bobbed more than it should.

Sara beamed. "Absolutely, ma'am. I've worked in both restaurants downstairs. I'm looking forward to the opportunity to work in the Imperial."

"Liam, have you had much experience?" Ella's senses prickled. But surely they wouldn't have hired anyone who didn't know what they were doing?

"Plenty, ma'am. Just not at this hotel. I worked at the Celestial on Suomen, and the Seaview at Bremer Island." He gazed at her steadily.

They were both first class restaurants, and she could only assume Ramira had checked with them. Oh well. Too late now. "Okay. It's an important night, everyone. Every night is important at the Imperial. Your guests should leave here feeling like they've had an audience with the Emperor. Okay?"

They all nodded, and she shooed them off, detaining Darius. "Are you happy with Liam?"

He mixed a nod with a shrug. "He's a late replacement. Ramira's approved him. We had another fellow booked but he'd had an accident. Apparently Liam's references are first class. I don't think he's as good as most of the others, but I've assigned him the table for four with the airball star." He grinned. "I don't expect Zoran will notice any slips."

Ella chuckled. True. Sometimes people came here just to show they could afford to do so. She wasn't much interested in airball, but from what little she knew, you didn't need to be high society to play.

The clients for the tables for two arrived within a few minutes of each other. Ella escorted them to their tables and introduced each couple to their attendant. Themazoren and his wife were next, trailing a gaggle of local luminaries, all resplendent in formal attire. As usual, Themazoren's wife dripped red jewels set in gold: bracelets, rings, and a magnificent necklace. For a change she wasn't a trophy bride, but she'd kept the good looks of youth. She could afford the treatments, after all. Ella didn't like the woman, who seemed to think everyone was beneath her, but she smiled and greeted them like old friends before she handed them to their table attendants.

It seemed Zoran and his party were disappointed they didn't have a table against the window. Ella smoothed the ruffles, explaining the step down limited the space available. But because of that very step, he and his party could see over the tops of the other diners' heads, thus enjoying the best views. She offered placatory drinks, aware of sniggers from Themazoren's table.

She returned to the desk in time to meet the last large group, five men and three women, all dressed in evening attire. While his companions chatted, one of the men approached her. He wore a high-collared jacket, the current fashion for male formal attire, not a uniform, but Ella would have bet a month's pay this man was military. The way he stood, the air of authority, she supposed.

"Ibbotson," he said. "Table for eight."

"Of course, sir. Welcome to the Imperial." She glanced over her shoulder to where the two attendants waited. "If you'll come this way." She hovered while he gathered his party, then led the way to their table. As usual, there was some discussion about where everyone would sit.

"The top end, Admiral," Ibbotson said, gesturing at a chair.

The man he addressed laughed and shook his head. "It's your birthday. You can do the honors for a change."

Ella's heart thudded. She knew that voice. She knew that man. Maybe not as well as she would have liked. Goran Chandler. He hadn't aged much, perhaps a little gray around the temples, an extra line around his lips. She fought the heat coursing up her body. It was all in the past, ancient history. He didn't even recognize her as the attendant helped him to his seat. Two of the women sat on either side of him, another opposite him. Ibbotson took the end seat, as directed, while the other men claimed the remaining chairs.

Mechanically, Ella introduced their two attendants, the new girl, Sara, and Timon, an older man with years of experience. One last smile. "It's our job to make this a memorable evening for you. If there's anything you need, please don't hesitate to ask your attendants, or me."

She walked away, her mind racing. Goran Chandler. Ten years ago he'd been a senior commander, and captain of the frigate *Antelope*. She had been Lieutenant Bulich then, and he'd kicked her off his ship.

'All hands, prepare for normal space.' Ella settled the harness over her shoulders and turned on her tracking display, ready to receive signals as soon as *Antelope* had transited to normal space. This was day twenty of the ship's patrol schedule, two days per isolated planet, waving the Imperial flag to assure the settlers they weren't forgotten. Telon Gar was one of the most isolated. According to the database the settlement was thriving, forging into fertile farmland.

Antelope shuddered as she adjusted to normal space, the deep throb of the drives replacing the whine of the shift engines. Telon Gar appeared in the center of Ella's display, the usual blue and white sphere smudged with licks of brown and green. From this distance, still outside the orbit of the innermost moon, the ship could have been anywhere, approaching one of the Empire's myriad populated planets.

"Captain on the bridge." Linnaes, currently officer of the watch, barked the words. Ella leaped to her feet, as did the rest of the bridge crew, a brief rattle of sound in the normally quiet bridge. She sensed Captain Chandler's presence without even looking at him.

"At ease."

Ella sat down. It was ridiculous how her heart started to race whenever he was around. She was hardly a star-struck teenager. The man must be ten years older than her, and married, too. For pity's sake, she was married herself. She'd never been one to fantasize over holovid stars like so many of her schoolmates, but she'd had a few fantasies involving him. He was her commanding officer, off limits. And he sure wasn't interested in her as anything more than a junior officer. Recently he'd become quite distant with her.

"What's that on the planet's limb, Bulich?"

She started. He was right behind her, leaning over her shoulder and she hadn't been paying attention to the job for which she was employed. Idiot. She directed the sensors. "A ship in planetary orbit."

What a stupid thing to say. He knew that. She pointed out the anomaly on her screen and asked the ship's system to identify.

'We're too far out to make an exact identification. It's a large ship, probably a commercial freighter.'

Ella risked a glance up at her CO. He stared at the forward view screen as if he could see the ship, which was not much more than a blip easing around from behind the planet. "I want confirmation as soon as it's eighty percent. Set an intercept course. All crew, amber alert."

Amber alert. So the captain thought this was a hostile. Ella concentrated on the data. The distant ship grew larger. A 3D display appeared over the projection panel, a ship rotating.

The ship appears to be a four-hundred-ton N-40 class freighter. In standard configuration it has two cannons on both flanks. The cannon ports on the model glowed red. *We are still too far away to give direct information about this particular ship.*

"Mister Judge, do we have any notification of legitimate commercial traffic for Telon Gar?"

The comms officer glanced over his shoulder. "No, sir. And the planet's communication satellite does not respond."

"That'll be a pirate or I'll hand in my commission. Contact Fleet Sector Control. We're going in." Chandler sat down in the command chair. "Sound battle stations."

The bray of alarms filled the bridge. Men and women straightened at their consoles. The dull thud was the bridge bay doors sealing shut. Ella's heart rate sped up. She'd never been in serious action before. They'd done plenty of drills, simulated encounters with Yrmak pirates included. It was a real and too frequent reality in this part of the Empire. She licked her lips. This is what she'd trained for, after all.

The unknown vessel grew in the display. As the ship's systems collected more data, the generic N-40 freighter was replaced with the target ship. The classification was right, unmistakably an N-40. There were thousands in the Empire, most used for inter-planetary cargo. Quite a few had been stolen by pirates. The ship looked like child's building blocks strung together, with a smaller rectangle at the front and below the cargo modules. This ship wasn't designed to enter atmosphere. It had large carrying capacity, but the cargo had to be brought into space. One of those building blocks contained atmosphere-capable barges to ferry cargo backwards and forwards. The smaller rectangle contained crew quarters, with the environmentals and engines taking up the last fifth of the space.

Ella looked for the cannon ports in the designated positions on the hull. They were there, but there seemed to be more. "Sir, there are at least four cannon ports on the starboard hull." She marked the spots on the display.

Chandler grunted. "I'll bet it's got more than two torpedo ports as well. Set speed to fifty. Mister Judge, initiate contact when we're in range."

"Aye, sir."

Antelope edged closer to the freighter, the 3D image growing more and more detailed. The ship was in geocentric orbit over the settlement. Ella chewed at her lip. That would be expected if it was a normal encounter. There was no space station to dock at. But she'd bet nobody on the bridge thought they were going to hear a cheery freighter captain welcoming them to Telon Gar.

"No response from the freighter, sir. We can't drag her ID. Ah. They're signaling."

Ella could just see the flashes from the freighter, the last resort when communication was down.

'*Communication down. Need help,'* the IS translated.

Chandler snorted. "Correct standard commercial traffic response. Well done, pirates. Mister Judge, ask them for the sector identifier."

Ella knew that one. Ask for assistance, lure the unsuspecting victim within range of their weapons and let them have it. But Fleet Control issued a secret code to every ship legitimately traversing the sector as an additional identifier.

"Bulich, can you see anything else on the ship that shouldn't be there? Suspicious ports? Possible gun emplacements?"

Ella examined the data, zeroing in on the oblong depression on the bow. "Looks like she has the torpedo ports, but they don't look right. They're too big," Ella said.

More signals flashed from the freighter. *A repeat of the previous message,'* the IS supplied.

On Ella's display the ship shifted suddenly, pivoting so its bow faced *Antelope*. Both torpedo ports opened.

"Shields to full. Pivot to attack position."

Chandler barely finished the order when the shields sparkled blue and the ship lurched, throwing Ella hard against her combat harness. Red lights flashed in maintenance control. Shields down ten percent. A glancing blow. They'd been lucky.

The freighter was shaping to make a run for it, firing every weapon it had at the frigate as it picked up speed, plunging past the advancing warship, firing as it went. *Antelope's* shields sparked at every hit, but the freighter couldn't match the warship's fire power. Two of the cannons on the port side were silenced. Two more torpedoes had been destroyed before they hit, the fragments disintegrating on the shields in a brief fireworks display.

"Weapons control, target the engines." The captain's voice was calm, controlled.

"Aye, sir."

The ship shuddered as missiles flew out of the bow ports, three pairs thirty seconds apart. The first pair damaged the shield but didn't penetrate the hull. The second pair finished the shields, and the third pair finished the engines. The freighter rocked and then an explosion sent fragments of hull and white-hot splinters flying. Ella pumped her fist. "Yes!" She wasn't the only one.

The freighter's control module had split open like an overripe fruit. Ella swallowed. Whoever had been in there, they hadn't stood a chance. The ship continued on its path, speeding away from the planet in an expanding cloud of debris. Some of the larger pieces looked like they might be bodies. Would they still be alive?

Chandler spoke from the command chair as Ella targeted one of the bodies. "I want a boarding party on that ship. We need to slow her down and get her back into orbit. And I want to know what's in the hold. Linnaes, see to it."

"Aye, sir."

Ella shut out the sound of Linnaes barking instructions to his waiting team as she adjusted the focus on a floating body. At this distance the features were grainy, but the green-scaled face was unmistakably Yrmak. He wore a survival suit, but no helmet. "They're Yrmaks, sir," she called over her shoulder.

Chandler nodded. "I expected they would be. And I'm more than a bit worried about what may be in those holds." He sounded grim.

"Sir?"

The captain looked straight at her. "Yrmaks love these small settlements. They're easy targets for collecting slaves."

Ella shivered. Slaves. The Yrmaks took mainly women to sell to the brothels on the mining platforms around asteroid belts. Men, kids, and old women were all extraneous to requirements. They might be left alive, but if the Yrmaks were in a bad mood, they were killed. She'd seen images, in fact they'd used a slave raid in one of the combat simulations. She'd had nightmares for a week.

The captain sent a reconnaissance droid first. It slipped into the hulk and sent back pictures of a ruined interior. The air had been sucked out when the hull ruptured, along with anything not fixed down. The droid floated through a broad space with chairs and tables fixed to the floor. The blast doors had slammed shut, but the droid had a flexible arm programmed to enable it to open the blast doors of most human freighters. The door slid aside and the droid powered down the corridor through cramped sleeping quarters. A pile of twisted bodies floated near a crack in the hull.

"Looks like they'd finished and were heading for home," Judge said.

"I hope you're right," Chandler said. "I'd rather not have to deal with a bunch of trapped Yrmaks in the settlement."

The droid had reached the engine room. The blast doors were breached. Ella registered body parts and tuned out. Judge redirected the droid to the bridge, moving back through the common room to the bridge blast doors. The droid opened the door, then it disappeared, replaced with crackle.

"Well, well," Judge said. "Seems someone's alive on there."

"Not for much longer. Weapons, put a contact mine on the bridge. Carefully. I don't want any more damage."

Ella looked around at Chandler. So did Judge and most everyone else, except the weapons officer, who bent to his task.

"Get on with your work," Chandler snapped. "If that's a slave ship, I want the slaves off asap."

Yrmaks fought to the death. It was a family honor thing. The only Yrmak prisoners Ella had ever heard about had been injured before they were captured, and all had tried to kill themselves later. It was a pragmatic decision to blow them up, but still.

The mine sped away, reporting progress via its sensors. The device slipped through the blast doors and disappeared when it exploded. Chandler immediately gave orders to launch the boarding party.

"Keep track of the boarding party, Bulich. If there's trouble I want to know immediately."

"Sir." Ella focused on the armored figures powering away from *Antelope's* external hatch. A trooper angled off to check a body, then moved on to a second floating figure, which wore a helmet. Ella could have sworn she saw a brief discharge from the trooper's weapon before he moved on.

The main group had reached the ship, the troopers carrying out the well-practiced drill of boarding a damaged hostile. A few anxious minutes passed after the troopers disappeared into the hull. Then the squad leader reported to the bridge, her voice sounding mechanical. "Nothing alive here, sir. We're sending a droid into the first cargo module."

Having reported nothing there but the landing barge, the team moved on through an activated airlock into the second module.

"Humans. A couple of hundred women and girls."

Chandler straightened. "All right, do what you can for them. Tell them we'll get them home as soon as we can."

"If we try to ferry them in our landing craft we'll take far too long," Linnaes said.

"Agreed. Land as many troops as you can at the settlement with our lander. We'll use the Yramks' barge to get the women down. How many licensed pilots do we have?"

Linnaes frowned. "The barge has auto pilot."

"Slaved to the freighter's bridge."

Linnaes nodded, shame-faced. "Of course. Sorry, sir." He rubbed his chin. "We need Wang for the lander." He glanced over at Ella. "Bulich? She's certified."

He exchanged a look with Chandler that Ella could have read from a mile away. 'We haven't got anyone else'. *Thanks very much, Linnaes.*

But her gut heaved. Yes, she had a current certificate for small ship transfers from space. But she'd have to suit up and cross to the freighter using a jetpack, then fly an unfamiliar barge with a cargo of civilians down to the ground. She felt Chandler's eyes on her. "Yes, sir. I'm up for a challenge."

Anything for a small smile of approval from her boss. That slight jerk of his lips, the approving nod went straight to her heart. Her cheeks heated. *You're pathetic, Ella. Simply pathetic.*

Linnaes shooed her off. "Get suited up and report to Master Sergeant Griffin in the hangar."

Praying Chandler hadn't seen the blush, Ella hurried down to the cabin she shared with Gillian, her fellow junior officer. Her survival suit was stowed in a locker, available at a moment's notice. Drills were run regularly, so she'd practiced suiting up a thousand times at least. Dressed, she took the elevator down to the hangar bay where Master Sergeant Griffin oversaw all extra-vessel activity. He checked her suit, drilled her on procedures, and made sure she knew where to go.

"You use this vector. Sergeant Monetti will meet you at the other end. Any problems, let us know asap. Got it, Mister?" Sergeant Griffin was probably born a sergeant. His grudging respect for a wet-behind-the-ears junior officer rang in his tone.

"Yes, all set. Thanks, Sergeant."

Ella stepped into the airlock and pressed the control to deploy the helmet from her neck pack. It rose smoothly, sliding over her head and securely into place, the air supply cool and tasteless. As the airlock's pressure indicator slid down to vacuum she made one more check of the vector and her jetpack's power needs. The door rose, revealing the same view of the planet and the freighter that she'd had from the bridge. Only now it seemed more immediate, and a long way away. Ella sucked in a deep breath and stepped into nothing.

Chandler made sure Ella didn't realize he'd recognized her, turning to his colleagues to discuss where everyone else was going to sit. They were all senior officers from his flagship, here for a private birthday dinner with Captain Ibbotson, away from the military, away from formal engagements representing Fleet. He'd had a chance to look Ella over, keeping his expression carefully schooled, when she had introduced the two attendants who would be looking after their group. She'd hardly aged. Those compelling dark eyes were just as compelling, her lips just as luscious. She'd grown her hair, but wore it tied back. The dark red uniform suited her, accentuating the brown of her skin.

"It's our job to make this a memorable evening for you. If there's anything you need, please don't hesitate to ask your attendants, or me." Ella beamed a smile around the table, although she brushed past him as though he wasn't there. Ibbotson thanked her, and then she walked away.

Ella. To start with she'd been just another junior officer, inexperienced but capable and willing. On a frigate the officers got to know each other, shared jokes and meals, sometimes even some leave time. She was fun, interested in everything, willing to try the food on any planet. He'd enjoyed her company more than he should have. Chandler wondered if she was still married. He had met the husband, briefly, when the man came to collect his wife for a weekend at home, but he couldn't remember the fellow's name, or what he looked like. What Chandler did remember was the feeling of jealousy, that this man was going to take Ella home and... have sex with her. That was when he'd realized he'd let himself get too close. He was her commanding officer. She was married. He was married, too, then.

She recognized him. Of course she had. But she'd decided not to let that show. Should he respect her unstated wishes? Let it go, put it down as a fond memory of things that might have been. Or should he talk to her? Tell her how much he missed her? How much he regretted what had happened?

An attendant leaned over next to him, a bottle of wine in his hand. "A red or a white, sir? Both excellent vintages."

He settled for the red and tried not to notice the slim figure moving between the tables.

Ella's heart raced. She'd done extra-vehicular trips before, several times, on training runs. She could do this. It was no different. Turn on the jetpack, not too hard. She moved forward, away from Antelope's flank. The suit's enviro-system had locked on to the target point where Sergeant Monetti waited. Some people loved this mode of travel; Ella wasn't quite there yet, but at least she didn't have to fight the urge to vomit like some of her fellow cadets. Never a good idea in a survival suit. She concentrated on the freighter, and from there the greater task of ferrying those women down to safety.

The cloud of debris surrounding the ship swirled aside as she moved, repelled by her suit's shield. Ella didn't dwell on what would happen if the shield failed. Some of those pieces were large and traveling as fast as the freighter had been. She dodged around a chunk of hull that went past her, headed for *Antelope*, where it would disintegrate against the ship's shields.

Close up, the freighter was a mess, its hull battered where it hadn't been split. At this point Ella had to reduce the suit's shield so she could maneuver. She took care to avoid getting snagged on jagged protuberances, using the jetpack to adjust her direction.

Monetti, waiting for her, pulled her into the freighter. "Okay?"

"Okay."

They floated close together in the darkness, the only light coming from their suits' headlamps. The beams spotlighted points of the walls as she looked around. Two bodies drifted nearby. For one heart-stopping moment Ella thought they were alive, their limbs moving. But they moved with the ship, just as seaweed moves in water.

"Barges are through here." Monetti used his feet to push away from a wall. "We've checked them out as best we can. The nearest one is ready to go. The one above won't be going anywhere any time soon."

Ella followed him. "What about the women?"

"They're ready. You check out the barge, and we'll get them on board. There's room for all of them, but it'll be cramped." He used his hands to stop his movement, landing against an air lock.

Ella slid into the chamber beside him. "You need to get out of here asap," he said as they waited. "The air supply isn't going to last."

Ella nodded, her nerves tensing up another notch. No pressure, none at all.

"The AG is working in here. Be ready when you walk out."

Ella angled her body so her feet were down and was ready for the jolt when she left the air lock. The boarding party had rigged a few lights in the hangar which threw multiple shadows. The barge sat squat and ugly facing the hangar bay doors. Many of the women huddled together near the barge's ramp turned to stare at her as she approached, their expressions a mix of fear and hope and anxiety. Some of them looked very young. All of them were dressed in night clothes.

The squad commander, Lieutenant James, met Ella near the ramp. "Glad to see you. The women are okay, but they're anxious to get home. I've warned them it won't be pretty." She glanced over her shoulder at the group. "We've received orders to come down with you. There's nothing more to do here."

Right. No pressure at all. "Monetti said the air supply's suspect. We'd better get moving." Ella hurried up the ramp through the empty cargo bay and into the barge's tiny bridge. She hadn't flown this model before, but the T-38 they'd handled at the Academy had been close enough. She familiarized herself with the controls and the navigation system, aware of voices and footsteps in the hold behind her. The most important thing was to be sure the cargo hold was aired up. That was okay. But the hold didn't have AG.

She went to the hatch and called the nearest trooper over. "They're going to float. There's no AG in the hold. Make sure they know that, okay? Gravity will take over as we go into the atmosphere."

The man nodded. "Yes, sir."

The squad commander came up to sit beside Ella in the cockpit, her armor reset to standard mode, and the helmet retracted into the neck pack. She scanned Ella with shrewd amber eyes. "Are you okay?"

Did she look as nervous as she felt? "I'm fine. Just want to be sure I do this right."

The woman chuckled. "I'm with you there."

Ella started the engines, warming them up for launch. Monetti waited outside, ready to begin the sequence to empty the hangar bay and raise the door. On the console a warning light glowed red. Oh, crap. This was serious. "Looks like the landing thrusters are damaged."

James looked at her. "Can you fix them?"

Without a maintenance section? Without tools, without really knowing the details of the ship? "No. How much time have we got?"

"Air supply? Not much. It's leaking through a crack. We did our best to repair it, but..."James shrugged.

She could call *Antelope*. But what could the ship do? Maybe fix the barge, but they'd have to ferry the woman over to *Antelope* and all the while time drained away.

"I'll take a chance. Even without landing thrusters, there are ways."

Ella sent Monetti the signal and waited until he was on board the barge before she raised the ramp. She'd have to do this fast. Weight in the barge wasn't an issue — it was designed to carry much larger loads — but the air circulation system wasn't designed for so many people. She contacted *Antelope*. "Loaded and ready to clear. ETA forty-eight minutes."

She'd barely received acknowledgement when the hangar bay door slid away. Ella nosed the barge out into space. Telon Gar glowed in the distance, a quarter of its surface in darkness, and farther away than she would have liked. She nudged the ship through the debris cloud surrounding the freighter, turning as she went to head back to the planet. It was mid-morning in the settlement. At least she could land in daylight.

On the console the red light flashed a warning; on off, on off. There wasn't a thing she could do about it but land as soon as possible. She gritted her teeth, and wished she'd had more time to check the barge before they left. But wishing didn't make a damn's worth of difference.

The red light continued to flash. The indicator light for the air supply in the hold continued to drop. The barge began its descent into the atmosphere. Ella fired the front thrusters, slowing the vehicle down. Despite the thick insulation on its base, the hull and the cargo hold would heat up from the friction. "Gravity will start to come back soon. And it's going to get a bit warm back there," she told James. "Better warn them."

James nodded and used her suit mike to talk to her team.

Below the hurtling barge a thick blanket of cloud obscured the ground. But ahead a towering storm cloud rose like a mountain. An alarm began to beep, a recurring, grating noise that pierced Ella's brain. The cabin lights went out. The display went dark.

Ella's heart thundered. The automated controls had failed. The cloud mountain blocked their path, lit up at intervals by lightning deep in its depths. The ship was heading through that storm cloud. Sometimes it would be nice to believe in religion, believe some god could change events. But there was only her. The only thing she could do was take over, bring the ship in manually. It wasn't a great option, she'd only done it in the simulators, but she was out of choices. She stretched down under the console's edge and pulled up the yellow yoke. "Better tell them to brace themselves, or hang on. It might get a little rough."

The barge plunged into total darkness. A bright flash lit up the cabin, the fear etched into every line in James's face briefly visible. Lightning, too close for comfort. The barge bucked and tossed, but not as much as Ella had feared. The ship's speed probably had a lot to do with it. And maybe there was a silver lining. The storm would slow the vehicle a little, keep it cooler. Maybe.

The windshield cleared, revealing a flat expanse of cloud. The barge dove through thick mist, then into clear air, flying over white-streaked gray ocean, heading for the coastline. Ella pulled on the yoke, raising the ship's nose and firing the forward thrusters to slow her down. This wasn't going to be pretty. The settlement was on a river, not far from the sea. Ella circled the town, looking for the landing area and slowing down. There, inland from the buildings, a tree-lined field. She angled the barge down, its nose raised. The ship hit too hard, smashing and bucking. Ella held tight to the yoke, jerking and bouncing with every lurch despite the seat harness. *Stop, damn you, stop.* The line of trees had looked a long way away when the barge hit. Now they were approaching fast.

Chandler cast a surreptitious glance at Ella as she left the bridge. He had to hope she'd be okay, he had no one else to send. He'd been reluctant but his own feelings about the girl — young woman — couldn't influence his decisions on the job. Meanwhile, he had a squad on the freighter and he'd have to send a squad to the planet. He'd go with that himself, help where he could, and talk to the mayor or whatever they had. If he or she was still alive. And he could meet Ella when she landed the barge. Strictly business, of course.

Leaving Linnaes in control of the ship, Chandler took his place in the lander with the rest of the crew he could spare. The pilot skirted around a towering thunderstorm and landed neatly next to the settlement. Rain clouds rolled on, moving away from the town. It, at least, was largely undamaged. Yrmak raiders had been known to raze entire villages, just because they could.

As the crew rose to disembark, Chandler called, "Take care, everybody. Activate your armor. The survivors are going to be on edge." There was no point in taking the chance of being killed by 'friendly fire'.

As it happened, they were safe enough. Three people approached from the shelter of the buildings. All of them looked haggard, their eyes reflecting deep pain. The leader, an older man nursing a damaged arm, said, "They've taken our women."

Chandler deactivated his armor. "We know. We intercepted their ship. Your women will be back soon."

Closing his eyes, the man sagged with relief. "Thank the gods. I thought... I thought..." He sobbed. The other two people, an older woman and a youngish man, hugged each other, and him.

Chandler could imagine, all too easily. The Yrmaks would have hit the town at night, in the early hours of the morning when most people were asleep in their beds. They would have snatched the women, and killed anyone who stood in their way. He let the man sob for a few moments, waiting until he was back in control. "I'm Senior Commander Chandler. And you are...?"

"Ah. Sorry." The man dashed a hand over his face. "Ted Hahndorf. I own the hotel." He jerked his head toward a larger building standing out among the utilitarian modules lining the streets. "They killed the mayor. And his wife when she tried to stop them."

Chandler nodded. A male, and a woman deemed too old. Typical. "How many are dead?"

"We're not sure. People are in shock. They only cleared out a couple hours ago." He spoke with the kind of twangy accent Chandler associated with back country farms on any number of planets.

Chandler directed the squad to help search the buildings. "Do you have a hospital?"

"We have," the woman said. She was gray haired, well past first youth, but her back was straight and her eyes held a steely glint. "I'm a doctor. But we only have six beds."

"A morgue?"

She shook her head.

"There's a cool room next to the hotel," Hahndorf offered. "We can put them there, give people a chance to..." he coughed, "identify."

Other people had emerged from the town, a few men, a few old women. Chandler called them over and organized for some to help the troopers collect bodies.

"Pity you weren't here yesterday." Hahndorf's eyes were narrowed.

Chandler had expected it. Get things moving, bring a touch of normality, then the accusation, the anger, started. "It wouldn't have made any difference. If the raiders saw a warship in orbit they would have gone elsewhere and come back later."

"We should have our own warship," the doctor snapped. "We're part of the Empire, aren't we?"

"Of course, ma'am. That's why we're here. But there are only so many ships, and this settlement is very small." In fact, Chandler had tried to argue that these tiny settlements deserved more protection, but the regional admiral wasn't interested in the opinion of a mere senior commander. Perhaps Chandler could make a bit more difference when he received his captains' stars in a couple of months.

A roar overhead caught his attention. The barge from the freighter, coming in far too fast. Chandler's heart thudded. Ella.

Something must have happened. The engines struggled as the ship looped around above the township. She'd angled the nose up, slowing it down, and now the ship was heading for the landing field.

Chandler ran.

The barge hit the ground, bounced once, twice, then slid to a grinding halt, ploughing up dirt, within a few body lengths of the line of trees. After a last splutter the engine died. The nose had tipped forward but the ramp hadn't come down. Chandler fumbled for the manual release and pulled at the latch with all his strength. People had gathered around him. Some had to jump out of the way when the ramp descended. The stench from the barge was dreadful, a mix of stale air, vomit, and sewage. Women in nightdresses poured out of the hold, shuffling down the ramp, some into the arms of loved ones, some shouting questions, looking around them. Chandler's troopers saluted as they exited.

The squad commander came down after her squad. And then there was Ella, stumbling, head bent. She slipped, landed on her butt and slid the remaining distance to his feet. He reached down to help her up, ignoring her reddened cheeks.

"What happened?" he asked when she was on her feet.

"The autopilot failed halfway down. So did the landing thrusters. I had to bring the ship in manually." She was trembling.

That must have been hard. She would only have done a manual takeover in simulations. "Is everyone here? In one piece?"

Ella exchanged a look with the squad commander, who said, "Yes, sir. A few bruises and a lot of frightened women, but they're home. The freighter was losing air when we left. We got out just in time."

"You did well, Lieutenant James. Take your squad to the hotel, the big building over there. The publican will give them a meal, then I want you to assist the recovery of bodies."

James saluted and went off with her squad.

Chandler wasted a bit more time looking the barge over while Ella dithered. It was pathetic, but he just wanted a little bit of time with her, even if he couldn't tell her how he felt. "Come on, Lieutenant. You probably deserve a meal too."

"I'm not really hungry," she mumbled, walking beside him. "Maybe I should have contacted the ship when I found out the barge's landing gear was damaged. But the freighter's hull was leaking air."

"So you made an executive decision. Sometimes you have to do what you have to, knowing it's not ideal. You did well." He said it again to reinforce the point.

"Yes, sir." Her voice was little more than a whisper.

The cloud was beginning to break up and sunlight glinted off damp roofs and shallow puddles. From here the town looked like any other.

"What's it like here?" Ella asked. "It looks so normal."

"They were lucky. Yrmak raiders operate in two ways. Quite often they just steal everything, kill everybody and set fire to the rest. But for the smarter Yrmaks it's a business. Leave the place intact, let the settlement recover, and in a year or two they can come back for another visit."

Ella paled. "Really?"

"Really." He'd seen both happen, back when he was a junior officer and the Yrmaks were more active. "We're not sure of the death toll yet. The troopers are helping collect bodies. They'll need to be identified."

They walked down a street lined on both sides with basic, modular houses, all with vegetable gardens planted in neat rows. Further along, the street opened out into a large, paved square, with the hotel on one side. A line of covered bodies in the care of two of the troops had been placed near the door of the cool room. Several women walked slowly along the line, pausing occasionally. One had obviously found what she feared, kneeling beside a corpse, sobbing, while others tried to console her. Another woman had picked up a tiny bundle, clutching it to her breast.

She spied Chandler and ran at him, the damp edges of her night gown flapping around her legs, her red-rimmed eyes wild. "You know what they did to him? Snatched him away from me by the feet and slammed him against a wall. He's dead. His father is dead. Why weren't you here yesterday? Why didn't you stop this from happening?"

"I'm truly sorry for your loss." Sorrow, then guilt, then anger. All a man could do was weather the storm.

"Doesn't bring them back, does it?" The woman turned to Ella. "And you. Were you trying to kill us? I thought I'd die on that trip to the ground." She burst into hysterical sobs. "I wish I *had* died. I wish I was dead."

Ella took a step backward. Chandler took her arm in a firm grip, trying to send the message. Do nothing, say nothing. An old woman hurried over and put an arm around the bereaved mother. She shot an apologetic glance at Chandler as she led the woman away.

Ella was staring at him, her beautiful brown eyes shining. He dredged up a hint of a smile. "Don't let it get to you. Right now they can't see further than their own problems. We'll do our best to help them. The battle cruiser *Starlight* is on its way. They'll be better able to assist." He only just stopped himself from putting his arm around her shoulders. "This way, Lieutenant. I don't want you fainting from lack of food."

Hahndorf had opened his kitchen with the help of some of the locals, and fed the recently arrived troopers. The smell of soup and fresh bread had Chandler salivating. He sat down with the squad and asked about the condition of the freighter until the food arrived. There had been some looting. Later he would send the lander up and retrieve what they could. After that he would send the hulk to crash on the nearest moon.

Ella drew patterns in the soup with her spoon, eating little until Lieutenant James said, "Bulich, the best way to get on top of this is to eat. Go on. It'll do you good."

Sighing, she scooped a spoonful into her mouth. When the plate was half finished she pushed it away. But she did perk up.

Chandler handed his empty plate to one of Hahndorf's people and stood. "Lieutenant, report to Lieutenant Arndt and help him collect statements." He would wander around, check on his troops, try not to worry about one junior officer.

Outside the women still walked along the row of bodies. The numbers had dwindled. When a corpse had been identified it was moved to the cool room. Many of the women had gone home to find out for themselves what had happened, and to dress. One came running now, tears streaming down her face. The older women met her, and Chandler sent troops to collect the bodies of her husband and son.

Chandler spied a trooper going into a house and hurried to catch up with him. He had to know what they were confronting. "Oh lord, look at this." The trooper stood at the top of the stairs, his face contorted in disgust, fighting the urge to vomit.

It had to be bad. These troopers were tough. Chandler ran up the stairs and into the bedroom.

The place stank of blood and guts and fear. Blood speckled the walls, or ran in messy streaks. The body of a boy of about ten lay on the blood-soaked bed. He'd been disemboweled, Chandler guessed with the knife used to spit the baby lying next to the crib. But the Yrmak hadn't taken this woman. The mother was dead, too, shot in the chest. She still held a gun in her hands, the gun she'd used to shoot the Yrmak. His body was sprawled on the floor beside the bed. Greenish-yellow blood was pooled on the floor and stained the covers.

"Captain, I —"

Ella had followed him. She stood beside him, eyes round. "Oh shit." She retched, turned and vomited up the food she'd eaten at the hotel.

Chandler shoved her out the door. "What the hell are you doing here?"

He'd shouted and she backed off. "Lieutenant Arndt sent me to tell you they found a couple of dead Yrmaks."

He rubbed his forehead. He'd yelled at her. Stupid. "Sorry. Sorry you had to see that."

She straightened. "Yes, sir. I'm an officer, sir."

It was a gentle rebuke, and she was right, even though her eyes glistened and she swallowed repeatedly.

"Okay. Where are these bodies?"

"On the edge of town. I can take you."

She almost ran down the stairs, then down the street and into the farmlands. Cattle standing in a group under a tree watched with interest, their jaws moving from side to side as they chewed.

A trooper stood guard beside two Yrmak corpses lying in a copse adjoining a field, killed with a pitchfork. The man who had killed them was dead, too, half his chest blown away. "Mister Hahndorf said the man was a farmer."

"A brave man. Looks like he knew his Yrmaks, too. The pitchfork would have pierced both hearts." Chandler turned to Ella. "Do some research. Use their patches and insignia to find out where they're from, which clan. It might give us some clues on where to find their base."

She saluted, then took images of the bodies from as many angles as she could. "Um. Should I do the other one?" She pointed a finger that wavered only slightly in the direction they'd come.

That would mean going back into the bedroom. "His patches were the same. There's no need."

"Yes, sir. Very good, sir." She tried hard to cover her relief, but didn't quite manage.

She walked away, shoulders back, back straight. What he really wanted to do was hold her in his arms, hug her tight and make everything better. But he couldn't.

He continued on his rounds, concentrating on making the villagers feel secure. No, he and his troops wouldn't be leaving. A battle cruiser was on its way, and the admiral would certainly provide them with whatever assistance they needed. More patrols? Beyond his power, but raise the matter with Admiral Hong.

The last light of the day painted the narrow band of clouds on the horizon red and orange. As it set, the sun sent up bright rays through the rents in the cloud, a final signal of hope.

Chandler went into the hotel and accepted a glass of beer from the publican. Hahndorf gazed up at Chandler, his face haggard with pain and sorrow. "There are guest rooms on the first floor. Might as well use them. Looks to me like your people could use some rest. You, too."

"Thanks. I'm grateful."

Tears welled in the older man's eyes. "Not as grateful as we are. But it sure is a pity you didn't arrive a day earlier."

Chandler nodded and rose to his feet. "Bulich, Judge, Ting, I'm going to avail myself of Mister Hahndorf's generous offer. Let's all get some sleep."

He pointed at the stairs amid the clatter of people standing up. On the landing a passage led in both directions, two rooms to the left, two to the right. Judge and Ting turned left. Ella took the end room on the right, Chandler took the next one.

Like everything else in the town, the rooms were easily-constructed modular units with a bed, a built in closet and a small washroom. A large window gave a view over the gardens behind the hotel. The sun had set and deep darkness settled over the settlement like a shroud. The stars blazed overhead, almost as crisp and cold as they were from space, uncaring spectators on the events of the last day. Images paraded before Chandler's eyes. The disemboweled boy, the old man with his chest blown apart, the baby with its head crushed, its blood smeared down the wall.

What a day. What a descent into hell. The conquering heroes finish off the nasty Yrmaks. Let's all have a celebratory party. Hurrah. But first we have to get these women down to their homes. To their dead husbands, slaughtered children.

Hell's teeth, this wasn't going to help. He undressed and turned on the shower. Hot water coursed over his body, sluicing away the aches and pains. He brushed his teeth, rinsed his mouth and washed his hair. The unit had a dryer function. Chandler waited long enough to ensure his hair was dry, then staggered to the bed.

He woke to screaming.

Ella. His heart hammering, he jumped out of bed, scooped up his service pistol and flashlight, and eased open the door. There was no one in the passage. He opened her door, keeping out of the entrance.

"It's all right." Her words were choked out.

She'd turned on the bedside lamp, sitting up, her breast heaving.

He came toward her. "It's Chandler. I heard you scream."

The fear had faded from her face but she was trembling, running a shaking hand through her hair. "It was just a dream. A nightmare."

Putting the pistol on the nightstand he sat down next to her. "You've had a very rough day."

"That boy on the bed. And the baby." Her lip quivered and tears welled.

Chandler put his arms around her and pulled her against his chest, stroking her hair. "You're allowed to cry. You're off duty and the adrenalin's drained. This is what happens next."

He let her cry. She was as naked as he was and his body was excruciatingly aware of her proximity. At length she drew away from him a little and looked into his face. "Sorry. You must think I'm a silly little girl." Tears still clung to her eyelashes.

He smiled. "You're not." He bent to kiss her forehead but she met him halfway, pressing soft lips to his. He knew he shouldn't, but he couldn't stop himself. She was here, where he'd wanted her for so long.

Her lips parted, her arms slipped around his neck and the kiss deepened. His hands roamed over her body, stroking, caressing. Ella lay down and he lay down beside her, fondling her breast, feeling the nipple tighten at his touch. His hand went lower, over her belly down between her thighs, dipping into warm wetness. She wanted him, he wanted her. He moved over, sliding into her. She sighed, her fingers clutching his shoulders. What was left of control evaporated. It was over too quickly. He groaned her name as he came. "Ella."

She smiled up at him, put her hand on his cheek. "Thanks."

Chandler spooned himself around her body, holding her until her breathing evened out. He'd loved it, every moment, but it should never have come to that. He was her commanding officer. He'd taken advantage of her distress. Sure, she'd enjoyed it, she'd encouraged him, but it was still wrong. What sort of senior officer screwed his staff? What if she changed her mind and decided to accuse him of sexual manipulation? Or worse, rape? He didn't for a moment think she would, he knew her better than that. But what if?

Careful not to wake her up, Chandler eased himself out of the bed and went back to his own room. The sheets were cold and comfortless, nothing more than he deserved.

Ella woke alone. Had that really happened? Had Senior Commander Chandler really made love to her? Would he know what that thought did to her? She'd loved it, she loved him. She slipped out of bed and into the washroom for a quick shower, then pulled on her clothes. Her suit sank of sweat, but it would have to do until they got back to *Antelope*.

She bounced down the stairs to the welcoming aroma of kaff and frying eggs. Chandler wasn't around. One of the troopers said he was out talking to the townsfolk, but he'd left orders for her to return to *Antelope* and start work on identifying the Yrmaks who had attacked the settlement. Ella ate breakfast and then hitched a ride back to the ship with the lander. On board the frigate seemed almost ghostly with so many of the crew down on the planet. She said good morning to Commander Linnaes, and set to work. During that afternoon the battle cruiser *Starlight* made planetary orbit, dwarfing the frigate.

Chandler didn't return to *Antelope* until the following day, when she was summoned to his office. He looked tense and grim, standing with his hands behind his back.

Ella saluted. "You wanted to see me, sir?"

"Yes." His Adam's apple bobbed, then he licked his lips. He didn't tell her to stand at ease.

A tendril of dread uncurled in Ella's stomach.

"Lieutenant Bulich, you're a very good young officer and I'm sure you'll go far in the service. What happened the other night in the hotel should never have happened. I... took advantage of you at a vulnerable time. I take full responsibility for my lapse in judgement. But it happened, I can't make it go away. As a result, you can no longer stay under my command. I've discussed the situation with Admiral Hong, and you will transfer to his flagship at once."

Ella sucked in a breath. He hadn't taken advantage of her. She'd taken advantage of him, encouraged him when she should have had the sense to back away. It wasn't his fault. She opened her mouth to speak, but he forestalled her.

"There is nothing to discuss, Lieutenant. This action has compromised both of us. The best thing we can do is pretend it never happened, and move on."

He was kicking her off the ship. Her spirits disappeared down a well of despair. He was right. She'd been an idiot, hadn't thought past her own libido. This could ruin his career, and hers. "Sir."

The tension in the lines of his face eased a little. "I'm sorry it has ended this way. I've announced to the crew that you've been transferred, and recommended for promotion. Pack your belongings immediately. Dismissed."

She saluted and executed a textbook about turn, blinking furiously to prevent the gathering tears. *Grow up.* Her roommate wasn't there when she went to her cabin, a small mercy. Packing didn't take long — uniforms, underwear, a few civilian items, and that was about it.

She passed a few people on the way down to the hangar bay. Linnaes ran after her in the corridor to wish her well, Gillian came down for a shared hug. Pretend it never happened and move on. *Yes, sir. Whatever you say, sir. What do I do about my broken heart, sir?*

"I must say, the food here is wonderful." Commander Smythe, sitting on Chandler's left, pushed her empty dessert plate aside, where it was swept away by one of the attendants. She eyed his barely touched plate. "Don't you like yours?"

"Hmm? Yes, it's delicious." Chandler dredged up a smile. "I guess I've just had enough."

Ella was at the table of four, two massive young men and their decidedly tipsy young ladies. Voices had been raised for a while now, as the two men had become steadily drunker.

"How long before the fireworks start?" the biggest of the pair asked.

"Just a few more minutes, sir," Ella said. "It's nearly midnight."

"Let's go down to the terrace, Emile," his girlfriend said, tugging an arm the size of a ham. "It's boring here."

Ella leaned closer to Emile, smiling, sending a completely inappropriate twinge of jealousy to Chandler's heart. "She's right, you know. Down there you're in the middle of it. Music, dancing. I'd be out there if I could."

That seemed to convince the rest of the party. "Come on, let's do it." The other young man stood. Emile, clearly outnumbered, paid the bill.

Ella escorted them all to the door.

Chandler watched them go. This was his chance. He had to talk to her. Murmuring, "Excuse me, won't you?" he followed her into the foyer. She'd taken the group to the elevator and was on her way back. She hesitated when she saw him, then plastered on a false smile.

"Good evening, sir. Can I help?" She pointed. "The gentlemen's washroom is —"

"I don't need the washroom, Ella. I want to talk to you."

She skewered him with a hostile glare. "There's nothing to talk about." She made to brush past him.

"Please, Ella. Just a few moments." He noticed a few stares. "Somewhere private?"

She hesitated for a moment, then, shrugging, she said, "Okay. In here." She stepped over to a door and opened it. Lights flicked on, revealing a large conference room with a central oval table surrounded by twenty or so chairs. It had that empty feel that unused conference rooms so often had.

Turning to face him, she gazed at him, one eyebrow cocked. "Well?"

"You look lovely. I like your hair like that."

Rolling her eyes, she shook her head. "Thanks. Now if there's nothing else...?"

"Ella, I'm sorry. I handled that situation very, very badly and I've regretted it ever since. You didn't deserve to be thrown away like that."

A sad smile played around her lips. "That's what I thought, too. But, as you said, best to pretend it never happened and get on with life. I gather you've made admiral."

He'd never been so tongue-tied in all his life. Sorry wasn't enough, let's try again wouldn't cut it. Not yet, anyway. Maybe not ever. She didn't even seem pleased to see him. "Yes. Made admiral. Are you still married?" He blurted the words.

"Chandler, that is none of your business." Frowning, she shook her head. "Look, I've got customers to look after. So if you'll excuse me —" Muffled explosions from somewhere outside cut her off. "They started the fireworks early." She stepped toward the door, but he grabbed her arm.

"That wasn't fireworks. It's shots, fired nearby."

Her eyes widening, she removed the comlink on her belt and flicked through several images. She groaned. "Look at this." She held up the device so he could see. Yrmaks, in the dining room he'd just left. All the guests were dead or dying. As he watched, an Yrmak casually shot a man who'd raised his arm. One Human was still alive, apparently talking to an Yrmak.

Ella grabbed Chandler's arm and dragged him toward the back of the room. "They're looking for you. That attendant was a late replacement."

Chandler put the rest together himself. Someone had organized for the Yrmaks to hit 'soft' targets on a night when fireworks would

be going off all around the city. They'd planted collaborators in the
hotel to help them get in. Ella opened a door and he followed close
behind into a cramped service area for the conference room. His
comlink buzzed. He didn't need Ella's hissed, "Don't answer it."

"Is there surveillance here?"

"No. Just in the public areas."

"So they'll know we were in the conference room." He opened a
cupboard and closed it again. Too obvious.

"What are you doing?"

"Looking for somewhere to put this to delay them." He shoved
his comlink into a cupboard under the sink. "Leave yours somewhere
more obvious. But before you do, check if we're being followed."

She nodded, flicking through images too fast for him to register.
"Looks like they've split up and are searching rooms. They're working
individually. Must think we're all easy prey." Her lip curled, she
switched the device off and put it into a cutlery drawer.

Chandler saw the glint of polished knives. "Are any of those
worth using as a weapon?"

She shook her head. "But there will be in the kitchen." She led
him through another doorway into a dusty corridor and broke into a
run.

Hurrying behind her, his nerves tingled. He could swear he'd
heard footsteps from the conference room. "Can they track your
movements?"

"Only through the comlink."

Good. They needed to get out of this building. He needed to get
to the president, and talk to his ship, get military help down here.
Ibbotson and six other senior officers were all dead, they probably
thought he was dead, too. But first he needed to get rid of the Yrmak
on their tail.

Ella opened another door and darted inside. The Yrmak murder
squads had already been here. Two cooks, their pale blue tunics

stained red with their own blood, lay slumped across a central bench. One of them still held a cleaning cloth in his hand. Broken crockery and glassware lay scattered across the tiled floor.

"Oh crap." Pain was etched into Ella's face.

Chandler put a finger to his lips. "Shh. There's nothing we can do for them. Carving knives, big ones, now."

She responded to his tone, crossing the littered floor to a knife block with six handles reflecting the soft light. She handed him the largest carving knife and kept a smaller blade for herself.

Chandler crouched down next to the door on one side, and motioned her to do the same. Miming, he described to her what he wanted her to do. He had to hope she understood. It was a risk, but if they didn't take the Yrmak out he would surely find them — or ask for help.

Time slowed. His heart thumped, but he calmed his nerves, preparing himself to react when he needed to. If Ella did her job, this should be easy.

His heart jolted when the door slid aside into the recess in the wall behind him. The barrel of a gun appeared, tracking from side to side. The Yrmak took one step, the heavy three-toed foot landed. Its other leg swung forward. *Now Ella.*

She dived, the knife held in her right hand, plunging the blade deep into the warrior's calf. It grunted and stumbled, trying to right itself. Chandler leaped on its back, forcing the Yrmak face-down onto the floor, driving the knife deep into its neck. If he could reach the large artery in front of its backbone, it would be over. The warrior thrashed, bucking and heaving beneath him. Chandler was losing the fight. The Yrmak tossed him off. Evil yellow eyes glared at him as it staggered to its feet. Chandler sidled away, the knife held in front of him. If the Yrmak wanted to kill him, he'd have to come and get him. Where was Ella?

Ella scrambled away from the fallen Yrmak, avoiding its flailing legs as it fought with Chandler. Its gun skittered away and lay among the fragments on the floor. She scooped the weapon up, scrabbling through her long-forgotten memories of how Yrmak guns worked. It couldn't be too hard. The warrior would have been ready to fire. Ah. Here near the left hand grip. Chandler was losing the fight, backing away on the floor as the warrior tried to stand. Ella aimed at the Yrmak's back and pressed the trigger. A blast of power lit up its form for a split second, then it toppled forward and lay still.

Ella glanced at the bodies of the two Humans, innocent people here doing a job. She wondered if they had wives, kids. *This one's for you, guys.*

Panting, Chandler dragged himself to his feet. "Thanks. And now we have a gun."

"My pleasure. I don't want to think of all the innocent people these things have murdered."

His face softened. "Just like Telon Gar." Shaking his head, he added, "Where to now? We can't use the elevator."

"We have to take a stairwell." But which one? "There's several. One escape route for guests in case the elevators are out, and one for staff to get things in the back door."

Chandler grunted. "That will be how the attackers got in." He frowned, chewing his lip. "Let's try that one. We have a gun if we get company. And you can bet the local authorities have been alerted, so they won't be far away."

It made sense. If the attackers had used the stairs they would have killed anyone in their way. The stairs were close by, to service the kitchens. Ella cracked the door to check the surroundings. Muffled noises percolated through from outside. Explosions, the sound of gunfire or fireworks. The hum of a low-flying aircraft, the dull roar of panicked people. But inside, this corridor was silent as a tomb. The metaphor came to mind too readily. For many people, the Majestic Hotel had become a tomb.

Chandler leaned over her, his body warm and close. "We have to go."

They did. She slid out of the kitchen and along to the stairwell marked 'staff only', listening for any sound, any hint of an enemy. She entered the code into the keypad on the wall and waited for what seemed like an eternity for the soft click, sounding loud in the silence, as the door unlocked. The lights brightened as she started down the stairs, treading carefully to minimize noise. They reached the first landing. Blood smeared the hand rail. Ella peered down the stairwell and saw a body spread-eagled on the floor. A thrill of unease shot through her without warning. She looked up and saw a figure two landings above them leaning over the rail pointing something.

"Chandler!" She screamed his name, raised the Yrmak gun and pressed the trigger, holding it down. Hot brightness grazed past her and splashed on the wall. Up in the stairwell somebody grunted. The figure toppled over the rail and fell past her to thump with an ugly splat onto the other body already there.

"Chandler?" He was sprawled on the steps, almost to the next landing. Her heart thundering, Ella ran down and knelt beside him. His eyes were closed and a deep scratch on his cheek oozed beads of blood. "Chandler, don't you dare die."

Chandler's lips cracked in a hint of a smile. "Keep that up and I'll think you care."

Damn his hide. "You're the only other person alive in this morgue. Are you hurt?"

He sat up, reached out his right hand to grip the rail, and pulled himself up. "Battered, no doubt bruised. I think my left arm is broken." He pointed to a point halfway between shoulder and elbow. "Is it much further?"

"One more flight," she said, leading the way. "Let's hope that was the only one waiting."

"And that he didn't tell anyone."

Oh, she needed that. But this stairwell ended in a lane beside the hotel, just off the main square. If the local authorities were busy, they should be safe. She hurried, moving as fast as she could while still keeping quiet. While Chandler covered the rest of the distance, Ella checked outside, using the spyhole in the door.

Chandler joined her, his attention on the two bodies behind them. "Do you know him? The one who fired at us?"

Ella noted the dark red jacket and black pants, the dark hair tied back in a ponytail. "That's Liam." She thought back to half an hour ago. He was the attendant at Emile Zoran's table. He should have been there when the party left. She'd made a note to discipline him. "He wasn't there to escort Zoran and his people out. He was probably here, letting the Yrmaks in."

Bastard. Why would a Human do that, help a squad of Yrmak warriors slaughter innocent civilians? Or maybe one table full of senior Fleet officers was the real target. Yrmaks seemed to take it out on everyone when they had the blood lust.

Even though she'd checked, Ella opened the door carefully. The square, decked out for the celebrations, looked like the aftermath of a battle. Mounds covered with sheets were everywhere. Lights flashed on vehicles. An ambulance took off in a shower of dust. Local troops helped people up the ramp into a second ambulance. Dead Yrmaks had been collected and placed in a pile under guard. There were no prisoners.

Limping slightly, Chandler took her arm in a firm grip and headed for the presidential palace opposite the hotel. The building still wore its flags and banners, the windows ablaze with lights. The perimeter had been secured, with armed troops manning the gates.

A soldier cradling a gun in one arm held up his hand as they approached. "On your way. You can't come here."

"I'm Admiral Chandler. I need to see the president."

The man sneered. "Yeah, and I'm Marilyn Fenton."

Chandler opened his shirt to reveal a readable disk, the sort all Fleeters wore. "Here's my credentials. Would you like to show me yours?"

The smile fading from his face, the soldier scanned the disk. His Adam's apple bobbed. "Shit. Uh — I mean. Just a moment. Sir."

Ella sniggered. "Ah, the impact of rank." But she felt a little bit sorry for the lad. Bumping into a Fleet admiral very likely hadn't been in the script.

The soldier returned with a junior officer, who performed an impeccable salute. "Come this way, Admiral."

Chandler still gripped her arm. Ella tried to pull away from him. Pretend it never happened, move on. "You'll be all right now. I better get on home."

He shot her a look through narrowed eyes. "You're not going anywhere." Tightening his grip enough to hurt he dragged her behind him.

"What happened to pretend it never happened and move on?" she said, stumbling over an empty bottle.

He pulled her closer to him. "I haven't finished apologizing yet. Now behave yourself or I'll have you arrested."

Behave herself? She'd just saved his hide. Twice. How about, 'thanks very much Ella, I'm glad you were there'? No. 'Behave yourself or I'll have you arrested.'

Six armed, uniformed troopers had formed up around them. It was amazing what a handful of stars could do to a group of soldiers. Ella stopped pulling and went with the flow. But she'd better get over this ridiculous notion that she'd like to hear his apology. She knew how it would go. Perhaps a two-night fling, then he'd be on his way, back to his wife, content that he'd done the right thing.

Chandler winced his way up the wide steps outside the palace, glad there were only four. His left hip ached and his arm throbbed, shooting agonizing pangs every time he knocked it.

Ella tugged at his shirt with her left hand. "Can you ease up on my arm, Chandler? I'm losing circulation."

"Sorry." He didn't release her, just loosened his fingers. He wasn't going to let her go, ever again. He walked between wide doors opening into a high-ceilinged foyer. A colonel of the local military waited for him, standing at parade rest. He came to attention and saluted as Chandler approached.

"Colonel Blick, Admiral. I'm delighted to see you. We feared you had not survived the terrorist attack." He glanced at Ella, a hint of a question in his eyes.

"This is Ella Bulich. I owe her my life. She got me out of the hotel. And she may be able to shed light on those responsible for the attack there. For now, though, I need to contact my ship. If the President wishes I can send troops down to assist."

"We would be grateful, sir. The terrorists attacked a number of places where celebrations were in progress. Our people are stretched."

"Why? There's quite a large Yrmak population here. I can understand them attacking Imperial Fleet officers, but why would they do this?" Ella said, shaking her head. "Why would Yrmaks want to slaughter innocent civilians? There were Yrmaks in the crowds, enjoying a festive day, just like the Humans."

"It's a good question." Blick ushered them to an elevator and selected a floor. "We've had good relationships with the Yrmaks on this planet for going on a hundred years. We've watched events on other planets and congratulated ourselves that it doesn't happen here."

It had now. Chandler suspected it had to do with the growing unrest resulting from a distant star going supernova. That star happened to be the eye of the Yrmak's mother goddess — or at least, it was in the constellation that bore her name. Fundamentalist Yrmaks had taken the event to heart, insisting the Mother was angry because they had strayed from her path. In their lexicon, Yrmaks were superior to Humans. Humans were natural targets, but so were Yrmaks who rubbed along comfortably with Humans. He'd bet quite a few innocent Yrmaks died in this night's rampage.

The elevator slowed to a halt, and Blick waved them out, directing them to a sitting room where he urged them to sit. "The President is on his way, but while we're waiting, if you have any clues as to who perpetrated these attacks?"

Chandler exchanged a glance with Ella. She looked tired. Strands of hair had escaped from the neat braid and a bruise had begun to color on her cheekbone.

"I've been thinking about it since we left the hotel," she said. "The Yrmaks probably got in via a staircase only used by staff. Someone would have had to let them in and I think that was a man called Liam who was a late replacement for my restaurant staff."

The Colonel's eyes narrowed. "And where is this Liam now?"

"I shot him. His body is on the floor in the stairwell at the Hotel Majestic." She tossed the line away, as though it wasn't important. Chandler hid his amusement at Blick's start.

Ella rubbed her forehead. "I've been thinking more about it. I shouldn't have been there tonight. The restaurant manager, Jose Ramira, stopped me just as I was about to go home and asked me to take his shift for him. He said his mother was in hospital, dying." She shrugged. "So I agreed. Ramira hired Liam. We were supposed to have someone else, but Ramira said that person couldn't come for whatever reason, so Liam got the job."

Blick's nostrils flared. "You think Ramira organized something with the Yrmaks?"

"Makes sense to me. He didn't like me. Liam's on the inside to open the door. Why stay around and risk getting killed? Yrmaks with blood lust aren't safe to be around." She frowned. "I just can't understand why he'd do something like that."

"Not everyone is happy to see Yrmaks and Humans living in peace," Chandler said. "You might find this Ramira person is a member of Humans First. They'd love to see an interspecies war."

"So a manufactured attack?" Ella raised an eyebrow.

"Yes. It's easy enough to hire a group of Yrmaks to do some killing. At least some of them are very likely from off-planet. But, of course, all Yrmaks will be blamed."

"I'll put out an urgent instruction to find Ramira." Blick's expression changed to obsequious in an instant as he bounced to his feet. "Ah. Mister President."

Oboko sailed into the room like a royal yacht, a vast man wearing a deep blue uniform with gold epaulettes and a golden lanyard across his chest. The high gold collar bit deep into the fleshy folds of his neck.

Chandler stood, jarring his arm. The pain was so severe he bit his lips to suppress a groan.

"Admiral Chandler. So good to see you. But you are injured." President Oboko towered above him, concern gleaming in liquid brown eyes.

Chandler fought the pain until it was an acceptable background ache. "A broken arm. I'll have it seen to shortly. Meanwhile, Colonel Blick says you could use our help?"

"We could. We are overstretched."

"Show me somewhere I can contact my fleet, Mister President, and I'll have things put into place. Meanwhile, if you would provide Miss Bulich with suitable accommodation, and collect the bodies of my officers from the Majestic Hotel, I would be most grateful."

"Easy on all counts." Oboko waved a hand glittering with jewels. A servant stepped beside him, head bowed. "Mister Lambo will see to the lady's accommodation. And Colonel, your office is suitable for a link to the admiral's flagship."

As Mister Lambo led Ella away she shot a glance at him over her shoulder. Chandler read calculation. She would try to leave, disappear in the chaos. When she'd gone, he said, "Mister President, while I want my companion to be comfortable, I also want her to stay where she is. Do you understand?"

Oboko's whole body moved when he chuckled. "The lady is not willing?"

Chandler shook his head. Was he so transparent? The last thing he wanted was a suggestion that she was being forced. The word 'rape' wouldn't go away. "Let's just say I don't want her to disappear before I get a chance to talk to her." He emphasized the word 'talk'.

Oboko chuckled again, sending the golden ornamentation on his uniform dancing. "I will make sure Mister Lambo understands."

Ella walked behind Lambo, hoping this would be a short trip. The adrenalin was wearing off, she'd been on her feet since dawn, and the aches and pains were beginning to sit up and ask for attention. Lambo never said a word, simply guided her to an elevator, then down to a lower floor and along a carpeted passage. He stopped outside a door and used his palm to gain access.

He bowed, gesturing. "If you will enter, madam."

Wow. This was a guest suite, rivalling if not surpassing the premier suites in the Majestic. The sitting room oozed understated elegance: pale wood, cream fabrics, a woven rug in forest colors. A large holovid receiver stood against one wall, opposite a three-seater couch. Matching armchairs completed the setting.

"You have a choice of bed chambers. Both have adjoining washrooms." He walked over to a cabinet against the wall and pressed a knob. It opened up to reveal drinks and snacks. "If you require anything at all — meals, drinks — press this," he pointed at a button, "and an attendant will come."

"A change of clothes would be nice," Ella said, plucking at her filthy tunic.

Tambo bowed. "I will have it seen to."

Ella yawned. Her eyes drooped. Right now, all she wanted was a shower and a sleep. "Tell them not to wake me, okay?"

The butler departed.

Ella selected the smaller of the two bedrooms, although it was still larger than the master bedroom of the average house. She expected Chandler would turn up sooner or later. This was a suite for an admiral, not a soon to be ex-restaurant manager. Pulling the clasp off her hair, she opened the door to the washroom. Golden fittings gleamed in soft light. A spa bath took up one corner. It looked inviting, but she'd probably fall asleep. Promising herself a long soak tomorrow, she settled for a shower, then crawled into a bed big enough to host an orgy. If she were into that sort of thing.

Ella woke stiff and sore. All the small injuries had formed a union and gone out on strike, complaining every time she moved. That spa bath was going to be a wonderful idea. She padded into the washroom and inspected her injuries in the mirror. Bruises on her hips and thighs, scratches on her face and hands. Nothing major. She found some Curall ointment in a cupboard and smeared it on her face, then lowered herself into the hot, bubbling water. Ah, bliss.

As promised, clothes had been left for her, draped on the sofa in the sitting room. She lifted a gown in various shades of blue, soft and feminine. Not her at all, but none of the others looked any better, more suitable for a courtesan than anything else. Oh, good grief. That's probably exactly what they were thinking: the admiral's piece of fluff.

She put on the blue gown, which at least more or less covered most of her, and found a news channel on the holovid. The terror attacks seemed to be the only thing on, with repeated footage of the carnage — minus the bodies, of course. The Hotel Majestic wasn't the only site hit. Yrmak warriors had decimated the packed crowds watching the entertainment by the lake, the sound of their weapons blending in with those of the music and the fireworks. They'd hit a popular outdoor food market away from the city center, and fanned out from there, killing anyone in their sights. Quite a few of the attackers had escaped, evaporating into the Yrmak areas of the city. A police cordon had been set up to protect the Yrmak population from the mob mentality blaming any Yrmak in sight. Ella noticed Fleet uniforms among the defenders. Chandler must have sent down troops.

Eye witness accounts were popular, with various individuals explaining how they noticed people screaming and running, and thought running would be a good idea. One man hid in an alley while an Yrmak who had already shot his wife and child searched for him. Tears gleamed in his eyes, reliving the horror as he talked. And there was airball star Emile Zoran.

He was dressed as he had been at the dinner, his hair disheveled and with smudges on his face. The cocky smile had gone, replaced with the haunted look of someone who has seen unspeakable things. "My friends and I were on the way to join the party by the lakeside. The shooting started just before we got there but we thought it was just fireworks. People started running, but we didn't realize it was serious until we saw an Yrmak shooting into the crowd."

His voice faltered. "Kids, old folks, anybody." He glanced behind him and Ella recognized the glittering façade of the Majestic Hotel. "Later we found out everybody in the restaurant where we had dinner had been killed. If we hadn't left early..."

Ella turned it off.

Her memories of the Yrmak slave raid on Telon Gar were always there, behind a shield that all too easily became translucent. She wondered where Chandler was, what he was doing. She sighed. Did she really want to go through all that heartache again? He'd be grateful this time, he'd apologize for kicking her off his ship, they'd have a lovely sexy night or two, and then he'd disappear back to his commission and his wife knowing he'd done the right thing by ex-Lieutenant Bulich. She'd cried enough tears over him. She thought she'd put herself back together, that he was just a distant memory. Until she saw him again in the Imperial.

The best thing she could do was leave. Disappear. She'd been going to do that, anyway, move on to another planet. The dress wasn't really suitable for day travel, but her apartment wasn't far away. She crossed the short distance to the door. It wouldn't open. Dammit, he'd imprisoned her. She smashed her fists against the locked door. Dammit. He had no right.

The door slid aside. Two troopers faced her, weapons held ready. Their eyes widening, they looked her up and down. "Is something wrong, madam?"

Ella lowered her clenched fists and put her hands on her hips. Let them look. "Why am I a prisoner?"

They exchanged a glance. "We have orders to guard the door, ma'am," the second man said.

"So I can leave." She took a step forward. "Stand aside."

The taller man shook his head. "You're to stay here. Orders."

Orders. Benighted orders. She couldn't take on two of them dressed in this frilly sack. "Okay." She stepped back inside and the door slid shut.

So she'd have to confront Admiral Goran Chandler. But she didn't have to play the game he expected.

Chandler didn't appear until the following day, late in the evening. Ella was reclined on the sofa watching the news when he came in without any announcement. Her heart skipped a beat. He wore the full dress uniform of a Fleet admiral, all white with gold stars on his epaulettes. The short jacket was cut close to his body, accentuating his trim physique and broad shoulders. She came within a hair's breadth of standing up and saluting, but changed the movement into turning off the holovid. "Admiral. I was about to get up and salute."

He sighed, shaking his head. "I don't want you to do that."

Still standing just inside the door he began to unfasten his coat, using only his right hand, sliding the gold buttons through the holes one by one. Ella, holding her breath from one button to the next, found the whole thing totally erotic. At last the jacket parted and he could ease out his arms, starting with the left one. He wore a short-sleeved white undershirt under the coat and as he drew his arm out she noted the flesh-colored casing around his upper arm. She'd forgotten he'd been injured.

"Does it hurt?"

"Not really. It's a clean break. The doctors injected nanobots, and a whole medicine cabinet full of pain killers." He finished taking off the coat and tossed it onto the back of a chair. The undershirt clung to his body, sculpting his muscles.

Ella caught herself staring again. This would not do. She would not allow him to play fast and loose with her heart. "You had me locked up."

He smiled for the first time, crinkling the fine lines around his eyes. " I told you. I haven't finished apologizing." He sat down in the chair at right angles from the sofa and stretched out his legs. The wound on his cheek had been repaired, but the scar remained.

Keep to the plan, Ella. "And after that, I'm free to go?"

"Of course. I would never do anything to you against your will."

The words came unbidden. "Except kick me off your ship."

He chuckled. "So. We've come full circle. Before we were rudely interrupted by a bunch of Yrmak terrorists I think I'd asked you if you were still married."

Ella examined her fingernails. "As I recall I told you to mind your own business."

"Or words to that effect. All right, I'll start. I'm single, have been for about nine years. Maybe a little more. My wife asked for a divorce after I blurted out your name while I was having sex with her."

Ella stared at him. His eyes twinkled and his mouth was stretched into the same half-smile she'd found so sexy all those years ago. His experience was a lot like hers. Her marriage to Ivan had been shaky at best. When she returned from Telon Gar on leave she suffered from nightmares that left her sweating and shaking. And it seemed she talked in her sleep. Ivan accused her of sleeping with her CO, which had to be why she'd been transferred, didn't it? That was the day she walked out. Not long after that, she left Fleet. "I'm divorced."

"How long?"

She shrugged. "About the same as you. Nine years. Why is this relevant?" Dammit, she was finding it very hard to keep up her animosity.

"Ella, I behaved badly after Telon Gar, but believe me, I had good intentions. We were both married, we did something we should not have done." He moistened his lips. "But I confess, my approaching chance of promotion to captain was a part of my reasoning."

The admission hurt, but it wasn't unexpected. "When I thought about it later, I figured that was part of it. Did you think I'd do something to sabotage you? Go to the promotions board and accuse you of sexual misconduct? Rape?"

He winced.

All the pent-up anger and frustration she'd felt for all those years bubbled up. "You did. You thought I'd do that to you. I love you, you idiot. I'd never do anything like that. And you didn't realize?"

Closing his eyes, he rubbed his forehead with splayed fingers. When he looked at her again, he said, "I realized we were becoming far too close. And Ella, that's not something a senior officer should do. At Telon Gar I worried about everyone's safety, but *especially* yours. And that meant I jeopardized my ability to make sensible decisions." He paused. "Maybe I should have told you some of that at the time. But I didn't. I'm truly, truly sorry."

'We were becoming far too close'. His words echoed in her head. She'd convinced herself he was sick of her, deliberately ignoring her. He was, but not for the reasons she'd thought.

"After my divorce I tried to find you. But you moved often. After the first two planets I lost the trail. But I've never been able to get you out of my head. Every new girlfriend I'd compare her to you, wonder where you were, what you were doing."

She swallowed. "I left Fleet behind. I didn't want any reminders. I found work where I could and soon found hospitality was a trade where I'd always find a job." And then, when they tried to promote her past her tolerance level, she resigned, and moved on. "I visited quite a few planets that way, got to see them from ground level."

She stood. "Can I get you a drink? They've got everything here." She padded over to the cabinet against the wall and pressed the button. The doors unfolded, displaying a range of bottles and glassware glinting in the light.

He'd straightened up in his seat, a smile playing around his mouth. "Nice dress."

The heat rose to her cheeks. The gown was semi-transparent, and all she wore underneath was a pair of panties. They were transparent, too. "It's not mine."

The smile widened. "I expect President Oboko thought it would suit." He came over to her, gazing into her eyes. "I don't want a drink, Ella. All I want is you."

She stepped back. She couldn't afford this, couldn't risk her badly repaired heart bursting apart again. "Look, Chandler, I'd rather not. Hot sex for a night or two, then you're on your way." She stared at her bare toes, buried in the rug. "No."

"Well then." He knelt in front of her, on one knee, and took her hand in his. "I love you, Ella. Would you do me the great honor of consenting to be my wife?"

Ella stared down at him, trying to find words to say. 'Yes' was too simple. She'd said yes once before, and look how that ended. "Ten years is a long time. What if we're both hanging on to a memory, something that doesn't exist anymore? What if we make love and it's ordinary, nothing like the passion we shared at Telon Gar?"

Still holding her hand, he stood. "I suppose there's a small risk. Why don't we try it and see?"

He slipped his right arm around her waist and drew her a little closer, bending over her to press his lips to her bare neck. He smelled of soap and a hint of cologne and her resistance was crumbling to dust as the pools of desire flooded her groin. Her hands moved almost of their own volition to his shoulders. His mouth covered hers, warm and gentle and seductive. The kiss seemed to last for an eternity as she molded herself against him, aching for the contact of flesh on flesh. She pulled back a little so she could push the undershirt up and away. She eased the garment up sliding her hands under the material and up over his body. He took over himself to remove the shirt from his left arm.

Oh, crap, she'd forgotten he was injured. "I'm so sorry."

"Don't be. Let's find somewhere a little more comfortable."

Her bedroom was the closest. While he kicked off his shoes and unfastened his trousers Ella discarded the dress and panties. The deep frown as he tried to take off his pants with his right hand showed his arm still hurt. Ella helped him, pausing to brush her lips against his erection. He laid a hand on her hair. "No. This isn't about me."

Ella gazed up at him. If she hadn't loved the man already, she would have fallen in love all over again. She straightened up slowly, sliding her hands up his body and pressing feather kisses to his stomach, his navel, his chest and then back for another long, deep kiss, pressed together. He urged her on to the bed, lying on his right side beside her, then took her nipple into his mouth. It was already tight, but his flicking tongue puckered it even further. She moaned, pushing her fingers through his hair. When he shifted his position to lie on top of her she stopped him. "Let me." She placed a hand on the dressing on his arm to signal what she meant. He nodded once, gazing at her with eyes dark with lust, as he eased over onto his back.

Ella straddled him, bringing herself down on his cock. He closed his eyes and sighed as she went deep, then slowly, slowly rode him; deep, hold, then up. "Oh Ella, that's delicious."

He pulled her down on top of him so he could kiss her while they moved together in that timeless lovers' dance. He drew his mouth away from hers. "Kneel for me."

Anything he wanted she would do. She knelt on the bed, listening to the rustle as he came to stand behind her, then slid his cock into her. His right hand slipped around her thigh to find her clit, strumming as he thrust, sending delicious quivers through her body. She came in a gush, arching her back and grunting incoherent sounds. Chandler pumped her, then sagged over her body groaning her name. He brushed her hair aside and kissed her neck. "Did I tell you I love you? Now roll over and let me cuddle you. I'm exhausted."

Ella did as she was told, lying with her head on his right shoulder, one leg thrown over his. "That was very, very nice."

His body bounced when he chuckled. "Rather better than the urgent coupling on Telon Gar, would you not agree?"

Oh yes. Yes indeed. This had been tender and gentle and caring and all about each other. All she said was, "Yes."

"So it's agreed then?"

What? "I just said yes."

"Good. I'm sure President Oboko would be happy to officiate at our wedding ceremony."

She raised her head so she could see his face.

He was grinning. "Well, I'd say we passed your criterion."

"I haven't a thing to wear."

"That can be fixed. I'll have one of my female officers bring some clothes for you and take you shopping."

"But..." Married. Just like that. She'd seen him again... was it really only two days ago?

Chandler disengaged her and stood. "I think I'd like that drink now."

She admired his lovely tight butt as he walked over to the drinks cabinet, visible through the open door. After taking a moment to look through the selection, he took out a bottle and twisted the top off. Then he picked up a couple of tall stemmed glasses and came back to the bedroom. He was gorgeous. Broad shoulders, narrow hips, strong legs and everything except his left arm in perfect working order.

He sat down on the edge of the bed and handed her a glass, which he filled with pale yellow wine that fizzed as he poured. "It's

Brookvale Estate. One of the top wine makers in the Empire." He poured a glass for himself and sipped. "Nice."

Ella moved around to sit beside him. "It's lovely." She chewed her lip. "You don't think this is happening too fast? It's been ten years."

"Exactly. Do you remember what I said to you when I kicked you off my ship?"

She did. The words were engraved on her soul. "Pretend this never happened and move on."

He nodded. "I've spent ten years kicking myself. Sounds to me you've done something similar. So I suggest we take that advice: pretend Telon Gar never happened and move on." He raised his glass. "Are we agreed?"

Smiling, she clinked her glass against his. "Agreed."

The Demon's Eye

This is another short, stand-alone story from the Dryden Universe. It has been published separately.

Krystina Merkos is reluctant to leave her home planet, but agrees it's best that her father doesn't have to concern himself with her safety while he fights a civil war. The journey on an Imperial warship becomes much more palatable when she discovers that Ben Paulsen, an old flame from her high school days, is a senior officer on the ship.

But it's not all plain sailing. The captain wants to seduce her, Ben's trying to keep his distance – and pirates want to sell her to the murderous sect waging war on her father.

When the frigate is attacked by a pirate fleet intent on capturing Krys, she faces impossible choices. If she hands herself over to the pirates, she will die a painful death. If she doesn't, everyone will die.

Unless she and Ben can contrive a way out for them all.

KRYS STRAIGHTENED HER BACK, SQUARED HER SHOULDERS, and smiled her public, so-pleased-to-meet-you smile before she answered the soft knock at her stateroom's door. The young man waiting there took a step backwards and cleared his throat, his eyelashes fluttering. Surely she wasn't *that* scary. And certainly the dress she wore wasn't especially revealing. A bit of cleavage, bare back that he couldn't see, it was cinched around the waist but fell loose to the floor. Not what she'd wear to seduce anybody.

Stepping into the corridor Krys put as much charm as she could muster into her tone. "I take it you're my escort?"

This lad was an officer? Lordy, they seemed to be younger every year. Krys could swear he still had pimples. But there was no avoiding the shiny bars on his shoulder boards.

"Yes, ma'am. Lieutenant Boll, ma'am." He ripped off a crisp salute, no doubt taking solace in established protocol. "If you'll follow me."

He marched in front of her, not too fast, probably afraid she couldn't keep up. Being tall enough to give most men a crick in the neck, she'd given up wearing nose-bleed high heels long ago. And her dress gave her plenty of room to stride in sensible, low-heeled pumps if she wanted to. Whatever. She let him set the pace and tried to get the funeral march out of her head.

The short passage opened into the elevator foyer, where Lieutenant Boll pressed the call button for a car, then dithered, looking around him, brushing a non-existent speck from his white dress uniform.

Krys didn't know whether to laugh or roll her eyes and settled for small talk, instead. "Have you served on this ship long, Lieutenant?"

Before he could answer, the car announced its arrival with a soft ping and a swish as the door opened. She stepped inside, with Lieutenant Boll so hard on her heels she could feel his breath on her back. Krys took up position in the left rear corner of the car while Boll selected a destination. He turned, put his hands behind his back and said, "Two months, ma'am. My first posting."

And his first important mission, by the looks; fetch Lady Krystina Merkos from the stateroom and bring her to the officers' mess.

It was a short trip. They'd barely started when they stopped again. The low rumble of voices was evident when the car door soughed open and Lieutenant Boll waved her forward. The noise faded into silence as soon as she entered, to find a crowd of men and women in white all staring at her. These days it was what she'd come to expect. Krys smiled around at them in greeting as Captain Saverill, commander of the Imperial star destroyer *Coromansa*, stepped forward to meet her.

"My Lady. We are honored by your presence." Clicking his heels, he made a formal neck bow.

Krys slipped on the public smile again while she ran an assessment. "You're too kind, Captain."

The man was a friend of her father's, someone he'd served with in his time as a Fleet officer. He looked a little younger than her dad, but then, her father ruled a planet, not a frigate. And although he was forcing himself to look at Krys's face, Saverill's eyes kept flicking to her cleavage. Typical.

Saverill moved to stand beside her and placed his hand on her back. Krys suppressed a shudder. Some men did that just to be friendly, although she had a notion Saverill wasn't one of them. Still, she'd give him the benefit of the doubt for now.

"Before we go in, allow me to introduce some of my command staff." The captain had a tenor voice, with the clipped accent of the Imperial capital.

Half a dozen officers had formed a line. Krys had learned in her skirmishes with public life that it was best to take them one at a time, concentrate on an individual for at least a few moments, and make them feel important, so she kept her attention on the first officer, an older man who swallowed and licked his lips as she approached. It seemed Lieutenant Boll wasn't the only man with a case of nerves.

Saverill stopped in front of him. "My executive officer, Commander Horton."

Plastering on a formal smile, Horton did the clicked heels, bow thing. Krys turned on her best, most winning manner. "Lovely to meet you, Commander. I'm very grateful to Captain Saverill for allowing me to travel with you."

Horton grinned, the sort of humorless grimace that didn't reach the eyes. "A pleasure to have you with us."

Oh well. She'd done her best, and it hardly mattered for what would be a relatively short trip.

"Commander Horton's a good officer and a friend. You can certainly rely on him if I'm not about," Saverill said as he moved on to the next man.

Krys's heart beat a little faster. Ben Paulsen. He'd filled out from the tall, skinny youth she'd known at school, but those smoky gray eyes and the strong jaw were unmistakable. The white uniform suited him, emphasizing his wide shoulders and flat abs, in stark contrast to Horton and Saverill, who both could benefit from some work in the gym.

"My master tactician and security officer, Commander Paulsen." Saverill's voice floated in, as if from a long way away.

Dragging herself away from memories of the library at high school, Krys gave Ben a genuine smile, but he didn't appear to recognize her, performing the routine heel-click and bow. Krys hid her disappointment, although there was no real reason why she should feel that way. They hadn't been an item, after all. Not really. But if that was how he wanted to play it, she could do that, too. Keeping her tone polite, but distant, she said, "Pleased to meet you."

Saverill propelled her on, his fingers pushing into her back. Her flesh crawled. She loathed being pawed. They'd reached the next person, the chief engineer, Commander Wong, and fortunately the captain took his hand away. Krys had almost lost interest in Saverill's officers by then, her thoughts returning to Ben. But she did her duty, responding to the officer's cordial greeting. The top of the woman's head barely reached Krys's shoulder, but her no nonsense manner and easy welcome hinted at strength of character. She asked Wong about her work before moving on to the last man, the officer commanding the ship's small marine contingent. She registered his name. Major Mill... no, Hill.

Saverill put his hand on her back again. "Please come through to the dining room."

Krys turned away from him just enough to force him to take his hand away and fixed him with a glare. "If you'll lead the way, Captain, I'll follow."

He blinked a couple of times, but at least he took the hint and walked ahead of her through a door into a room with three long tables set horizontally, with a shorter table at the top. While Saverill fussed over her, pulling out the chair next to his in the middle of the top table, the rest of the officers took their places amid a din of conversation and scraped furniture. Krys tried not to notice Ben taking a place at one of the other tables, but his tall, powerful frame was unmistakable.

Dinner was interminable, a series of particularly fancy courses which she was sure had been chosen to impress her. Krys oohed and aahed at the right places and tried not to be too bored at Saverill's endless tales about his and her father's exploits at the Fleet Academy. She was sure he was leaving out a lot of the details.

Her own father made no secret of being a party-goer and womanizer before he'd married her mother. Which led her to her mother, sequestered in the palace with her father. She hoped her mother would be okay. Dad had wanted her to leave with Krys, but there was no way she could have escaped without anyone knowing. Besides, she point-blank refused. Small and slender she might be, but her mum was much tougher than people realized. She and dad had been through some turbulent times together. This would be just another one. Krys hoped.

Saverill had stopped talking. In the lull in conversation, while the steward topped up the wine, Krys got a word in edgeways. "I notice a couple of the officers you introduced are sitting at the side tables?" She let the question hang.

Saverill took a gulp of wine before he put his glass down. "Only Paulsen and Wong. They seem to think they need to mix with their underlings, even here." His shrug said it all. Krys thought it was a smart move, cementing the relationship with the team, but she wasn't going to say so. Saverill was clearly an elitist. Rank mattered.

Refusing another glass of wine, she sent the steward away with a shake of her head. "You'll forgive me, Captain, but it has been a trying few days. I'm tired." And that was true enough.

Saverill rose to his feet as soon as she did. The man could certainly handle his drink; he hardly even swayed, even though he must have gone through a bottle by himself. "Of course. Let me escort you to your stateroom."

There was an unmistakable glitter in the captain's eyes. He wasn't bad looking as far as it went, about Krys's height and elegant in his dress uniform. But he was always touching, invading her space and she had no doubt that seduction was high on his agenda. It sure as hell wasn't on hers. "That's kind of you, but it's just up a few levels and then down a corridor, isn't it? I'm sure I can find it. Or you can send Lieutenant Boll with me."

A chair scraped and Ben rose to his feet. "I'm on duty shortly, sir. I can escort Lady Krystina to her quarters on my way."

Saverill's eyebrows came together.

Before he could say any more, Krys turned to Ben. "Thank you, Commander... Paulsen, wasn't it?" When he nodded she hurried around the table to where he waited. "I'm sure that's much better than intruding on the captain's time."

Ben gestured toward the exit to the foyer and followed behind her as they made their way to the elevator.

"I couldn't leave you to Slimy Saverill's tender mercies," he murmured as he summoned a car.

Her heart skipped a beat. Damn, that was so immature. "So you *did* recognize me."

"Of course. But our captain doesn't need to know we're old friends."

The car arrived and he bowed her inside. He stood fairly close to her, both their backs against the wall. "So. What's happening on Novastora?"

Krys stared up at him, searching the hard lines of his face for any signs of duplicity. "You know that, surely? The Warriors of Sundara have started a civil war."

"The bare facts, yes. I hoped you might be able to tell me more. Like why you're here?"

The lift pinged as the door opened. Ben strode beside her for the short walk to her door. She felt a bit like she had all those years ago, coming home from a date.

"Come inside?" she asked.

He hesitated for a second, then shook his head. "Saverill will check on me. Just quickly...?"

"Why am I here? Aria Arachonis is a right wing, misogynist bastard who would try to use me against my father if he could get his hands on me. *Coromansa* was up at the space station on a routine visit. Dad attended military college with Saverill. He trusts Saverill to get me to the Empire."

Frowning, Ben nodded. "I've got to go. Duty and all that. Maybe I can catch up with you tomorrow."

"I'd like that. And... it's great to see you." She could have sworn he flushed as he turned away.

The stateroom was as well appointed as a top class hotel, with a three piece lounge suite, a refreshments dispenser and a superior entertainment unit. A wall-sized screen showed a starscape, an image of what they'd be looking at if the ship was in normal space. The screen looked like a viewport, but she didn't have to be a space scientist to realize that down here on level six it had to be a projection.

Krys flopped onto the couch, kicked her shoes off and propped her legs up on the low table. She was tired. Sneaking out of the city and getting onto the ship had been exhausting. But her brain wasn't tired.

Ben Paulsen. He'd certainly grown up to be quite a man. He'd been tall at high school, but all arms and legs and skin and bone. He'd filled out, adding bulk to that framework. She wouldn't mind finding out what was underneath that dress uniform now. The material strained just a little across his chest and the slope on his shoulders hinted at solid muscle. Now she thought about it his response to her had been in character. He'd always been a bit distant. Not shy exactly, more self-contained, a loner. That used to annoy some of the alpha male bully boys.

Krys cast back, trying to remember the name of the good-looking boy everyone but her wanted to date. Lex somebody. Not that it mattered. Lex tried to tease Ben, but Ben never reacted, just stared back with a faint smile on his lips. Krys had intervened once, in the library, when Lex and his gang had Ben in their sights. She'd asked him for help with her math homework, even though she really hadn't needed it.

Lex had loomed next to her, hanging over her. "I can help you. You don't need to waste your time with this loser." He'd spat the words, his lip curled as he eyed Ben.

She'd told Lex to fuck off.

Krys rarely swore and it had been worth it to see Lex's slack jaw, the startled eyes.

Lex had stomped off in a huff.

She'd dated Ben a few times, but he'd been two years ahead of her, studying hard for his final exams and she wasn't going to spend too many free nights on her own. Krys and her girlfriends had found a few boys more willing to hang out in dance clubs and weasel their underage way into bars. And then, of course, Ben had disappeared, straight into the fleet academy, which he'd always said was his aim. He'd done well, too. Commander at about thirty.

Unable to keep the yawn down Krys stretched, then rolled off the couch and headed for the washroom. She hadn't lied to Saverill; she'd had a very busy few days.

Ben came to visit the following afternoon, ship time. He stood at the doorway wearing his day-to-day gray uniform, looking tense as if unsure of his reception. Just like a teenage date. "May I come in?"

It was good to see a familiar face, someone she knew she could trust. Krys stood aside and flung her arm out. "Of course. I've just been catching up on the news."

He sat in one of the armchairs with his weight forward, his hands crossed over each other in his lap. "It's not up to date. We pulled the latest data when we left Novastora, but that was a day ago."

"Yes. I'm worried about my father and mother." She sank down onto the couch opposite him, enjoying simply looking at him.

"Understood. But as far as we could tell your father has the loyalty of the armed forces." There was a hint of an upturn on the last few words, so he wasn't certain, and he was probably right. Loyalty could be a negotiable commodity.

"We think so. But these rebel extremists seem to be very popular with the impressionable young. It's scary."

He lifted a shoulder. "The idea of the Warriors of Sundara is attractive to many young men." He raised a fist and chanted, "Go forth and slaughter the non-believers. We will establish a new order based on the True Believers of the Way of Sundara."

She almost grinned. Ben had made a very good imitation of Aria Arachonis, the leader of the WoS. But he and his movement weren't funny. "What gets me is that some young women have become involved, too. Women are just chattels to them. For sex and children."

The very thought made her blood boil. How could any self-respecting woman allow herself to be treated in that way, hidden behind shapeless bags of dresses, and in separate compounds? Girls—children, really—married to men twice their age and more. She loathed the very idea.

"Is that why your father sent you away?"

The sound of Ben's voice startled her. "Yes. I can look after myself, but if I'd stayed, Dad would have been far too distracted. So I agreed to leave."

"You don't have an escort?"

"No. Dad and Saverill are old friends. So when Arachonis started his rebellion a day after your ship docked at the space station, Dad saw that as a great opportunity to get me away. He's afraid they'll target me because of him. And they wouldn't be nice about it."

She swallowed bile, recalling the news footage she'd just watched, showing the bodies of women and children in a country village. Their only crime had been that they hadn't belonged to the Sundaran sect. The news reader said 'violated' and 'beheaded'. Her imagination could fill in the rest and provide words like 'rape' and 'torture'.

"He doesn't trust your own bodyguards?" Ben asked.

It was a good question. She hadn't altogether trusted her bodyguards, either, especially the new ones. "There may be a bit of that. We had an incident in the palace a few weeks ago, concerning a guard who turned out to be a member of WoS. They've infiltrated many places. So the people we trust are there keeping up appearances, pretending that I'm living in my apartments at the palace." Marina, in charge of Krys's protection force, hadn't been happy about the arrangement, but she recognized that if she tried to leave with her, Krys would be easier to track.

Ben pursed his lips. He'd relaxed a little, sitting back in the armchair. "I suppose it makes sense. I think I'm the only person on this ship who hails from Novastora, and the Warriors of Sundara movement is isolated to that planet, so you should be safe on a fleet warship."

"Captain Saverill told Dad he would take 'most excellent care' of me." Krys rolled her eyes.

Ben snorted. "I'll bet he did. Up close and personal at every opportunity."

Krys stood and went over to the dispenser in the corner of the room. "Fancy tea? Or something stronger?"

"Tea would be good."

She pushed the selector buttons and placed the cups under the spout as the machine did its thing, hissing softly. While she waited she turned to face Ben. "You don't like Saverill, do you?"

Ben grinned, just like the eighteen-year-old she remembered. He had dimples in his cheeks. "No, I don't. He's a womanizing, social climbing, incompetent drunk."

She laughed carrying the cups back and put one in front of Ben. "Why don't you tell me what you really think?"

"I'm thinking—hoping—I've been posted to this ship as a trial so I can see what not to do. I imagine some admiral somewhere is having palpitations at the idea that Saverill's out here representing the fleet."

Ben lifted the cup and sipped, the steam rising around his face. "And Horton's not much better. Anyway, that's not your problem. Getting back to Saverill, what will you do when he makes a pass at you?"

Not 'if', 'when'. "I'm a level eight at Karindo. So he'll be tossed on his ear. If he's lucky." Krys drank some tea and watched Ben's eyebrows shoot up.

"So you really *can* take care of yourself."

"I'm a good shot, too." Krys pulled her Cobar 47 out of the holster under her shirt. It nestled into her palm, the butt warm from her body. "Small but deadly."

"I'm impressed. I'm a Karindo practitioner, too."

Stowing the gun she said, "Really? What level?"

"Four."

"Wow. Super impressed." Level eight took hard work and time, but level four and up took more than she had to give. "Would you spar with me? I haven't practiced for a couple of weeks, what with everything."

Ben rubbed his fist over his mouth. "I don't think Saverill would like it."

"Stiff. It's none of his business."

Ben's lips quirked in a half-smile. "His ship. His rules. And yes, he likes me as much as I like him."

Her muscles tightened. If Captain Saverill thought he could dictate who she could talk to, he could think again, her father's friend or not. "He doesn't make the rules for me. I'm not a prisoner."

"All right, all right." Ben raised his palm in the traditional stop sign. "When do you want to do this? Saverill is on the bridge right now."

Gulping down the rest of her tea Krys stood, a surge of adrenalin shooting through her body. "Right now will be fine. Give me a minute to change."

"Fine. Wait here, I'll be back." Krys waited until Ben had disappeared through the doorway before she went into her bedroom.

She hadn't brought too many clothes with her in her scramble to the spaceport, just what she could shove into a duffel. She couldn't look like her father's daughter. She had to be just another refugee getting the hell off Novastora in front of the growing escalation. Sundara fighters had already carried out a number of suicide bombings and the population was jittery. While the richer people escaped off-planet, those with less resources at least got out of the city. The roads and sky lanes were all busy, and she'd blended right in, just another anonymous person in the crowd, carrying all her possessions on her back.

One of the essentials in her wardrobe was a figure-hugging training suit that she took everywhere with her, the sort of garment that could be shoved into the bottom of a bag and yet would shake out as good as new. The soft fabric clung to her body, flexing with her as she moved, rather like a second skin. She was ready in five minutes, limbering up in her sitting room, shaking out her legs and rolling her shoulders. She hadn't sparred in a few weeks and she was looking forward to it. Although a little voice in her head wondered if that was because she'd get up close and personal with Ben Paulsen. She'd enjoyed his kisses all those years ago. They'd even had sex once, one of those messy encounters between two inexperienced people. She hadn't been a virgin and she was pretty sure he hadn't been either. But neither of them were very good at it, and the backseat of the skimmer he'd borrowed from his father hadn't exactly been romantic.

Ben walked in, wearing a suit rather like hers, just as she was finishing a calf stretch. He stopped short, staring at her, probably the same way she was staring at him, licking her lips to stop the drool. He was everything she had imagined. Wide shoulders tapering to narrow hips, well developed pecs, flat stomach, and long-muscled, sculpted legs. He was an athlete, not a body builder. Just looking at him was enough to have the butterflies practicing a salsa in her stomach, sending delicious swirls of warmth through her body. Krys couldn't resist a quick glance at the interesting bulge at his groin. Even though part of that was the extra protection in the suits, designed to keep the crown jewels safe and secure, she knew what was in there, after all. He'd been well hung at eighteen. That wouldn't have changed.

Ben cleared his throat. "Well. If you're ready?"

The words 'for what' danced on the tip of her tongue. His eyes had darkened and there was a tension about his stance and the flexed fingers that hinted at something other than exercise. It wouldn't have been the first time Krys had seduced a man. But somehow the idea of a quick fuck didn't sit well. She wasn't sure why. Maybe because she knew too much about him to just see him as a relief for an itch. "Sure am," she answered with enthusiasm. "Let's go."

The tension drained a little as he turned and led her to the elevator while she enjoyed the view of his broad back and lovely tight ass. He wouldn't look at her as they stood in the lift together, so she tried conversation. "Level four Karindo is impressive. How did you find time?"

He grinned. "Travelling in space is boring, especially in shift space. That means plenty of time for exercise. The bigger ships all carry marines, who spend a lot of time training. Even if they don't know Karindo they know hand-to-hand fighting, and they don't pull their punches. But I've been fortunate to have been posted with a few

Karindo masters, so I've learned the correct moves from them, and from vids."

The elevator slowed and stopped. The journey had taken much longer than the short trip to the mess level, descending into the lower regions of the ship. Here the corridors were strictly utilitarian, with hard floors and gray walls lined with widely spaced doors. The sound of the environmentals was a little louder here, a quiet whoosh that would fade into the background soon enough. They passed the number twelve followed by an S or a B several times, painted in large, raised letters on both sides of the passageway. She knew enough to know that with the black letters and the S on her right, she'd be heading for the stern, the white letters and the B to the bow.

Twice doors were open. Krys heard the sharp bark of commands and tramping feet from one, and the grunt and heave of people working out from the other.

"These are all training rooms and gyms," Ben said, his voice sounding loud in the unshielded passageway. "We don't need any equipment except mats, so the small one down the end will suit us fine."

"Sure." Krys was very aware of him, striding along beside her. She'd never married, although she'd had her share of affairs. Her father had introduced her to a number of aspiring young men—and not so young men—whom he deemed suitable for his little girl, but she'd never really clicked with any of them. She'd certainly clicked with this one. She wanted to know everything about him, where he'd been, what he'd done since last she saw him all those years ago. Her heart jolted and she almost stumbled. What if he was married? Had kids?

He slowed down, a concerned frown on his face as he caught her arm. "You okay?" The touch of his hand sent lightning bolts through her nerves.

She plastered on a grin. "Yeah. Fumble feet."

"We're here." Ben slapped his palm on a sensor, which opened a door revealing a largish room, its floor covered in mats. The walls were padded halfway up as well, obviously a space configured for unarmed combat.

The door closed behind them and Ben started a stretching routine, a set of exercises that Krys recognized. He smiled and nodded as she copied his movements, going through the basic Karindo sequence. She watched him from the corner of her eye as they both worked, extending muscles and tendons, arching backs and pulling in core muscles. It became a stately dance, matching without touching, mirror images. It was almost erotic. After ten minutes she was hot, and not just from the exercise. She wondered if he felt the same. When they finished the sequence and he straightened up, she couldn't resist a peek at his groin. Was that bulge a little more pronounced?

"I think we should work through the basic moves for your level. The falls and rolls, and then we can practice some of your attack and defense moves." Ben raised his eyebrows in silent question.

"Sounds great."

Krys performed the basic rolls, then the combat stances. He was fast. Faster than she was. Krys had to work hard, watching his body rather than his eyes to judge the next move. She jerked her head back to just avoid a fist that whistled by so quickly she felt the slipstream. If that fist had hit her she would have been unconscious on the mat.

Ben stopped, frowning down at her. "You're off balance."

He grasped her waist and altered her stance. Thankfully, he let go before she dissolved into a messy puddle on the floor in front of him. "Now place your feet like this." He showed her, pivoting his body easily on the balls of his feet.

Krys copied him while he nodded. "Let's try that again. But this time, get your mind right. Focus on my movement and nothing else."

He moved into position while she steadied myself, calming her mind, concentrating on his hands, shutting out everything else. The attack came as if in slow motion, giving her plenty of time to move smoothly out of the way, pivot, and follow through to use his momentum to trip him. He rolled and bounced back onto his feet, grinning. "Much better."

She beamed, exulting in the small victory. "It was like slow motion."

His eyes positively sparkled with delight. "Good. Fabulous. Rest assured it wasn't. But that's where you want to be, where you can almost see what your opponent is going to do before he does it."

He switched the exercises to attack moves, with him dodging, then correcting her mistakes. She was tiring, her legs a little shaky, her breathing too heavy. In one last lunge she almost had him, but he pirouetted while gripping her arm and Krys found herself hard up against his body, staring up at him. The air between their locked gazes fairly sizzled. His eyes darkened, he swallowed and then his lips parted. She was ready and waiting, longing for him to kiss her. She would have put her arms around his neck, but she was trapped with no way of breaking the hold and keeping the contact.

"Krys." Ben almost groaned her name and her heart missed a beat. Releasing her he stepped away, his shoulders heaving as he sucked in a huge breath. "Sorry. It won't happen again."

Before she could open her mouth he looked up at the chrono on the wall. "Fuck. Is that the time? Shit, I'm due on the bridge in five." He dodged for the door. "If I'm late, Saverill will have my balls."

Krys stood in the middle of the room staring at the empty doorway. Just like that. "I wasn't sorry," she mumbled at the uncaring walls. Damn it, she wouldn't have been sorry at all.

Anger and frustration took over. Krys slammed her fist into the padded walls hard enough to hurt. She made her lonely way down the length of the corridor back to the elevator foyer. Damn it. She was certain he felt the same way she did. Maybe he was married. Maybe he had a mess of kids somewhere. The car arrived with the usual soft ping. Somebody got out. She got in and pressed the button for level six, waving the temporary authorization she had been given to allow her access to that level. No response. What the hell?

She finally noticed the two young men standing against the wall, one carrying an armful of boxes. "It's going down," he said.

"Oh." Feeling silly she conjured up a grin. "Looks like I'm coming for the ride."

A few numbers rolled past, before the car slowed and stopped, and the two ratings stepped out. The door was beginning to close when one of them shouted and sprang back. Krys put her hand in the entrance to stop the door from closing.

"Thanks," the kid said. "Did I drop a tag?" He heaved a sigh of relief as he scooped up a cylinder from the ground.

She watched him walk toward a door marked in large red letters 'Engine Room. Authorized Personnel Only'. He and his companion went through. It was probably start of shift for them, too.

The elevator car hadn't moved. No level had been selected. Of course. She'd canceled the request for the sixth level when she held the door open. Shaking her head at her own stupidity, she pressed the button again. Just before the elevator door closed the engine room door opened again and someone stepped out. Krys thrust out her hand to hold the car up again, but too late. Oh well. That was life.

The car stopped four times before she reached her level, crew going on or off shift. Caught up in her own cogitations she didn't take much notice of the comings and goings and her fellow passengers did little more than give her a brief nod or smile before they retreated to their corner of the car, although a couple of the men gave her a surreptitious once-over. That simply irritated her. She almost felt like giving them a come-on so she could dump them on their butts.

Frustration does that to a girl. It was looking like she'd fallen for Ben Paulsen all over again.

As soon as she reached her stateroom she slouched off to the washroom, sloughing off her suit as she went.

Later, washed and dried and wearing a leisure suit, she emerged into the sitting room where the ship's communication system said, *"I have a message for you, madam, from Captain Saverill. He would like you to call him at your earliest convenience."*

Damn. Her spirits tumbled and crashed with a resounding splat. She'd hoped for a lovely moment it might be Ben. She didn't want to talk to Saverill, or to the damn machine. She'd tried to tell the thing to call her Krys, but it wouldn't be swayed. She was madam. It was stupid to be annoyed but she was, anyway. She poured herself a glass of water and gulped down a mouthful before she answered. "All right. Put him through."

The captain, immaculate in his day uniform, appeared as a hologram. A slight frown etched parallel lines between his eyebrows. "Lady Krystina. I was concerned."

"About what?"

"You weren't in your room." He waited for a response.

"I went down to a gym to do some exercise. I try to keep myself fit." She didn't try to hide the sharpness in her tone. Who did he think he was? Her guardian?

"With Commander Paulsen, I believe."

She pushed down the irritation. Of course he knew. "He's an exponent of Karindo. So am I. I asked him to practice with me and he obliged. Is there anything else, Captain?"

His eyelids flickered. He swallowed whatever he had intended to say. "I promised your father I'd take special care of you. Would you honor me by dining with me this evening, in my private dining room?"

Oh, Lordy. Just what she wanted. Not. But it wasn't an unreasonable request. As the daughter of a head of state, she was due a little more than the usual niceties. Which, of course, was not why he'd asked. But she was confident of being able to hold him at bay, and she might be able to find out a bit more about Ben. "Of course, Captain. What time would you like me to arrive?"

He smirked. "Eighteen hundred. I look forward to it."

Krys put on the smile again. The feeling wasn't mutual, but what could she do? "Thank you. I'll be there."

His image disappeared as suddenly as a turned off light.

"Ahhhh damn." Krys stared at the starscape, which hadn't changed from the last time she looked. Lordy she hated all this protocol nonsense. If she wasn't her father's daughter she'd tell him to... to... But she was. So she'd perform, up to a point.

Saverill probably expected her to dress up. Well, that wasn't going to happen. She thought about wearing her training suit but figured he was stupid enough to see that as a come-on. Her leisure suit would do, loose, comfortable, and all-concealing.

Eighteen hundred came all too soon, but she was prepared to be punctual. The door to the captain's cabin opened as she approached. The captain, positively glowing in his white dress uniform, greeted her in his sitting room, although the smile slipped a little as he looked her up and down. "Lady Krystina. So nice to see you."

"I do hope casual dress is acceptable. I'm sure you'll understand that I didn't have time to pack much and I wore my only formal attire to the mess last evening." Krys chewed on her lip, hoping she looked contrite.

Saverill manufactured a smile. "Not at all, not at all. I quite understand. And you look lovely just as you are. Please, sit down." He gestured at an armchair, then turned to a soft-footed steward who had appeared from an adjacent room. "I'll have the usual, Trent. And madam? A glass of Sheridan?"

Krys sat where indicated. Sheridan was a top of the range, very expensive sparkling wine, obviously chosen to impress. Okay, she was impressed. "Thank you, no. A glass of Wertsford, if you please."

Saverill's eyebrows rose. Wertsford was a non-alcoholic wine, not Krys's usual beverage of choice, but under the circumstances tipsy was something she didn't want to be. "Are you sure?" he asked.

"Quite sure."

The steward fetched the drinks while Saverill seated himself opposite her. Saverill drank from a heavy-based glass, the amber liquor about a third of the way up and apparently with no mixer. Hopefully he'd drink himself under the table soon.

After a couple of drinks and some inane conversation about what was happening at the Imperial court, Krys managed to fit in a question about Fleet life and marriage. No, Saverill wasn't married. Anymore. His eyes had lit up at the question, no doubt misinterpreting to imagine that meant she was interested in him. Good lord, perhaps her father had entertained some misguided notion that she and his old friend might make a good match? She would have to have a stern talk with her father.

"And Commander Wong? Is she married?"

"Wong? I don't think so. Horton isn't. Neither is Paulsen." Saverill shrugged and snapped his fingers at the steward, his empty glass held out for a refill. "Fleet and family life can be difficult."

So Ben wasn't married. Although she wouldn't have been surprised if Saverill simply didn't know. Before she could say anything more the steward announced dinner and she preceded her host into the captain's dining room. The large area sported a table which could have seated twenty. Two places were set, one at the head of the table, for him, and one to his right. A picture window on one wall showed a beautiful landscape of fall woods around a lake, with white-capped mountains in the background.

Dinner was nice, a starter of seafood followed by a roast with fresh vegetables, no doubt sourced in the markets of Novastora, and a light, fruity dessert.

Through it all Saverill entertained her with stories about the places he'd been and the people he'd met, name-dropping at every opportunity. After the main course plates were cleared, the landscape gracing the wall disappeared, replaced with the image of a battleship in space. Krys wondered why until Saverill told her all about his efforts as gunnery officer on the *Emperor Minkara* in a battle between the Empire and an Yrmak force. The green-scaled aliens were the bad boys of the neighborhood, notorious as pirates and mercenaries. Krys had met a few on her diplomatic journeys with her father while he was still an ambassador. Like most species, some individuals were pleasant. And some were not. It seemed the *Emperor Minkara* had happened upon an Yrmak attack on a colony world. Things had looked grim on the planet.

"By the time we'd finished," Saverill said, waving his glass, "three of their ships were drifting hulks. The other two made off as fast as their engines could take them." He drained the last of the Sheridan in one gulp. "Thieving bastards, Yrmaks. Can't stand 'em."

As soon as the steward took away the dessert plates, Krys seized her chance, rising to her feet. "Thanks so much for dinner, Captain—"

"A night cap before you leave," he said, standing.

"No, really. I must—"

"I insist. Trent, I'll have brandy."

He herded her out to the dining room and tried to direct her to the couch, but Krys aimed herself at the door. Before she got there the ship lurched, the engines screamed a protest and the lights flickered and dimmed. Krys staggered against the couch with Saverill's arm around her shoulders while alarm klaxons blared and dull thuds attested to blast doors locking into place.

"Fuck." Saverill breathed alcoholic fumes all over her as he straightened. "Status report!"

A voice Krys didn't recognize answered. *"Sir, the ship has emerged from shift space prematurely. Engineering is investigating. No sign of hull breaches at this point."*

Swearing under his breath, Saverill lunged for the door out of his cabin. Krys's pulse pounded. Even without any technical knowledge she knew ships weren't supposed to do that. The klaxons still blared, sawing into her mind. Not quite the way she would have chosen to avoid Saverill's advances but still, there was a bright side to everything. She slipped out the door and headed for her quarters.

The sound of running feet startled her and she turned, falling automatically into fight stance. Recognizing Ben, she sighed with relief.

Putting his hands on her shoulders he said, "Are you all right?"

"If you did this to get me out of Saverill's clutches, it worked." She grinned, trying to make a joke of it. It didn't go down well.

He frowned down at her, his eyebrows locked together, his eyes narrowed. "For a ship to jolt out of shift space is vanishingly rare. This may not be an accident."

She gaped at him. "You think it was deliberate?"

"I don't know. But if it's deliberate, then why?"

Why indeed. Why would anyone do that? "Sabotage? Something to do with WoS?"

"I don't know. Stay with me. We're going to the bridge. There's a row of seats down the back, near the entrance. Sit there and don't move, got it?" He had her arm in a firm grip, propelling her along with him as he spoke.

Krys put two and two together as he hustled her down the corridor past the captain's quarters. "You think this is about me?"

"Could be. If it is, I want to know where you are." He stopped at a closed doorway, where he paused to identify himself to open the doors.

She had never been on a warship's bridge before. It looked as though the curved line of workstations were set against a viewscreen, but the bridge was on level six, so it had to be a display, just like the picture window in her stateroom. The stars blazed out there, hard and cold and multi-colored, a little different from what she'd seen in her own room. She guessed this was the real thing. Over to the left a white, star-studded mist must be a nebula. To the right the galaxy formed a glittering, almost solid mass, a little like a multi-stringed necklace interspersed with pools of darkness.

Ben shoved her into a chair, muttered, "Stay here," and walked on to where Saverill stood, a picture of indignant rage. His head was lowered, his stance stiff. "Where the hell have you been, Commander?" he demanded.

"It's not my shift, sir. Commander Horton has the watch." The man himself stood a little behind Saverill. Horton wasn't happy with being ignored, although he tried to hide the microsigns.

"It's a general alert. That means here." Saverill stabbed his finger at the floor. "Straight away." Saverill was swaying slightly, finally showing the effects of all that alcohol.

Ben's jaw tightened. "I got here as soon as I could." He turned to one of the people working on the displays. "Have we run a sweep with long range scans?"

Saverill waved a hand. "I told them not to bother. We're nowhere near any system. It's an engineering problem and Wong's people are working on it."

The bridge staff glanced at each other, looked at Saverill, and kept doing what they were doing.

Horton noticed Krys at last, directing a glare at her. "What's she doing on the bridge?"

The look of surprise on Saverill's face signaled he hadn't realized she was there. Krys debated whether to give a little smile and a finger-wave and talked herself out of it.

"I thought it best to keep her where she can be safe, sir," Ben said.

Horton's eyebrows came together, then he looked down at his boots and stifled a laugh.

Saverill chuckled. "I suppose it hardly matters. Of course you can stay, Lady Krystina. Have you been on a warship's bridge before?"

Lordy, the man was such a patronizing prat. "That's kind of you, Captain. No, this is my first time on a bridge."

Stepping toward her, Saverill said, "Let me show you around."

He'd hardly finished a pace forward when a tech called over his shoulder, "Sir, five marks have come out of shift space."

Looking at the viewscreen Krys couldn't see anything different. But then again, without a nearby sun to illuminate the ships' hulls, what would she have seen, anyway? A row of running lights, perhaps?

An image had appeared on a 3D display in the center of the bridge, two larger ships and three smaller ones. Krys wondered at the detail, then guessed the system must have matched the sensor data from outside with information held in the database, and projected an enhanced version on the bridge.

"It's an Yrmak fleet, sir," a tech called.

Saverill staggered a little as he turned. One glance at the incoming ships was enough. He stiffened. "Yrmaks. Sound red alert. All crew to battle stations."

As distant alarms brayed, he sat down in the bridge's command chair. "Get me close-ups."

The display changed, zooming in on a gray, wedge-shaped vessel while the images of the other ships disappeared into nothingness. "An old Imperial Vertorn class frigate, probably modified. See the missile launchers on the second level?" The tech used a pointer to indicate the objects he was talking about. To Krys they didn't look any different to the rest of the ship.

The display zoomed out, then zoomed in again on a different ship, smaller and more streamlined. A stylized death's head had been painted on the black flanks. "This one's an ex-Jort frigate."

The other three ships were smaller patrol ships. The tech pointed out the blank plates covering the missile launchers. Krys didn't know much about weaponry, but it was enough to make her nervous. One ship against five?

Ben rubbed his hand over his lips. "We're out-gunned. We can match the Vertorn, but the Jort ship will outclass us."

Saverill glared at him. "This is an Imperial frigate with state of the art weaponry. They're just a rag-tag bunch of pirates."

Ben's chest heaved as he sucked in a breath. "With respect, sir, that's Imbol Raakt's fleet. Or a part of it. He runs a well-disciplined outfit."

Saverill shrugged. "We'll outrun them anyway."

"Er, no." Horton shook his head. "Commander Wong says an explosion damaged the compression flow to the main engines. We have all systems running, but we can't pick up speed."

Purple with rage, Saverill let fly with a string of expletives which would have embarrassed a navvy. "On my ship. Explosions? How did this happen? Wong? Get Wong on the line."

The techs were exchanging glances, eyeing the senior officers.

"Perhaps we should take this to the ready room, Captain?" Ben said.

Saverill used his arms to propel himself out of the command chair, stumbling on the raised platform. Ben steadied him, which earned him a black look. The captain shook off Ben's hand and strode to the ready room.

Ben collected Krys as he went past, taking her along with him into a room just off the bridge. A conference table almost filled the narrow space, and status screens on the walls showed the same data as on the bridge. They could run the ship from here, and have a private conversation.

The officers sat round the table, Saverill in the top chair, Horton on his left, Ben on his right. A woman about Krys's age sporting lieutenant's bars sat opposite Ben, and Major Hill of the marines sat beside her. Krys sat next to Ben and read the woman's name tag. Lieutenant Dharma.

Saverill glanced at Krys and dredged up a smile. "This has nothing to do with you, Lady Krystina. It's probably best if you return to your stateroom."

"With respect, sir, this may well have something to do with Lady Krystina. In my role as security officer I would prefer to have her where I can see her," Ben said.

Saverill's eyebrows nearly hit the ceiling. "Why would it have anything to do with her? We've had a malfunction at an unfortunate time. It's part of space travel."

"The Yrmaks will work for anyone for money. Including the Warriors of Sundara. I find it a little coincidental that we should find ourselves jerked out of shift space near an Yrmak fleet."

Horton shook his head, frowning. "You're guessing. What do we have that the Yrmaks would want?"

Ben jerked his head at Krys. "Her. Merkos's daughter. The Warriors of Sundara would pay a fortune to get their hands on her. They'd love to make an example of her, tear her apart—literally—in a public broadcast for Merkos to see."

Krys's gut roiled but she managed to keep the bile down. It was bad enough imagining that happening to another person.

Saverill rubbed his mouth.

Blinking rapidly, Horton swallowed, sending his Adam's apple dancing. He scowled at Ben. "Nobody knows she's on this ship. No-one was told."

Ben wasn't fazed, gazing at Horton in just the way he'd gazed at the bully-boys at high school. "If they found out, it would be well worth their while to intercept us."

Horton leaned forward, a hint of menace in his tone. "You seem to know a lot about it."

"I come from Novastora. I keep my ear to the ground." Ben spread his hands. "I could be wrong. But it's a scenario. And I think we should plan for it. Don't you, Captain?"

It was like watching a dropball game. Saverill and the two commanders stared at each other, while the others waited for somebody to blink.

Saverill blinked. "You're seriously suggesting this attack on the engines is sabotage?"

"That's ridiculous." Horton's lip curled. "Some sort of bad joke."

Ben didn't smile. "I don't make jokes about that sort of thing. Why don't we ask Commander Wong?"

Saverill had the AI contact Commander Wong. She appeared in the room as a hologram, an irritated scowl on her face. Her explanation left Krys floundering but it included words like 'bearings' and 'fiddly' in the discussion about the shift drive. The damage to the main engines was caused by a build-up of compression and a clogged valve. Or something.

"Was this a normal accident?" Ben asked. "The sort of thing that comes up often?"

Wong pursed her lips. "No, it's not normal at all. Damage to the bearings is rare, although not impossible. And having a compressor failure at the same time is a bit odd. Why do you ask?"

Ben leaned forward. "Could this have been sabotage?"

Wong's eyes narrowed. "Hmmm. Let me take a look. I'll get back to you." Her hologram disappeared.

To say Krys was worried was an understatement. If the ship had been sabotaged, somebody still on board had it in for her. Just as well she was here and not alone somewhere. Thanks to Ben.

"I think I'd better arrange for a guard in engineering." Major Hill bent over his comlink.

Saverill nodded. "Good idea."

Krys glanced over at the screen displaying the advancing Yrmak force, with a timer underneath counting down the seconds. Sixteen minutes and forty-three... forty-two...

Wong returned, her face grim. "Definitely sabotage. If you hadn't mentioned it, we wouldn't have noticed it. There was a timer involved. If it had all gone according to plan, we would have been a lot closer to that advancing fleet when the hyperdrive failed."

"Can you fix it?" Saverill asked.

"Damage is isolated to the cross bearings, so we're lucky. It's not as bad as I feared. But it's precise work. We're fixing it as quickly as we can."

"Time?"

"Rough estimate, fifteen minutes. And no sir, I can't do it any faster. And no sir, there are no workarounds."

"What about the main engines?"

"We can do that faster, I've got a team working on it, but even when we've made the repair we'd be pushing our luck to try to push her to maximum power."

"So we'll be limping." Horton had a laser pointer in his hand, turning it end over end, over end, over end.

"Yes. Will that be all? Sir?" Wong looked harassed, constantly glancing over her shoulder. She disappeared as soon as Saverill dismissed her.

Krys's mind had fixated on fifteen minutes. That pretty well coincided with the time of arrival of the pirate fleet. Her stomach churned as she remembered those horrible images from the news bulletin she'd watched. Rape. Torture. Her. The seconds rolled past, going backwards. Nineteen... eighteen... seventeen...

Someone's hand touched her arm. Ben, his concern evident in his eyes. "Are you okay?"

"Of course," she lied.

Patting her arm gently he said, "It's okay. We'll get out of this."

"You have a suggestion then, Commander Paulsen?" Horton's voice dripped sarcasm.

Ben's jaw tightened as he turned away from her. "We need to buy time for Wong to fix the engines."

Horton shifted his gaze around the table. "You all know we can't fight off two ships our own size and three patrol ships. We've sent a signal to HQ, but this was a good place to drop us out of shift space. We're out of contact here. Even if we weren't, nobody could get here in time to help us."

Krys was caught between a black hole and a cosmic storm. The situation reminded her of a book she'd read a few months back. Prince Talmud, a Golden Age hero, had sheltered in a hilltop monastery which was surrounded by an army. The attacking general offered to spare everyone if Talmud was handed over. Thinking their position was impenetrable, the monks refused and smuggled the hero out. The general, enraged by their stance, destroyed the monastery and slaughtered all the monks. She felt like she was Talmud and *Coromansa* was the monastery. Unless the engineers could make this ship work before the pirates arrived, a lot of people might die because of her. She couldn't just sit here picking lint out of her navel.

"Look, if you can't fix the engines and they catch up with us, then you have to send me over. I'd never be able to live with the notion that all the people on this ship could die because of me." She wouldn't live, anyway. If worse came to worst and she was sent over to the pirates, she'd kill herself in the capsule. Or maybe she could take a bomb with her; something that would explode when she got there.

Somewhere in the fog she heard Ben say, "Krys, Raakt's fleet will attack us anyway. If they get you first, it just makes it easier for them."

Major Hill leaned forward. "It may not come to that. If the engines are repaired, we might be out of here before we need to fight. I've sent a platoon down to engineering. No-one will get in or out without our approval, so there won't be any other attempts at sabotage."

"Unless it was an engineer," Horton muttered. He had a point. It was the obvious conclusion.

Saverill raised his hands. "Thank you for your offer, My Lady, but it is our job to protect you, and let's remember, this may not be about you." He gazed around the table at his officers. "Let's prepare for an attack from the five ships we know about."

Saverill was starting to look tired, the worse for wear. His eyelids drooped. He waved his hand at Ben. "Get on with it, Paulsen. You're the tag... tagtics man."

Ben had the AI place a 3D chart in the middle of the table with *Coromansa* at the center. Then he used scaled models of the five pirate ships to plot possible attack formations, with Horton and Dharma adding suggestions.

Krys hoped the captain would do them all a favor and keel over so Ben and Horton could take over. By the end of the briefing he was nearly asleep, resting his face in his palm, his elbow propped on the table.

Saverill's hand slipped and he jolted awake. His eyes were bloodshot. "Where were we? Finissshed?"

The time had ticked by. The pirate fleet was eight minutes away. The officers around the table exchanged looks. "Probably best if we tuck him into bed," Ben said.

Horton nodded. "Agreed. Hill, Paulsen, why don't you help the captain to bed?" He stood. "I'll get back to the bridge."

Ben dragged Saverill's limp body out of the chair and looped the captain's arm around his shoulder, Hill took the other side. Krys went first, opening the doors in front of her. Basically, they threw Saverill on his bed, contacted medical, and hurried back to the bridge.

Krys sat down in her seat at the back of the bridge. Horton had taken his place in the command chair. The atmosphere fairly thrummed with tension, stiff-backed staff bent over workstations, concentrating on their jobs, Horton gripped and released the arm of the command chair, Ben paced behind the techs, and glanced over their shoulders at their displays. The hologram in the center of the bridge continued to show *Coromansa* in the middle with the approaching Yrmak fleet closing in. Krys had managed to work out what some of the numbers on the screens meant. Too far to fire at the frigate yet, but the raiders were spreading out, probably working at being able to fire at *Coromansa* from many sides, just like a pack of sharks homing in on an injured whalfish.

"The approaching vessel is requesting contact, Commander Horton."

"Accept contact."

A green-scaled Yrmak appeared, its eye ridges orange. The creature spoke in its own language, leaving the translation to the ship's systems. "Nice to talk. I am Imbol Raakt. You are Captain?"

"Yes. What can we do for you?"

The creature smirked as only an Yrmak can smirk, revealing a mouthful of teeth. Somebody once told Krys that rasping sound was the Yrmak equivalent of a laugh. Her heart beat a little faster. It the situation amused the alien, this didn't augur well.

"I offer you a deal. You are outgunned. We can destroy your ship, yes? You are... how you say... stopped."

"What sort of deal?"

"You have a human female." Raakt looked at something below the level of his image. "Klystela Mullkess."

He mangled the pronunciation but it was obvious who he meant. Krys wiped clammy hands on her thighs.

"If we hand her over?" Horton sounded perfectly reasonable. Ben, seated at a command console, spun his chair around, staring at Horton, his expression watchful. Krys's heart thudded so hard it hurt.

Raakt raised both clawed hands. "Give woman. We go. Easy."

The tension drained out of Horton's shoulders. If that message was a relief to him, Krys was even more nervous than she'd been before. But she *had* offered, and the offer had been genuine. One life for hundreds.

Ben rose out of his chair, his hands making the T sign, left hand horizontal over his vertical right hand.

Horton's nod was barely perceptible. "Give us a few moments to consider."

Raakt held up one clawed hand. "This long." One hand was four minutes. His image disappeared.

"She offered. You heard her. One woman for the good of the ship? Sounds fair to me." Horton rose to his feet and stood so that he and Ben were toe to toe.

Ben's jaw jutted. "If we hand her over, he'll take the ship anyway. How do you suppose he got the frigate?"

Horton waved his hand. "It's immaterial. We need time for Wong to get the hyperdrive fixed. If we can delay them for a little while, send them the woman, we'll be able to make our escape."

"Look, I agree we need to buy time. So we'll send over a survival capsule." Ben's grin was feral, without humor. "With a bomb in it."

It sounded like a plan to Krys, and it certainly made her feel better. She nodded, while sending every good thought she could to Wong and her team in the engine room.

Horton shook his head. "They won't buy it."

"We can at least try. After all, every delay buys us minutes."

Horton shrugged. "Open the line to Raakt."

Raakt appeared. "Well?"

"All right. We'll send you the woman."

Raakt clicked his claws together, but his features remained unchanged. With a human Krys might have read the body language. But Raakt wasn't human. "When?"

"Give us a few moments to organize a pod for her."

The pirate's eye ridges went red. Not happy. "No pod. You think me stupid? Use suit. Survival suit."

Krys's heart sank. That meant it had to be her. Survival suits were used when people went outside the ship. The helmet was clear, like a goldfish bowl, giving maximum visibility for the wearer of the suit—and anyone on the outside looking in. Although the level of transparency could be reduced, depending on the circumstances.

"And helmet must be clear," the Yrmak added. "If I cannot see face, we fire. I give you this much." He opened his claws twice. "If woman not in space then, I fire." With that he disappeared. No discussion. No negotiation. No options.

Krys closed her eyes and gritted her teeth, willing the bile in her throat to go back to where it belonged. They were out of options, but she could buy them time and trust that her time had not yet come. There was something to be said for the Sundara cult. Everything they did was for a future life, cavorting with houris in Sundara's garden. For her, all she could pray for was Commander Wong and her engineers.

"Krys, we'll get round it." Krys opened her eyes. Ben stood in front of her.

She forced a smile. "It has to be done, Ben. It buys us all time. I can do it. And there's no choice, is there? They're sure to have facial recognition technology, and if they knew to come after me, it was easy enough to get a picture of me." She pushed herself out of the chair. "Come, on, let's get moving. We don't have very long."

"Krys—"

Shutup shutup shutup. She raised her hand. "Now."

"She's right, Paulsen. Take her down and make sure she's out of there in time. We have a ship and crew to think of."

Horton could be such a pompous, righteous, holier than thou... words failed her. Might as well get on with it.

Ben went down to the hangar bay with her, summoning the elevator car, pressing the buttons for the hangar deck. "Have you been in a suit before?" he asked as the elevator descended.

"Once." It had been years ago, a drill on a trip with her parents to the Imperial capital. She didn't mind admitting the experience had scared her, even though she was safely tethered. Space is very, very empty.

Down in the spartan hangar bay the ceiling soared into the dark. Harsh lights cast even harsher shadows and every movement echoed and clanked. Ben pulled a suit off a rack in a closet and handed it to her. The garment was surprisingly smooth and soft, a one-piece with an opening at the front. The material would stiffen when subjected to vacuum. She shucked off her clothes and climbed into the suit while her nerves danced to their own orchestra.

Pulling down the helmet from a shelf, Ben said. "We'll fit you with a tether. That way we can pull you in when Wong has the engines fixed."

She nodded. *When.* Keep thinking when, not if.

After she had fastened the suit, she clipped her pistol onto the belt.

Ben helped her put on the back pack with the power jets and oxygen supply, and fitted the neck lock which held the helmet in place. "Show me you know how to use the jets."

It wasn't so different from the suit she had worn all those years ago. The controls were on her wrists; she could angle the power cells any way she wanted, and turn by toggling the power from one side to the other.

He nodded once, then opened a small airlock, one of the ones specifically fitted for allowing people to exit the ship. The look on his face touched her heart: tortured, wounded, sad. "I'd do this for you if I could."

She blinked away the wetness from her eyes. "Well, you can't. But hey, we can have a lovely reunion when I get back."

"When." The grin didn't work. "Click the tether on the back pack when you're ready to leave the ship."

Krys stepped into the airlock and gave him a small wave as the door closed.

Time to concentrate. Time to get the heart rate down. Time to live for the moment. She put her mind to work on the suit, checking her grip, rehearsing the controls so that she could react if she needed to. The air gauge in the airlock read zero. The external door slid aside. The view was the same as it was on the bridge, to the left a distant nebula, straight ahead the river of stars. In the middle ground a dark shadow spangled with running lights was silhouetted against the starscape. One light on its flank flared red and steadied.

Krys swallowed. The eye of the demon. She remembered reading a horror story like that once, where a glowing red eye in a statue lured a woman to her death.

Ben's voice sounded like he was right there with her. "Aim for the red light. But take your time. Fumble a bit. And don't forget that tether."

She found the tether at the exit and clipped it onto her back pack. "Won't they see it?"

"Hopefully not for a while."

Krys took a deep breath and stepped forward out of the ship. She drifted along beside the hull with her feet over nothing. Her nerves flared with panic but she fought against it, shoving the monster down into the depths of her consciousness. *The red light: concentrate on the red light. Don't look down.* Wherever that was. Using her hand she pushed away from the airlock. The pressure was enough to send her tipping forward and her attempt to stop the motion with her legs sent her into a gentle tumble. The ship, then the stars: the ship then the stars. Something tangled with her arm, sending her heart into a frenzy. The panic monster lurked in the shadows, ready to take over at the first opportunity. Her fingers closed on something long and thin. The tether. She breathed a little easier. At least it was there. Ben had said to fumble a bit and she wasn't even trying.

"Use the jets," Ben said in the helmet. "Very gently against the roll."

The buttons on the wrist bands were large to make it easy for gloved hands and they had their own illumination. The galaxy moved around her as she fumbled for the control. Her stomach churning she forced herself to fixate on what she was doing. Lower the nozzles, fire gently. Don't be sick. It took her a couple of tries but eventually she was stable, aimed at the dark shape against the stars and the demon eye. If she ever reached it, that would be the start of hell. *Please, Wong, work a miracle.*

"Wong's nearly there, Krys. You're doing great. But they're getting impatient. Move toward the black ship. Not too fast."

Ben's voice brought her back from the abyss. She was tethered. Wong was nearly finished. It would be over soon. Very soon. She raised her left wrist and used the buttons to lift the jets to waist height, then put on a short burst of power. There was no real sensation of movement, since she had nothing to judge against. If the black mass with its evil demon eye became larger, it was so slow the change didn't register. The stars blazed on, cold and hard against the velvet darkness. She was alone inside her helmet, listening to the too-fast double beat of her heart. Lub-dub, lub-dub, lub-dub.

Moistening her mouth as best she could, she croaked, "Are we there yet? Is it finished?"

"Hang on, babe, nearly there." He paused, and then hissed, "Yes! I'm pulling you back. Use your jets. We'll be out of here as soon as you're back."

Krys whooped for joy, out there in the privacy of her helmet, and waited for the tug of the tether. Nothing happened. The panic in the shadows gained shape, dark and ugly. The red devil's eye gleamed against the stars, lidless, unwinking. "Ben?"

"Hang on, Krys. I'm coming to get you."

He was gone. "Ben?"

Fighting down the fear, she groped around to where the tether attached to the harness and pulled. It wasn't taut, floating freely toward her. She was out there on her own. Trying to ignore the leering shape of panic clawing at her nerves, she focused just like she had when she sparred with Ben in the gym. A part of her wondered what had happened to him, but she shoved that aside. She'd find out soon enough. She concentrated on the jets, rotating herself to face the wall of the frigate with its row of lights. Too far. The wall revolved slowly away from her. Gritting her teeth, she tried again, putting some power into the back jets, while she tried not to even contemplate being left behind.

Now that she had something to judge distance against, she could see she wasn't too far away from the ship. She'd moved sideways a little, so the open airlock was at an angle to her left. She toggled the jets, alternating power with course. Too far again. The panic clawed closer. Krys pivoted and out there in the middle distance the black shape and its demon eye taunted her. It had sucked her in, unable to escape, like the girl in the novel.

"Stay calm, babe. I'm coming to get you." Ben's voice anchored her.

Krys forced herself to breath, in through the nose, hold, out through the mouth. Where was he? She rotated again, firing the jets one more time and caught a glimpse of something coming toward her. Her heart hammered so hard she thought her ribs would burst. She fumbled for the pistol on her belt. They weren't going to get her without a fight. She'd half-turned again. The frigate's side wall rose in front of her, close but too far away to touch.

Something jerked her backwards.

"Krys, I've got the tether. Turn the jets off. I'll get you back."

Ben. Her hands were shaking but she managed to force her fingers to turn off the jets as she swung around on the end of the line like a fish. She watched the red demon light apparently swinging from side to side as she was hauled back.

She collided with something behind her, sending her nerves into overdrive again. "Got you."

Ben. Tears welled up into her eyes. "Just stay where you are. I've got to get us back to the ship before it jumps. As long as we're holding onto her, we'll go along for the ride."

Before it jumps. They could be left out here, easy pickings for the pirates with *Coromansa* gone. Ben's arm slung around her, turning her away from that demon eye.

The airlock in the frigate's side grew larger. Please, please. Krys risked a look over her shoulder. The demon eye hadn't moved.

Her body jerked as she hit something hard. Lights flashed and her head spun.

When she looked over her shoulder the pirate ship had disappeared. So had the galaxy. Straight in front of her was brightness. But Ben still held her. Maybe she was dead. Maybe he was, too.

"Come on, Krys. Turn off the jets. We have to get on board." Ben's voice was urgent, grounding her enough to obey his command. She pressed the button on her wrist, then hit the bulkhead in front of her and bounced off. A hand grabbed her shoulder and pulled her around. She nearly cried with relief. She was floating in the airlock and Ben was staring at her through the helmet of a space suit.

"Straighten up. I'm going to turn on the artificial gravity." He moved to the control panel while she forced herself to line up with the floor at her feet. The AG came on gently, so her feet pressed into the floor. As the pressure increased she sagged to the decking, unable to bear the weight on her trembling legs.

"Krys? Are you okay?" Ben's voice held a note of panic.

"Present." She knew she whispered the words.

"Thank the Mother." He sighed with relief. "You're safe. *Coromansa* has gone into shift space. I'm sealing the airlock. It's airing up now."

It seemed to take forever before the gauge showed full and the internal hatch into the ship cracked. Krys gathered herself together but, before she could stand, Ben was there, helping her onto the deck where crew waited to help them both out of the packs and suits.

Now the weight of the suit was gone Krys's legs trembled, her body aching with fatigue. She closed her eyes, sucking in deep breaths. She never, ever wanted to do anything like that, ever again.

When she opened her eyes Ben stood right in front of her, his eyes searching her face, his body tense. "Are you all right?"

She tried a grin. "I'm fine. Really. Just a bit shaken up."

He brushed a stray piece of damp hair away from her face. "Understandable. Let the medic check you."

A woman wearing a medical patch on her uniform fastened a monitor to Krys's neck and frowned at the instruments. After a few moments she looked up, smiling, and removed the sensor. "Looks like you just need a bit of rest."

Ben thanked the medics and stood them down. "I'll take you to your stateroom." He had his arm around her waist as he guided her to the elevators. Krys wasn't arguing. It felt good, safe and warm.

She waited until they were in the car and moving up, then said, "You came to get me. You could have been left behind."

He shrugged. "Yeah, well. I wasn't going to leave you to Raakt's tender mercies on your own." He wouldn't look at her, his lip caught between his teeth.

Her heart swelled. He'd risked his life for her. One thing for sure, she wasn't going to let him out of her sight again. With her hand on his shoulder she leaned across and kissed him on the cheek. "I'm forever in your debt. And I hope you'll give me a chance to say thank you in any way you'd like."

His arm tightened around her and he stared into her eyes. "I'll take you up on that. But first I'd like to know who released that tether."

"Released?"

He nodded. "I checked the end. It was intact. And I checked the connector in the airlock."

"Who?"

Ben's jaw clenched. "I don't know. It was released from inside the ship. It can be done from the hangar bay, and from the bridge. It's a safety feature in case there's something out there we need to drop."

"Like me," she mumbled.

He squeezed her shoulder. "I wish I knew who did it. Horton might have dropped the tether, for the sake of the ship." He rolled his eyes. "But who sabotaged the shift drive? Someone who knew you'd be on the ship. Saverill is the obvious choice. But I can't see him pulling a stunt like this."

The car slowed and halted with the trademark soft ping. The door opened. A scene flashed into Krys's memory. The gym, down on the level of the engine room, somebody coming out, her hand stretched out to stop the lift doors.

She gasped. "Oh. It was Horton. Horton was down in the engine room after we finished sparring."

She stepped into the foyer, Ben frowning at her. She explained what had happened, what she'd seen as she made her way back to level six, the unintended journey down to the engine room and the figure coming out. "He looked familiar, that's why I tried to stop the elevator. But then I figured he was just somebody else changing shift."

His eyes narrowed and she got the notion she wouldn't want to be on the wrong side of Ben Paulsen. "He's the exec, so he can go anywhere. But I can't imagine why he had to go to the engine room at that time. And he's great friends with Saverill. Hmm." He shooed her along in the direction of her room. "You go along. I'll see what I can find out."

Krys grabbed his arm as he made to turn away. "Oh no, you don't. I'm staying with you." She felt safe with him. The prospect of being all alone in her stateroom didn't sit well. Not right now, anyway. Besides, she'd just promised herself she wouldn't let him out of her sight.

The elevator car stood open in front of them. After a momentary pause he nodded. "Okay. I'll feel better if I know where you are."

Ben's office was two levels down, a small, neat space fitted with a large desk and several screens. Pointing at a visitor's chair, Ben said, "Sit. Let's see what the surveillance files has to tell us."

Ben started up his system with voice recognition and an eye scan. Krys pulled the chair around so she could see over his shoulder as he entered a location, date and time. The display showed an engine that Krys didn't recognize in an empty compartment.

Nothing.

"Hang on." Ben pointed his finger at the date and time on the display. "Let's try that again." He rolled the image back. "Note the time. Now forward."

Krys peered at the screen and her nerves tingled. "It's been cut." She exchanged a look with Ben. "About forty seconds at about the right time. How many people can fool around with the logs?"

Ben grinned. "Horton has the authority. But would he have the knowledge?" He leaned back in his chair and requested a connection to Commander Wong. The chief engineer appeared as a hologram. "This had better be important. I'm a tiny bit busy right now."

"I wouldn't bother you if it wasn't important, Sella. You know that."

The woman folded her arms, a mock frown on her face. "Well?"

"Two things. One, did Commander Horton come to ask you about the schedule at the end of third shift?"

Wong pulled a face. "No. Should he have?"

"You didn't see him?"

She shook her head. "But then everyone was busy." Her eyes narrowed. "Why?"

"Second thing. Apart from an engineer, who could have fooled with your shift drive?"

Wong nodded slowly. "You mean knowledge required? Obviously my own people. But if you're meaning Commander Horton, he has some background in engineering. I've had many a technical chat with him. But why? Why would he want to give Lady Krystina to pirates?"

"Money." Ben leaned forward, his expression somber. "These are just investigations, Sella. Okay?"

"Understood." The chief engineer passed her finger across her mouth. "My lips are sealed."

Krys scratched her hair. It felt awful; lank and damp. "Okay, let's say it's Horton. How did he tell the Yrmaks where we'd be?"

"If he called someone from the ship, we've got him." Ben rose and crossed the two paces to the opposite side of the room, where he opened tall doors, revealing a workstation.

"We have a second record of the logs—and all transmissions." Ben logged in, using iris scan and voice recognition.

"Horton would know that, surely?" Krys said.

"Access is strictly limited to this room and triple secured." Ben placed his hand on a sensor for DNA scan. "The captain and I are the only ones with access, and it has to be done here. Horton probably figured he was safe enough with the daily log fixed."

Ben asked for the backups of the daily log, specifying date and time. The empty engine compartment showed on the screen. Then a figure entered, glanced around and bent over the engine. It was over in seconds and the camera never caught a good image of his face. Damn.

"Let's see if there are any messages from Commander Horton off the ship." Ben entered the dates when *Coromansa* was docked at Novastora.

No results.

Krys's heart sank. She leaned her elbow on the desk and supported her head in her hand. Damn. She'd been so sure.

"Don't give up yet. Let's see all the messages from anyone that day." Ben edited the search criteria.

A list appeared on the screen. Saverill was mentioned several times.

Krys looked at Ben. Saverill? Surely not.

"Play Captain Saverill's messages," Ben said.

The first two were straightforward, Saverill talking to the station controllers, arranging docking, then a call to Krys's father's office. Then another call, a few hours later. But this time, the voice was different. Horton, talking to somebody Krys recognized.

"Well, well. Leskor Planck." Krys wasn't surprised. "He owns the Lady Luck Casino, apart from a whole swag of other businesses. He's always one step ahead of the law. My father has been trying to pin him down for a while."

Horton sounded nervous. "I can pay you, I'm sure of it. My ship will be carrying something valuable."

"How valuable?" The gravelly voice oozed distrust.

"I'm not sure. But very valuable. So valuable we'll be pulling out soon."

The expression changed to bored. "So why are you telling me this?"

"I can organize for the ship to be at a place and time. Please. You'll get your money, I'm sure of it." Horton gabbled the words, his panic obvious. "These are the coordinates."

Ben punched the air. "Yes! Slime ball. He used Saverill's office to make the call. And his voice will be in the records." To the ship's AI he said, "Identify the speaker."

The response was immediate. Commander Horton.

Ben swept Krys around in a bear hug, a huge grin on his face. "That's enough for me to arrest him." He waved Krys out of his office and into the elevator foyer, where she pressed the button to summon a car. It was already on its way down.

Placing a hand on Ben's shoulder, she said, "I'm glad that's over. It was pretty scary, not knowing who."

The door swished aside. Her heart lurched. Commander Horton stared at her, an unreadable expression on his face. He stepped out, assembling a smile on his face. "Ah... Lady Merkos. So glad to see you. I was afraid we'd lost you."

Ben grinned. "I'm sure Mister Planck will be disappointed, too. I'm placing you under arrest."

Horton's eyes widened. Krys could almost see the cogs meshing as he realized he'd been caught. Time seemed to slow. His hand rose and extended toward Krys, the fingers hooked to grab. With all the time in the galaxy she knocked his arm aside, then shoved the heel of her hand in a blow to his chin that flung him hard against the wall. He grunted, the air knocked out of him. Krys followed up with a kick to the groin which produced a satisfying gasp of pain. Bastard.

"That'll do, Krys," Ben said, gently tugging on her shoulder. His pistol aimed at Horton, he made a short call on his comunit.

Horton skewered him with a gaze full of hate.

"Coming down here to get rid of the evidence?" Ben said.

"No comment."

"It's all in the logs. You must have owed Planck a lot of money if you were prepared sacrifice everyone on this ship for a bounty on a woman's head."

Horton's eyes glistened. "I never meant it to get that far. I didn't know it was her. Saverill carried drugs. Did you know that? Drugs. I thought he must have made a special pickup." A sob wracked his body.

Krys felt a pang of pity. But only for a moment. He didn't change his commitment after he found out he was selling a woman to the Yrmaks. He could rot as far as she was concerned.

"You'll be court martialed, you know that."

Horton nodded.

"But we might be able to do a deal in exchange for information."

The sound of boots rang in the corridor. Two armed marines. They helped Horton to his feet and escorted him to the ship's cells. The man was broken, his head bowed, his shoulders slumped. He refused to make eye contact with Krys.

When they were alone Krys asked, "What was that about drugs? And information? You're surely not going to let the bastard off the hook on a technicality?"

"Ah." Ben scratched his nose. "That was why I was assigned to this ship. Admiral Stakpole had private suspicions. She wanted evidence to get Saverill. I'd say Saverill suspected as much, so he never put a foot wrong. This changes everything though."

Krys glowered at him. "If Horton gets off—"

"He won't." Ben made to put his hands on her shoulders but thought better of it. "He's finished in the fleet. But he might get a shorter sentence if he helps us get Saverill. Don't worry, Krys, they'll both pay. Trust me."

He looked so sincere, like a puppy who thinks he's done something wrong. She melted. "Of course I trust you."

Ben had his arm around Krys all the way back to her stateroom, where he urged her inside. The look he gave her was pure predator and it sent delicious shivers through her body. He put his hands on her shoulders. She moved forward, ready to be crushed against him, but he kept her at a distance. Damn his eyes. "Ben..." She wasn't above pleading.

He bent his head and brushed his lips over hers, sending shivers of longing through her body. She wanted more, but he pulled away. "I'm going to be acting captain. I have duties to attend to. Have a shower, sweetness. It'll make you feel better." His fingers trailed down her cheek.

Before he went through the door he turned, a spark in his eyes. "I'll be back. Very soon."

Then he was gone. But the delicious tremors didn't go away. If anything, they intensified. Her nipples were so tight they hurt. But she did need a shower. She'd sweated in that suit and her hair was plastered to her skull like strands of rope.

Krys took her time standing under the warm water. The shampoo wasn't the fragrant type she would have preferred, but at least her hair was clean. She'd just finished drying her hair when Ben cracked open the door to the washroom and put his head around. "Finished?"

"Finished? We haven't started yet." Her nerves dancing a tango she emerged naked as the day she was born.

So was he. Wide shoulders, flat abdomen, muscles defined but not heavy. And he had all the right equipment, in the present arms position. She lifted his balls in her hand, then slid a finger up his cock, reveling in the way his pupils expanded and he sucked in a breath. "Where would you like to start?"

Ben was gone when Krys woke up. His side of the bed was cold, so he'd been gone a while. Just thinking about him was enough to make her smile. Fancy getting together again, after all those years, and in such a dramatic way. She wiled away the time watching a series of holovids until he came in. He had dark circles under his eyes, but a slight smile flicked around his lips.

Krys stood. "Hiya. Tea? A drink?'

Smiling properly now, he came over to her and tenderly brushed the hair away from her face before he brushed her lips with his. She put her arms around his neck before he could escape and kissed him properly, drinking in his warmth, his taste, his smell.

"Nice to know you're still pleased to see me," Ben said when they finally disengaged.

She almost rolled her eyes. Men could be so insecure. "I'm hoping we'll be getting to know each other for quite a while. Now. Tea?"

When he nodded she went over to the dispenser and pressed the buttons.

"Horton has been interrogated."

She picked up the cups and brought them to the couch where Ben sat on one side, leaving her space next to him. She handed him his cup and sat. "So that's where you were?"

"I didn't do the interrogation. I left that to the experts." He took a sip of tea. "It didn't take long for him to fold."

"What did he say?"

"He's got a gambling problem. Spent way more than he should have in a casino at Novastora. Planck owns the Lady Luck and he wanted his money, or else. Horton's great mate Saverill let slip that *Coromansa* would be carrying a very special cargo back to the Empire. He didn't tell Horton what it was, but Horton guessed it would be very valuable. So he figured he'd organize for the gangsters to pick up the cargo while we were en route."

"So he set up the sabotage."

"Yes. He knows enough about engineering and the ship's systems to blow her out of shift space without too much damage."

She gazed down into the greenish-brown depths of her cup. "So he didn't know the 'valuable cargo' was me."

"Not until he saw you, no."

She drank a little more tea. It tasted of herbs and warm afternoons. She hoped Ben wasn't implying that was some sort of excuse. "Didn't stop him, though. He was still willing to hand me over to the Yrmaks."

Ben drained his cup and put it on the table. "Yes. He was. To save his own miserable hide." The words were clipped, harsh. "He'll be court martialed. He won't serve on an Imperial ship, ever again."

Serve him right, as far as Krys was concerned. "What about the drugs?"

"Horton was more than happy to put his dear friend in the frame if it meant a reprieve from the Emperor's prison settlements. I've already sent the information to Admiral Stakpole. She's a happy woman."

So... all tied up neatly. Except for one thing. "How did the pirates know, to ask for me, though?"

Ben shrugged. "Who knows? Maybe Planck worked it out? He could well have had informants at the space station who identified the mysterious guest on *Coromansa*. Or an informant at the palace? Someone who knew you weren't really there?"

She nodded. Fair enough. There were lots of possibilities, especially for those prepared to take a guess. Anyway, it didn't matter now. "How's Saverill?"

"Oh. I forgot to tell you. Horton said he added a little extra to Saverill's brandy bottle before your dinner date. Just to make sure the captain would be out for the count when we arrived at our unexpected stop, and Horton would be acting captain. Saverill is recovering in sick bay. I'll be acting captain until we dock."

She grinned. "I hope they have the sense to make that a permanent arrangement."

He pulled her against him, with her head resting in the hollow of his shoulder. "I'm hoping so. Maybe your father would think about accepting a Fleet captain as a son-in-law."

Krys sat up. Ask her father for her hand? "What? You think my father would have anything to do with my choice of husband?"

He laughed. "If the very idea was impossible, you would have said so. Now I've got something to work for."

She felt squirmy, wanting some more loving. Running her fingers through his hair, she said, "Is there anywhere you need to be for an hour or so?"

He relaxed, moving around so she could fit more comfortably against him. "What did you want to do?"

He knew. His eyes had darkened and his grin had becoming decidedly predatory. She stood, pulling him to his feet with her. They stood a hands breadth apart, gazing into each other's' eyes. "I was hoping we could have a bit more getting to know each other."

"Sounds good to me."

They went into the bedroom together, their arms around each other.

Don't miss out!

Visit the website below and you can sign up to receive emails whenever Greta van der Rol publishes a new book. There's no charge and no obligation.

https://books2read.com/r/B-A-VPC-GLDCD

Connecting independent readers to independent writers.

Also by Greta van der Rol

Black Tiger
Black Tiger
White Tiger
Black Tiger / White Tiger

Dryden Universe
Eye of the Mother
A Dryden Collection
Ella and the Admiral
A Matter of Trust
The Demon's Eye
For the Greater Good
Retribution
The Search for the Crimson Lady
The Thunder Egg
Imperial Agent Collection

Morgan Selwood
Supertech
Morgan's Choice

Morgan's Return
Kuralon Rescue
Rescuing Romila
Escape from Shar Burk
A Victory Celebration
Ink
Morgan's Misfits

Ptorix Empire
The Iron Admiral: Conspiracy
The Iron Admiral: Deception
Starheart
Crisis at Validor
The Stuff of Legend
The Admiral and the Rebel
The Complete Iron Admiral

Standalone
To Die a Dry Death
Shorts

Watch for more at https://gretavanderrol.net.

About the Author

Greta Van der Rol crafts intricate space opera worlds with epic quests that captivate readers from the first page to the last. Her books will keep you reading in one sitting!

Read more at https://gretavanderrol.net.

Milton Keynes UK
Ingram Content Group UK Ltd.
UKHW010639290424
441924UK00005B/406

9 798224 986569